Just My Type
Henderson Family Book 1

SYNITHIA WILLIAMS

I0638161

Copyright © 2024 Synithia Williams
ISBN: 978-0-9975729-3-3
Originally Published by Crimson Romance
June 2014
Cover Art by: Mae Phillips at Cover Fresh Designs
Synithia Williams
Columbia, SC

ACKNOWLEDGEMENTS

They say it takes a village to raise a child. Well, it takes a great group of people to polish a book. Many thanks to Liv Rancourt and K.M. Jackson for asking the questions about Freddy and Janiyah that made me dig a little deeper into their characters. And a huge thank you to Jess Verdi for sending back editing questions that really made me think. All of that thinking really made this book shine. Thank you to all of the readers who've pushed me along and asked when the next book was coming. You guys kept me going when I thought about hanging up the writing cap. And, as always, thank you to my husband, my biggest supporter as I blunder my way through this part of my life.

CHAPTER 1

Janiyah Henderson sang along with Bruno Mars about sex and paradise as she swung her yellow Camaro into the driveway of her parents' three-story brick home. She was there for another random family meeting. Another chance for her dad to evaluate his children's lives. Another chance for all of them to somehow disappoint him.

She wasn't overly concerned about disappointing her father. Her dad loved his kids; he just didn't quite understand them. His disappointment never came with threats to disown them, or rants about them ruining his legacy. Instead it was entwined with bafflement that his kids had grown up to be the complete opposite of him. Janiyah was pretty sure he still expected the four of them to one day miraculously evolve into the Cosby kids.

She glanced at the time and cringed. This impromptu family thing was going to make her late meeting her friend Liz. They were going to the young professionals mixer. Not a party, but a place where bankers, accountants, bureaucrats, and other nine-to-five clones met to "network." Janiyah called it for what it was: an excuse for people under forty to drink and flirt under the pretense of doing business.

She didn't attend the mixers regularly. As a virtual assistant, she wasn't a part of the normal nine-to-five crowd. She loved the flexibility of her job. Working on a variety of projects, talking to clients on the phone from her living room while wearing pajamas, and completing an assignment in the middle of the night as she indulged in infomercials which made her aware of items she'd never realized she had to own immediately. That was ten times better than stuffy business suits, rigid work hours, and days full of meetings.

She was only going because Liz had begged her to come and break up the monotony. And since Janiyah couldn't deny attending a party, even if it was a suit and tie party, she'd agreed. Janiyah had bet Liz fifty dollars that she'd make it to this event on time. That was before her dad called his family meeting. She was going to be handing over that fifty if she didn't get out of here in under thirty minutes.

After putting the car into park, she reached into the back seat to grab the red dress still wrapped in plastic from the dry cleaners. Picking up her black clutch and patent leather heels she got out of the car and continued singing as she strutted up the drive, past the vehicles that belonged to her brothers, to the front door.

She sang to herself as she breezed through the door and hurried down the tastefully decorated entryway into the main gathering place. Her brothers were already situated around the large sunken living area. It was her favorite part of the house. So cozy and welcome with leather couches, an entertainment system that was really more a home theatre, and a wet bar in the corner.

The oldest, Kareem, sat on the floor in front of the large wraparound sofa. Headphones covered his ears as he sketched in a notebook. His shoulder length dreadlocks were pulled back in a ponytail, and he was dressed in his standard all black—something he'd started after getting out of jail several years ago. He'd tried to redeem himself by opening his own barber shop, but it wasn't like jail was something the family could easily forget. He glanced up when she walked in, and threw up his hand as a greeting. A quirk of his lips that made the scar along his upper lip twitch was his attempt at a smile.

David, the middle brother, was on his phone in a corner; the smile on his face meant he was probably talking to a woman. He leaned against the wall like a Ralph Lauren model with his perfectly faded hair, neatly trimmed beard, and wrinkle free grey three piece suit. Seeing David dressed nicely wasn't anything new. Her brother always left the house as if he had a photo shoot. He'd taken up the reins of Henderson Automotive, the family business, after Kareem went to jail, but quickly discovered that the pressure to run the business the way their dad wanted it done didn't leave room for anything else.

Janiyah grinned when she saw the youngest brother, Aaron, on one of the couches. They'd talked a few times during the week while she helped him with the final touches for a business proposal he needed, but she hadn't seen him in over a month. His fingers furiously went across the keyboard of his laptop as he spoke on his cell phone. He ran a hand through the short twists on his head and frowned.

He looked up and smiled. "Hey, Janiyah." The voice on the other end of his cell picked up. "Good, then try that route. We can't mess up our first haul with this provider."

For Aaron to be that agitated he had to be talking to one of his drivers. He'd dropped out of college and started driving big rigs. Which would have been crazy if he hadn't turned that need to roam into his own trucking business.

Well, the gang's all here. The reformed, the martyr, the roamer, and her: the baby. At least her brothers appeared just as unconcerned about the impromptu meeting as she was.

She turned to go upstairs at the same time her dad came down. Roger Henderson's light brown eyes filled with affection. Tall and thin, with reddish brown skin and graying hair, her dad was a handsome sixty something gentleman. She'd never seen him in jeans, and today was no different: slacks, golf shirt, and loafers.

"Hey, Daddy," she said, giving him a quick hug. The comforting fragrance of Old Spice and Dax moisturizer surrounded her.

"Hey, baby girl." She may not be as sweet as one of the Cosby kids, but her dad always sounded like seeing her was the highlight of his day. "Now that you're here we can get started."

"Just give me a few minutes to change," she said, going up the stairs.

"You're already ten minutes late." The familiar bafflement entered his voice. "I have something important to talk to you about."

"Okay, just a second, I promise. Go ahead and start with the guys and fill me in later." She reached the top of the stairs and rushed down the hall to her old room while humming the lyrics from the song.

She tossed the dress on the bed, still covered in the pink and green comforter she'd had as a teenager, and crossed the room to the adjoining bathroom. There was a knock on the bedroom door soon after she took her clothes off in the bathroom.

"Janiyah, hurry up, your father is waiting," her mom's voice called.

"I'll only be a minute," she called from the bathroom.

"I don't understand you kids. Your dad calls a family meeting and none of you are showing any type of interest."

With a sigh, Janiyah hurried to get dressed. She opened the door and met her mom's frustrated gaze. "I've just got to put on makeup."

Loretta Henderson looked regal in a deep purple wrap shirt and black slacks. The frown on Janiyah's mom's heart-shaped face didn't take away from her poise and beauty. The complete opposite of Janiyah, Loretta was rarely ruffled, arranged tasteful dinner parties, and remembered to send a thank you card to the mail man at Christmas.

Her mom's expression became pensive. "Do you have another date?"

"No, I'm meeting Liz for a party."

Her mom didn't relax. "Well, that's not much better."

"You see, most mothers want their daughters to date." She came out of the bathroom and grabbed her makeup bag off the bed.

"I would if I thought you were doing it seriously and not for fun."

"I'm not dating for fun. There's nothing wrong with going to dinner or a movie with an interesting guy when he asks," Janiyah said, though she'd repeated this to her mom a hundred times. "Besides, casual dating does not mean casual sex."

"Oh, Janiyah, please," Loretta said, waving her hands as if to shoo the words away.

"Well, it's true. You'll be happy to know most guys don't make it past one date."

"Maybe they would, if you dated some really nice guys," Loretta said. "Like that music teacher. I liked him, but all of a sudden he was out of the picture."

"Out of the picture because he thought I was only good for one thing." *You're a joke, Janiyah.* The words he'd uttered right before they broke up played in her mind. She pushed them aside.

Loretta grunted and scowled. "To hell with him then."

Janiyah grinned and kissed her mother's cheek. Loretta didn't play when it came to someone disrespecting her kids. "My words exactly."

"Enough of this," Loretta said, effectively changing the conversation away from Janiyah's dating life. "I'd better see you heading down those stairs in five minutes."

Janiyah hurried back into the bathroom. "I'll be there in four. Promise."

Her mom's "What am I going to do with you?" came through the door.

"Love me," she called back.

Fifteen minutes later, she'd put on makeup, teased the riot of curls she'd forced her shoulder length hair into, and donned her dress. When she came downstairs, her dad was pacing the length of the family room. Kareem still sketched, David was checking his watch, and Aaron tapped his finger on his cell phone.

"Ready to grace us with your presence?" her mom said with a raised eyebrow.

Janiyah smiled and walked over to lean against the edge of the couch Aaron sat on. "I told you to get started."

"What are you dressed up for?" Aaron asked.

"The young professionals mixer."

"And you're wearing a red dress?" She couldn't tell if there was admiration or disbelief in his voice. She decided to go with admiration.

Janiyah straightened and brushed the edges of her outfit. The off shoulder cotton dress fit her upper body like a glove and flared out into a mini skirt. The instant she'd seen it at a consignment store the week before she knew she had to buy it.

"Red is bold," she said.

"And bright," David said from across the room.

Her dad held up his hands. "That's enough. I didn't call you all here to waste time talking about Janiyah's dress."

"Do you like my dress, Daddy?"

"You shouldn't wear red to a professional event," he said.

Not surprising. Roger was old school through and through. To him, work meant getting up every day and going to an actual location. Which meant he thought Janiyah's job as a virtual assistant was a real as Super Mario's Mushroom Kingdom.

Janiyah's phone buzzed. It was a text from Liz. *I'm almost there, how far are you?* She cringed and glanced at her dad. "Can you fill me in on the details of this meeting later? I really gotta go."

David stood. "I've got someone waiting on me, too."

Aaron checked his phone. "And I really need to check on Joe to make sure he's back on track."

"And I need to get back and close up the shop," Kareem said, referring to his barber shop.

They each made moves to escape before the lecture began. Any guilt she would have felt about skirting out early was kept at bay by her brothers' attempts to leave as well.

"I'm selling Henderson Automotive," Roger said over the sound of his kids' escape attempt.

Janiyah swung around. Aaron plopped back into his chair. David looked as if he'd been slapped. Her mind swirled with dozens of questions, but the main one was why would he even say something like that? Her dad had started Henderson Automotive in the seventies. Through hard work and dedication, he'd turned a struggling used car dealership into a successful franchise with five locations. He always said the business was like one of his kids. Now suddenly he wanted to sell it. It made no sense.

Though she'd never aspired to take an active role in the business, not wanting to work there didn't mean she didn't want it in the family.

"What are you talking about? I run the business," David said in a tight voice.

"Not for much longer," Roger replied.

"Why would you sell it?" Aaron blurted out when David looked ready to argue. "You've preached to us for years about the importance of the legacy you built. Now you're ready to let it go?"

Roger crossed his arms; he suddenly looked as if he had the weight of the world on his shoulders. "I started Henderson Automotive with the hope that one of you would take over, but none of you are interested in that."

David stepped forward. "I've busted my butt for years to help out."

"No, you've sacrificed yourself," Roger said slowly, as if he regretted saying the words. "You don't really want to be there,"

"Who are you selling to?" Kareem asked. Surprising, since he was the one most adamant about not being involved with the dealerships.

"I've got interest from a few other automotive groups. It's time to settle things. Make sure my hard work isn't wasted."

"And you don't trust us to do it?" David asked, not bothering to mask his scorn.

Janiyah felt the tension in the room rise with each word. She didn't know what to say to make things any easier. She agreed David wasn't thrilled when he started working there, but he was as proud of it as she and the rest of her brothers. How could their dad just toss aside their family legacy to some strange company?

Roger looked at each one of them. "Honestly, I don't. Kareem doesn't want anything to do with it, Aaron has his own business, you never wanted to run it, and Janiyah can't. You all have your interests that I can help secure if I sell. It'll put you three in a position to look after your mother and sister when I'm gone."

Janiyah froze. *Hold up, did he just say Janiyah can't?* "What's that supposed to mean?" she asked. "Why can't I run the business?" True, she'd never wanted to. But it didn't mean she couldn't.

"Baby girl, I love you to death, but you're not cut out for it; you don't really work," her dad said.

"I do work," she said slowly. "I'm a virtual assistant."

"That's not a real job." He said it as if it were some universal truth. Like 'the sky is blue' or 'it snows in winter'.

"It is a real job. I make money."

"And I supplement your income. Who's going to do that if I'm gone? You're not trying to find a husband."

Holy crap, now he was throwing in the husband card. This meeting had gone from inconvenience to pure B.S. in no time. "Number one," she held up a finger, "you supplement my income because I let you. Number two," she held up another finger, "what does my marital state have to do with any of this?"

"I admire the fact that you've tried to start your own business. I'll even admit that you might make enough money doing your online stuff, but let's face it, Janiyah, you're not ready to have a real job."

She threw out her hands. "Where in the world is this coming from? Just because I don't want to be another corporate America clone doesn't mean I couldn't make it there."

Loretta stood and placed her hand on Roger's shoulder. "Let's settle down. We didn't bring you all over here to start a fight."

"No, you called us over here to insult my intelligence," Janiyah said. Her heart pumped high octane indignation through her system. The spark of one more insult was likely to make her explode.

Aaron groaned. "No one's insulting your intelligence, Janiyah. Dad's just making a point."

She swung around to face her brother, the one she'd thought understood her better than anyone. The pain of his words hurt worse than her dad's. "I don't see you sitting at a desk every day, Aaron, but I'd bet he'd trust you to run Henderson Automotive," she shot back.

David stepped forward. "I run Henderson Automotive."

"Enough!" Roger said loud enough to cut off the potential sibling argument. "The point of this meeting is to settle things. I won't be here always. I want to make sure you're all taken care of."

"You can't sell the business, Pops," David said.

Roger put his hands on his hips and spread his legs in a defensive stance. "The last time I checked, I don't need to get my kids' permission. My job is to protect and provide for my family.

This is the best way to do that. I want to make sure your future plans are secure so that you can look out for your mother and sister."

Janiyah clenched her fists. "So, not only am I incapable of," she made finger quotations, "working for real, but I'll need my brothers to look out for me."

Loretta sighed and rubbed her temple. "Janiyah, don't be so dramatic."

Her phone chimed again. *Where are you?* Liz texted.

She looked at her parents. The indignation in her system grew hotter with each passing second. Out of all of their kids *she* was the one they said couldn't handle running the business? Forget that Kareem went to jail, David lived in a world of regret, and Aaron couldn't stay in one place for more than a week. *She* was the one who couldn't handle it. As if sitting at a desk would really prove that she was more responsible?

If she stayed there a minute longer she would end up saying something she would regret. "Screw this," she said, turning her back on her family.

"Where are you going?" her mom asked.

She spun around. "I don't need to stay, seeing as how Daddy and my brothers are going to plan out the rest of my life."

Her sarcasm wasn't met with any arguments. What the hell was up with that? Then it hit her. She'd indulged in being the baby girl of the family for far too long. Okay, she was often late. And, yes, she did accept the money her dad gave her, but he always insisted on helping her out. She'd taken it because of that, not because she couldn't survive without it. She wouldn't have taken it if she'd realized he gave it to her because he thought she wasn't able to support herself. Did they all really think she was so useless?

She looked at her dad and brothers, and got her answer. She was the little girl they needed to coddle, not a grown woman they could trust to run the family business.

You're a joke, Janiyah, the asshole's voice taunted.

Did her family view her as a joke as well?

She shook the thoughts from her head. No. She would not go there.

But the words swirled around her brain. Tears burned the back of her eyes. Yeah, breaking down and crying would really make them respect her.

Her cell rang. It had to be Liz.

"I'm out of here," she said.

On her way to the car her ex-boyfriend's condescending words replayed in her brain. *You're a joke.* Three words that left her doubting herself. Something she hadn't done since she was a teenager and she damn sure wasn't ready to start doing again. That ended tonight. She was not a joke.

She went back to singing about sex and paradise in an effort to block them out. Her life was perfect. No life-sucking nine to five job, no demanding husband, no kids to chauffeur to soccer and ballet practice. She took care of herself just fine and would continue to do so. The pitiful Janiyah looks her family threw her way flashed through her mind. To hell with that. She wasn't wallowing in self-doubt anymore. She pushed her discomfort aside and sang louder.

CHAPTER 2

Panty hose, blazers, and ties in varying shades of navy, beige, and black as far as the eye could see, along with a band playing '90s pop music, was the normal welcome to the young professionals mixer. The only thing that changed was the monthly location. This time it was in a trendy bar she'd frequented on late nights and weekends when the young and carefree crowd took over. All of the trendy artwork and eclectic signs on the walls seemed out of place with so many suits in the building. Someone really should shake this party up a bit. That someone would probably be her.

Liz waited for her at the door. Her friend, who worked at a brokerage firm, blended in perfectly in a grey pantsuit. Her red hair was twisted in a sleek knot at the back of her head and she wore stylish, but sensible, black heels. Janiyah and Liz were complete opposites. Thrown together in a dorm room in college, somehow they'd hit it off instead of killing each other. She'd dragged Liz out to parties and forced her to have a life, while Liz ensured Janiyah studied for her exams and made it to class on time. The only thing that hinted at Liz's willingness to cut loose with Janiyah were the purple and pink framed glasses she wore.

"I'm here!" Janiyah said, slipping her arm through Liz's.

"Finally," Liz said with a smile. "I thought you bailed on me."

"No, this stuffy party can be kind of fun." Several people shuffled past them to sign their names onto sticky nametags and join the rest of the crowd in the bar.

"Only when you're here. You always find a way to liven things up."

Janiyah tilted her head to the side and patted her hair. "Well, that's me, life of the party, dahling," she said in an exaggerated haughty voice.

Liz laughed. "That you are, but you still owe me," Liz said, tugging Janiyah where their arms were connected to the registration table. "Leaving me waiting for twenty minutes is adding to your debt."

"Not my fault. Daddy called a family meeting."

"Oh yeah, and what's the emergency?"

Janiyah fought hard not to roll her eyes. "I don't have a real job. My brothers will have to take care of me until I find a husband." She didn't mention his threat to sell the business. Regardless of what her dad said, she couldn't imagine him actually going through with it.

Liz laughed and tightened her hold on Janiyah's arm in a modified version of a hug. "I love your dad, but he's as old fashioned as they come. What did you say?"

"I stormed out."

"Brilliant. That's exactly how to prove to your family you're a functioning adult."

"Shut up, Liz."

Liz only smiled and filled out a nametag. With a sigh, Janiyah scribbled her name on a tag and pasted it onto her chest. Maybe storming out wasn't the best way to convince her family she was more than the baby of the family. She just got so frustrated when they did that. From the moment she'd graduated from college her parents expected her to either become some focused career woman or marry a guy that would pamper her the way they had. Of course there was no outright pressure for her to do either; it was just insinuated in conversations and offhand comments. In their minds, women found husbands or jobs in college, and Janiyah had found neither.

Someone tapped her on the shoulder. She turned and came face to face with a broad chest. She leaned her head back and met a pair of dark eyes. The guy had to be at least six feet tall, dark skinned, with a Colgate Total smile. She'd never seen him here before.

"Excuse me," he said in a very sexy voice.

It was automatic. She gave him her best flirtatious grin. "No problem at all." She stepped out of the way so Mr. Tall, Dark, and Handsome could get to the registration table. He gave her body a quick once over, taking his time admiring her legs before raising an appreciative brow.

Yeah, her dress would make her a bull's-eye in the middle of the after work crowd. Exactly what she needed to get her proverbial groove back after the ego bruising she'd suffered.

After giving Mr. T.D.H. just as thorough a look, she turned to Liz and followed her further into the bar. If he were interested, it wasn't as if wouldn't be able to spot her.

"So let's see what we can get into." Janiyah glanced around. The bar served a variety of beers and had a small kitchen that made appetizers. Several wooden tables with stools filled the space. A back door opened up to a deck with more seating and a second bar. Pictures of locals who'd sampled every beer they served aligned the walls.

Several people greeted her and Liz as they walked through the crowd. Liz tugged on her arm. "There's Diane and Marlena. Let's go say hi."

"Do I know Diane and Marlena?"

"I think you met them once. Diane works in the mayor's office and puts these things together. Marlena works for the municipal association. They know everything happening in the city."

Janiyah vaguely remembered the two women. They were dressed in tailored business suits and nursed glasses of white wine. Both had impeccably stylish and über-conservative hair, nails, and makeup. They were the kind of women who found jobs and husbands in college. Probably weren't troubled by fathers believing they pretended to work.

Or ex-boyfriends who said they were a joke. She shook her head. Enough of that.

They went through introductions, before the women dived into conversations about city politics—a subject Janiyah had no interest in, so she tuned out and looked around the room for a distraction. She caught the eye of Mr. T.D.H., who smiled and raised his glass. Distraction found. Mr. T.D.H. with his suit and tie wasn't her normal type—she usually didn't fit well with the conservative kind—but he did get bonus points for looks, and she hadn't fared too well with the artsy music type before.

"What do you think, Janiyah?"

Janiyah turned away from her distraction to look back at her companions. Crap, she had no clue what they were talking about.

"This party could use a makeover. Have you ever considered doing themes? You know, Mardi Gras, casino night, something like that?"

Silence. And confused stares.

Liz recovered first with a laugh. "We were talking about the money the city spent on that new building."

With a shrug she said, "I really don't follow that type of stuff."

Diane shook her head. "You really should pay attention. It is your tax money at work." She said each word slowly as if it would somehow mean more.

"Got it. Pay attention to what politicians are doing with my tax money."

Liz chuckled. Diane and Marlena exchanged a glance. Janiyah wished she'd ordered a drink before this conversation. *You're a joke, Janiyah.*

"So what do you do, Janiyah?" There were all kinds of judgment in Marlena's question.

She squared her shoulders and lifted her chin. "I'm a virtual assistant."

They actually winced. She would laugh if it weren't so infuriating.

"So, how does that work exactly?"

Liz placed a hand on Janiyah's shoulder. "She's great at getting people organized. And you should see the presentations she puts together. I think she even helps a few authors out with blog posts and giveaways."

Another judgmental glance between Diane and Marlena. Liz's support sounded more like a weak justification.

Crap, what was wrong with her? At this rate she might start questioning her abilities, too.

"It keeps me busy. I have a range of clients from corporate CEOs to artists who need extra help with planning events, putting together proposals, or researching items. I brought up the idea of the theme for this mixer because I recently helped one my clients increase the attendance to his organization's quarterly conference by incorporating a fun, interactive theme." She gave Diane a smile. "Think about it."

"Maybe I will." But her tone of voice said, *Not in this lifetime.*

Janiyah didn't really want to help with this mixer, but it was nice to put Misses Tight and Tighter in their place.

"So, have you seen the latest top forty under forty? Number one is no surprise," Diane said, changing the subject.

Marlena waved her hand. "Yes! It's amazing what he's accomplished in such a short time. Once he snagged Nebulas Pharmaceuticals, I had to vote for him." She leaned in. "You know he recently broke up with Desiree."

Janiyah's ears perked up. Desiree? That name sounded familiar.

"He's here tonight," Diana said. "I just might buy him a congratulatory drink."

"Hold off and let us single gals buy him a drink," Marlena said.

Liz grinned at Janiyah. "I think he'd like it if Janiyah did."

Janiyah perked up. Could Mr. T.D.H. be the man they were discussing? Liz had probably noticed their not-so-subtle eye flirtation. He was new here, to Janiyah at least, and had the young and successful top forty under forty look going on.

Marlena bounced on her toes. "Oh, there he is. And he's coming this way."

Janiyah turned in the direction Marlena indicated, but her guy was nowhere to be seen. Instead, she made eye contact with a pair of light brown eyes that sent a familiar jolt through her system. It was the jittery feeling she got—and tried to ignore—whenever it came to Fredrick Percival Jenkins, aka

Freddy. He was her brother Aaron's best friend, and he'd spent so much time in her house as a kid he was like a brother.

He'd always been there. Hanging around playing video games with Aaron. Helping her with her math homework whenever she got stumped. Helping her go through college applications before graduation. Handing back her heart, crushed and broken in his hands, when at seventeen, she'd tried to give it—and her virginity—to him.

She would forever be embarrassed for throwing herself at Freddy back then. But thankfully, they'd made an unspoken agreement to never bring it up. Now they shared a close, but strictly platonic, friendship. They lived across the hall from each other. He teased her about the men she dated or her choice of colorful outfits, and she gave him grief about his exciting life of PBS documentaries and button up shirts.

She turned back to Liz. "You all were talking about Freddy?"

Liz sighed. "Don't you know about his recent success?" Liz must have read the WTF look on her face. "You live right across the hall from him, but know nothing about what he does all day."

Janiyah shrugged; it didn't push away the discomfort that she'd somehow done wrong for not taking more of an interest in Freddy's job. He was an accountant, for goodness' sake. How interesting can it be looking at numbers all day?

Marlena grinned. "He's smart, successful, and fine as hell. In other words, Columbia's most sought after bachelor."

Janiyah looked at Freddy then back at the woman. "Freddy?"

Then it hit her: Desiree was that woman Freddy broke up with a few months ago.

Freddy strolled over. "Hello, Janiyah, bright as usual." His toffee colored gaze slowly roamed over her.

There went that damn feeling she tried to ignore when he looked at her like that, a stomach flutter followed by a slight clench. No matter how much her brain understood, her body sometimes forgot that she and Freddy were incompatible with a capital I. Freddy was as straight laced as they come, and even she would snort if someone used those words to describe herself. A complete turn off for a guy like him.

She tried not to care; he wasn't really her type. Granted, he was good looking. If she were into conservatively dressed, light skinned guys, with sophisticated square framed glasses. He was five foot ten, taller than her, but not exactly towering. He made up for his lack of height with muscles. And, boy, did Freddy have nice muscles. He lifted weights routinely, the most exciting thing she thought he did. He also had a dimple in one cheek going for him. It only made rare appearances if she could coax a full blown smile out of him, and the canine tooth on his left side was crooked in a cute kinda way.

She gave him her brightest smile and bumped his shoulder with hers. "You love my dress, admit it."

"You look like a stop sign," he said in his usual voice that was part lecture and part teasing. In other words, the same tone her brothers used.

"And like that sign, I stop traffic."

The corner of his mouth twitched. Dimple appearance a negative. "That you do." He looked to Liz. "How are you, Liz?"

"I'm great, Fredrick, and yourself?"

"Never better."

Diana quickly picked her jaw up, which had nearly hit the floor when Freddy came over to tease Janiyah, and jumped in.

"Never better I'm sure. We were just discussing your deal with Nebulas Pharmaceuticals. Congratulations."

"Thanks, Diana. I'm very excited about the opportunity."

Janiyah frowned. He already knew Diana. Though that shouldn't be surprising. Freddy frequently attended these types of stuffed shirt events.

"So what are your plans now?" Marlena asked.

Freddy shifted beside her and put a hand in his pocket. "I'm expanding my staff. I'm wrapping up the last few interviews for a new accountant, then I'll be ready to look for a new administrative assistant. My current assistant is doing the job of two."

The way the two women pushed their shoulders back so that their breasts were thrust forward was laughable. It couldn't be more obvious that they were trying to catch his attention. Freddy could do better than both of them.

"I'll keep my ear to the ground," Liz said. "If I know of someone good I'll send them your way."

"Thanks. I'm hoping to start interviewing in a week or so."

Janiyah bumped shoulders with him again. "You can always hire me."

Diana and Marlena both laughed. Janiyah cut her eyes at them. The comment was said in jest, but that didn't mean they had to laugh. She looked back at Freddy to find enough of a smile to elicit a slight dimple appearance.

"Sure, Janiyah," he said as if placating a child. "I see someone I need to speak with. Liz, Diana, Marlena it was good to see you." He looked at Janiyah. "Make sure you don't break too many hearts here tonight." He patted her shoulder, and then walked away.

No he didn't just act as if her working for him was silly! Freddy knew she was a good virtual assistant. He had no reason to just brush off her suggestion. Even if she wasn't serious.

Diana and Marlena gushed about how great he looked as soon as he left. Liz must have noticed the funky look on her face, because she excused them and led Janiyah to the bar.

"Why's your face all screwed up?" Liz asked after they ordered drinks.

"Did you see how Freddy just brushed off my suggestion?"

Liz's hand froze halfway to the peanut bowl. "You were serious?"

"No, but that didn't mean he had to brush it off."

"Come on, Janiyah, we both know you couldn't work for Fredrick."

"Oh really? Why?" She turned in her chair and propped a hand on her hip.

Liz grabbed a handful of peanuts and laughed. "Okay ... number one, you and he are constantly at each other's throats."

"Friendly banter, that's all."

"And Fredrick is too structured. You'd drive him crazy in two days."

"I'm structured. I am responsible." Man, she sounded like a teenager protesting that she could stay home alone for the weekend.

"In your way, you are. You're just not ... office material." Liz cracked a few of the peanuts. "I love you to pieces, Janiyah, but let's be real. You're not the nine to five, navy pant suit type."

"Then why do you invite me here?"

"Because, you're my best friend and you make everything fun," Liz said, reaching over to place her arm around Janiyah's shoulder and giving her a quick squeeze.

She really wasn't in the mood to make tonight fun.

There came another tap on her shoulder. She glanced over her shoulder to find Mr. T.D.H. standing behind her, an inviting smile on his handsome face.

"I hope you don't mind, but—"

She spun her barstool around, cocked her head to the side, and gave him her practiced, *yes I'm interested* smile. It was what she was here for anyway. Break the funk that she'd had ever since the asshole ex called her a joke. "Janiyah Henderson. Five, five, five, six, seven, six, five."

His eyes widened, and his smile softened at the edges giving him a seductive air. "Gerald Westlock, and I'll remember that."

"I hope you do." She gave him as thorough a once-over as he'd given her before turning back to the bar. She'd guessed correctly that he'd seek her out. She gave it three days until he called.

"That was a record," Liz said after he walked away.

"He took longer than I expected," she said with a wave of her hand.

Liz laughed and popped peanuts in her mouth. Janiyah caught Freddy's gaze from across the bar. She could almost hear the disapproval running through his head. She wouldn't be surprised if he called Aaron to tattle on her. So what if part of her reason for coming tonight was to find someone to snap her out of the dry spell she'd willingly entered after her last breakup. There was nothing wrong with that. But Freddy's stare made her face burn as if she'd done something wrong.

He didn't have to look so upset. With just a word, he could end her single girl status. The thought brought her up short. Where in the world did that come from? Freddy was not interested in her, and thoughts like that were nothing but a big ole shoe box of trouble.

The bartender handed Freddy a glass with cola in it. She knew without asking that there was no alcohol in it. Freddy didn't drink. He raised the glass her way when Marlena came up behind him and placed her hand on his shoulder. Janiyah ignored the clench in her stomach and turned to Liz.

"Let's find something to get into."

CHAPTER 3

A familiar knock on the door—one, two and, three, four, one two—interrupted Fredrick's plans to relax after the mixer with a new book. He hated the networking events. He'd rather spend his time away from the office not thinking about work. And especially not listening to idle chit chat disguised as work in an effort to snatch up a new date. They served their purpose though. It was at a mixer he'd first learned that Nebulas Pharmaceuticals was on the lookout for an accounting firm to handle their books, leading to him landing the biggest client of his two-year-old accounting firm. And tonight he'd met the head of a local restaurant chain looking for someone to handle the audits of their books and possible payroll. He didn't need it, but he wanted the restaurant's business. His dream of laying the foundation for a stable future was finally in sight, something he'd vowed at the age of thirteen when he started screening calls from collection agencies for his dad.

The knock came again, followed by "Come on, Freddy, I know you're in there." With a sigh, he put his book face down on the coffee table and got up from the couch. No surprise Janiyah had decided to pay him a visit after the mixer. Most nights she stopped by his apartment for something, mostly food, before going home for the night. He opened the door and gave her a smirk. "Is there no one else you can bother?"

Despite his words, she smiled. Like she always did whenever he hinted around that she should find another person to hang around. He'd bet money that if she didn't find some way to get under his skin during the day she considered it a failure.

She cocked her head to the side, a teasing glint in her brown eyes. "You know you love my visits."

The corner of his mouth lifted. "Yes, the younger sister I always wanted who comes over to watch my television, eat my food, and pester me." He turned and walked into the apartment.

"Ha, ha."

Janiyah popping in on him had been a given from the moment he'd moved in across the hall from her. When Janiyah returned to Columbia after college, she chose to live forty-five minutes away from her family. Not far really, but enough to make her dad worry about her being too far away for anyone to help if she needed it.

When the lease to his old apartment was up, his plans were to move to this side of town. He had never planned to move so close, but she'd not so casually mentioned in front of her father that the apartment across from her was available, and since Freddy was looking for a new place, he might as well move there. The solution had brought immediate relief to her dad, whom Fredrick admired almost more than his own father. So here he was, unofficial brother/watcher of Janiyah Henderson.

Too bad he was very aware that Janiyah wasn't his sister.

They went into the living room where he sat on the couch. She plopped down beside him. The too short skirt of her red dress billowed out then settled high on her thighs. She'd kicked off her shoes somewhere and tucked her legs beneath her on the couch. She smelled like vanilla, reminding him of cake and making his mouth water way more than it should.

"I can't believe you wore that tonight."

"What's wrong with my dress?"

Not a damn thing. No man in his right mind would be able to concentrate on anything but seeing her out of that dress. Which was exactly why she shouldn't have worn it to a professional event.

"It was a business mixer."

She blew air between her lips and waved a hand. "Bullcrap! Call it what you want; that was a meat market for the nine to five crew. I was hit on at least six times."

"Wasn't that the intent of the dress?"

"No." She grinned when he raised a brow. "Okay, yes. But I'll try to wear something less eye catching next time."

"So how many numbers did you come home with?"

"None. My mood was off." Her pensive expression said there was more behind that story. Then she smiled and waved a hand. "But I did give one guy my number."

He remembered the tall, dark skinned guy she'd made eye contact with all night. "I bet I can guess who."

She sighed all girlie like and leaned heavily into the couch. He'd seen that look before. She'd set her sights on that college professor. He felt slightly sorry for the guy. Janiyah made it easy for men to fall in love with her. She loved new things and a new boyfriend was like a new toy. Fun, shiny, and exciting, until the newness wore off. As soon as the poor schmuck fell in love she lost interest, usually leaving the guy scratching his head and wondering what he did to lose her so quickly.

He knew from experience, though he'd never really had her. The summer before she was to go to college she'd kissed him, and tempted him far more than he cared to admit to take it further. Common sense kicked in and he'd pushed her away. But it didn't stop him from wondering about maybe, after she'd experienced college and grew up a bit, asking her on a date. That plan was quickly shot to hell when a few weeks later he and her brother Aaron found her wrapped up in the arms of some wannabe thug.

"His name is Gerald Westlock," she said, oblivious to his trip down memory lane. "Doesn't that sound so dignified? Tall, dark, handsome, and since he was at that thing tonight, gainfully employed. You guys were talking. What do you know about him?"

"Not much. He's a new professor at the university. I met him briefly at the last networking mixer. I'm surprised you're so interested. Are you growing tired of starving artists, struggling musicians, and wannabe businessmen?"

"Don't hate because I date interesting people. You, on the other hand, must meet your women at stuffy women dot com."

"Stuffy?"

"Yes, stuffy. Remember that ... what, dental hygienist you dated a few months ago?"

He'd noticed she never would call his ex-girlfriend by her name. Janiyah hadn't liked her, said he needed someone less stiff. He'd brushed it off, until he'd caught Desiree alphabetizing his canned goods. But he wasn't going to give Janiyah the satisfaction of knowing her observation had led him to break things off. "Desiree wasn't stuffy."

"I wanted to go to sleep after two minutes of listening to you two talk about some rebellion overseas."

"You'd do better to pay more attention to those rebellions. Libya's the country and the citizens were—"

She held up both hands. "Not now."

"Fine. But it's not as if I enjoyed listening to you and that music teacher talk about what Dwayne Wade wore during the NBA All-Star Weekend."

Her chin lifted. "Remember, we're not talking about him anymore."

Anger flared inside, which he swiftly tamped down. He hadn't liked that guy from the start, and didn't know what he'd said or done to hurt Janiyah. Her assurance that it wasn't physical was the only thing that kept him from going down to that music studio and beating the crap out of him until he found out.

"Fine, I won't mention him. But I did want to fall asleep while listening to you two."

She reached over to tug the collar of his shirt. Her small fingers brushed the underside of his chin and caused an unwelcome tightening in his groin. He pushed her hand away.

"You'd do better to know more about men's fashion," she said. "D-Wade is fly."

"I dress conservatively. It never goes out of style."

She waved her hand. "Look, I didn't come here to talk about the sticks in the mud you date—FYI, stay away from Marlena."

He cocked a brow. "What's wrong with Marlena?"

"I don't trust her."

"Why not?"

"She's just not right for you. A gold digger." She pointed and tried to look stern. "Stay away."

It usually worked his nerves when she tried to give him love advice like she did her brothers. In this case he agreed with her, but wouldn't let her know. She already thought she had to put her seal of approval on the women he dated in the same way she did her brothers.

"Stay away from Gerald Westlock," he said, knowing she didn't like getting relationship advice from him any more than he liked getting it from her.

Janiyah grinned; she was always pretty, but beautiful when she smiled. "A stalemate then."

He shook his head. "Can we get to the point of your visit, Janiyah?"

"Fine. Why did you brush it off when I mentioned hiring me as your assistant?"

Fredrick picked up his book. "Because it's not happening."

She scooted closer and grabbed his arm then squeezed his bicep. He tried to ignore the satisfaction the movement caused. He accepted that most women viewed him as the quintessential good guy. Always delegated to the friend zone. Hell, that's where he was firmly stuck with Janiyah. And exactly where he needed to remain. On the rare occasions he thought about having more, he only had to remember her tendency to change boyfriends like shoes and get over it. But he did enjoy the rare moments when Janiyah noticed there was something beneath his sweater vests and oxford shirts.

"Oh, come on, Freddy! Give me one good reason why you wouldn't hire me."

"Number one, I won't have you skipping around the office in party dresses and calling me *Freddy.*"

"I wouldn't skip in the office. And, again, you like my dresses."

"Forget the dresses. It wouldn't work out."

"Do you think I can't do it? You know I'm a good virtual assistant."

"Virtual assistant and real assistant are two different things. You set up meetings and work on presentations in your Hello Kitty pajamas with infomercials playing in the background. You can't do that in the office."

"I know that. I'd buy work appropriate clothes."

"Is that it? A job in an office means you can buy a new wardrobe?"

She glared. Her nose crinkled and her mocha colored eyes flashed with irritation. "You're not as funny as you think."

"And you're not as cute as you think." He got up and went into the kitchen. The sound of her sucking her teeth followed him.

He tried to imagine Janiyah getting up every morning to go to work. She was an early riser, but he never saw her in anything other than pajamas before noon. He grabbed a carton of vanilla ice cream out of the freezer.

"No, Freddy, no ice cream," Janiyah said, rushing into the kitchen.

She reached for the carton and he held it out of her reach. She glared and jumped for it. "You shouldn't eat sugary snacks after eight."

He held it higher. "You sound like a mother."

She jumped for the carton again. Her body bumped against his. Electricity sizzled over his skin when her breasts brushed against him.

"Okay, that's enough." He took several steps back.

She planted her hands on her hips and pouted. Janiyah was as cute as she thought. Cuter. Smooth cinnamon skin, soft brown eyes swirled with darker hints that reminded him of espresso. A heart shaped mouth that could keep a man up for hours imaging it doing all types of inappropriate things. With perky breasts that often didn't require a bra—something he wished he'd never noticed—and a perfect backside and thighs. She was a sexy, tempting—high maintenance and flighty—ball of fire.

"You don't need the ice cream," she said.

"Don't you know you can't order your boss around?"

Her arms dropped to her sides. "You're not my boss."

"Just pointing out another reason why I wouldn't hire you. You don't listen."

"I listen to you. I would make a good administrative assistant, or associate, or other similar professional title."

"Where is this coming from? I thought you liked the freedom of being a virtual assistant."

Her pretty pout transformed into a frown. "I'm tired of people thinking I can't take care of myself. I'm smart enough to do the nine to five thing like everyone else if I needed to."

The steely determination in her voice surprised him, but not as much as the slight hesitation. Almost as if she were uncomfortable making the declaration.

"I know you're smart, Janiyah."

"Well, today you and a few others made it pretty clear the idea of me working is funny." She slapped her hand on the counter. "I'm tired of being considered a joke."

Her uncertainty was unsettling. She was always the first to dive headfirst into any situation. Janiyah might be carefree and impulsive, but he never doubted her intelligence.

"The only way to change the way people think is to show them something different," he said. "If you want to prove that you're ready for a real," she cut her eyes at him, "sorry, *regular* job, then prove it."

She crossed her arms over her chest and pursed her lips as she thought about what he said. "I need to let that idea roam around my brain for a while. Time to go home, take off this dress, and get in the tub with the newest issue of *OK! Magazine*."

"How is that going to help?"

She grinned. "It's where I do my best thinking. Which reminds me, I need to clean the tub. You got any bathroom cleaner?"

And just like that, she was off to another topic. As exasperating as it was, he could never view her as predictable.

He took a big bite of vanilla ice cream and enjoyed the creamy goodness more than he should. "In its usual place."

She breezed out of the kitchen and down the hall. A few minutes later, she returned with the bathroom cleaner he kept under his sink. She walked over and poked him in the side. "Put the ice cream down or you'll gain twenty pounds."

Instead of answering he put another huge spoonful in his mouth. She rolled her eyes and headed for the door. "Whatever, Freddy. You won't stay sexy sitting up eating ice cream every night."

The door shut behind her. He stood there, breathing in her vanilla perfume, and staring in the direction she'd gone for several seconds. "Damn, Janiyah," he mumbled before throwing the ice cream in the trash.

CHAPTER 4

It took five hits of the snooze button before Janiyah could drag herself out of bed. Getting up early wasn't new, but the night before she'd stayed up way too late in order to finish a project for a client. It was all Freddy's fault. She'd lounged in the tub for over an hour thinking about what he'd said. She did need to prove that she wasn't a joke, or a tragically single woman. She'd only been out of college three years.

She cringed. Three years. When did that happen?

It seemed like she'd just graduated and still had the freedom to explore her interests and figure out what the hell she was supposed to do with her life. Everyone had expected her to have a plan the second the degree hit her hand. For the first six months, everyone was okay when she said she was taking time to figure out her next steps. A year later the questions came with a tinge of *what's the hold up*. Eighteen months after that, *what's the hold up* turned into *she must not want to work*. Until finally she was considered hopeless, regardless of the fact that she made enough money to cover the majority of her expenses from her virtual assisting clients.

Honestly, she didn't know what she wanted to do with her life. She liked helping people, and working on a variety of projects. She was pretty sure she didn't want to become one of those people chained to a desk, punching a time clock, and so accustomed to the mundane that being stuck in a routine was expected.

But as much as the idea scared her, if she wanted to prove that she was more than the pampered baby girl, she would have to come up with a plan, a serious plan, for her future.

She shuffled from the bedroom to the kitchen. Bypassing her pantry, she grabbed a bowl from the cabinet and a spoon from the drawer then left her apartment. She knocked once on Freddy's door before opening it and walking in. He always unlocked it for her in the morning. It was either that or have her knock every ten minutes if she needed something.

The living area was empty, but his cologne mingled with the scent of coffee. She hated coffee, but liked his cologne. The comingled scents always energized her in the morning.

"I'm getting cereal," she called.

His muffled voice came from the back, but she couldn't make out what he said. She went into the kitchen and helped herself to a bowl of corn flakes. Taking a banana from the counter, she broke off a few chunks, dumped it in the cereal, then poured milk on it from the fridge.

She picked up the bowl and frowned. Step one for proving herself would be stocking her own pantry with food. Freddy would appreciate it. No matter how often she offered to repay him for groceries he refused, even though her food preferences frequented his grocery list. The man hated bananas. Which was crazy. Who hated bananas, honestly?

Stocking her pantry meant she needed to get a handle on her budget. She rarely overspent her income, but payments from clients were so sporadic she didn't have a clear idea of what came in and out. She'd need to sort that out—along with refusing any more money her dad tried to give her.

Freddy rushed from the back into the living room. Janiyah walked over to lean against the bar separating the kitchen from the living area and watched him run around grabbing his watch, wallet, and other accessories. His muscles flexed and tightened beneath his dress shirt with his movements. She didn't need to imagine what he looked like without the shirt. Thanks to her family's pool parties, she'd had plenty of opportunity to silently drool over his washboard stomach, defined chest, and strong shoulders. But if he ever found out she appreciated his body, he'd laugh from here to California. Freddy made it perfectly clear she was the last woman he'd ever be interested in.

She didn't know what she'd do if he ever became interested. Her warm and fuzzy feelings for Freddy were packed up, padlocked, and stored deep in her heart, all in an effort to accept that he only saw her as a friend. Daydreams of more led to impulsive decisions—and the last time she was impulsive with him it hadn't gone too well.

"Someone else sleep late?" she asked.

He snatched his laptop bag from where it was propped against the couch. "Something like that."

"You never sleep late."

"I couldn't sleep." He nailed her with a penetrating stare. "Unwanted dreams."

"Don't look at me like that. I wasn't running around in your head." She slowly slid the other half of the banana into her mouth.

He cleared his throat and turned away. "No ... you weren't running."

Now that was interesting. Heat crept up her face. Could he have possibly dreamed about her? She shook her head. Rein it in, girlfriend. No need for foolish fantasies to take hold. Any dream Freddy had about her would involve exasperation and scolding.

"Can you do me a favor?" she asked.

He bent over to pick his laptop bag off the floor. "Do I have a choice?"

"Not really, so go ahead and agree."

The corner of his mouth lifted, she got a hint of the dimple, and it made her morning.

"Okay, what's the favor?" He walked over to get his keys off the bar in front of her. He smelled nice. Acqua Di Gio cologne. She'd smelled it on other men; it was always better on him.

"I want to develop a portfolio or something. You know, show I can manage money and be responsible."

He froze in the middle of putting the lap top bag strap on his shoulder. "Portfolio?"

"Don't look so surprised. I can't eat your bananas for the rest of my life."

He looked at his watch. Freddy was the only guy she knew who still wore a watch. It was kinda cute. "You don't need me to help with a budget."

She could see the refusal in his eyes. She reached over to straighten his tie, and smiled prettily. "I know, but you're apparently the best accountant in the area. I always want the best."

He gently pushed her hands away, but smiled. Bingo, full dimple appeared. "Fine, we'll create a budget."

"Good. And to show my thanks, I'll buy you dinner tonight."

"I'm working late."

"Then we'll eat late."

Another appearance of the dimple. She was on a roll today. He turned away from the counter. "Lock up after you leave."

"Yes, brother."

He shook his head and hurried out the door. Janiyah got up and went into the kitchen to pour coffee into the silver mug sitting beside the coffee maker. She put in three heaping spoonfuls of sugar and stirred. When Freddy burst back through the door, she was waiting on the other side with the coffee in hand.

"Thank you," he said, grabbing the mug then rushing out.

Janiyah grinned and went back to finish her cereal. When she left a few minutes later, their neighbor Mrs. Driggers poked her head out of her door. Her blue-grey eyes brightened in her wrinkled face when she spotted Janiyah. It wasn't even seven in the morning, but Mrs. Driggers was dressed as if she were going to church in a classic navy and white polka dot dress.

"Oh, good, you've had breakfast," Mrs. Driggers said.

"I did. Do you need help with something?" Sometimes she helped Mrs. Driggers with odds and ends around her apartment.

"Actually, I do."

Janiyah tugged on the corner of her boy shorts. "Give me a second to get dressed and I'll be right over."

"Oh, no need to get dressed up for me. Just come as you are."

Janiyah pointed at her door. "How 'bout I brush my teeth first?"

Mrs. Driggers paused to consider then nodded. "That's a good idea."

Ten minutes later, Janiyah was settling in at the desk in the bedroom Mrs. Driggers had converted into an office.

"So what can I help you with? Are you having trouble with your internet connection again?"

"No." Mrs. Driggers rubbed her hands together. She hurried to the bookshelf next to the door and pulled down a large box. "I need help with my business."

"Business? I didn't know you had a business."

"Something I started a few months ago. I had some success, but I need someone to help me branch out."

"Why would you think of me?"

"Because you're an assistant."

Janiyah scratched the back of her head. "Virtual assistant. I don't work for people I know." It was less pressure and fewer expectations when she worked for people she only knew online. People who knew her personally always expected her to screw up or not take things seriously.

"Well, now you can start by working for me. I really need your help, and I know you can do it, because I went to your website. And before you say no, remember that you're supposed to mind your elders."

Why not help Mrs. Driggers? For her to ask meant she wasn't expecting Janiyah to screw up and that she viewed Janiyah's abilities as useful.

"Okay, so what's this business?"

Mrs. Driggers eyes sparkled with excitement. She held out the box. When Janiyah reached for it, she pulled it back.

"I don't want to shock you."

"I doubt you will."

"We'll see." Mrs. Driggers handed over the box.

With a grin, Janiyah grabbed it and pulled off the lid. Her jaw dropped. She looked at the hesitant smile on Mrs. Driggers's face, then back to the box.

"Not what you expected?"

"Not at all." She'd expected makeup, Tupperware, or even crocheted scarves. What she got was mind blowing coming from her elderly neighbor—the box was filled with sex toys. Slowly, she took out one of several vibrators. The soft, purple shaft curved up to a long, tapered tip. She turned it to the left, right, then upside down.

"That's the g-spot stimulator," Mrs. Driggers said. "I'm selling sex toys through Nancy's Naughty Novelties."

"I've seen the infomercials." Janiyah picked up another one. It was clear, with beads, bumps, and two different appendages. She flipped the switch. The toy vibrated, gyrated, and spun. Her eyes widened. Cool.

"I have a catalogue that customers can order from, and I've held a couple of parties for my seniors group. These are my samples, except for the lingerie. That's in the closet. I've done pretty good, but my team leader thinks I'd do better selling online. They gave me a website, but I don't know how to set it up. I figured you could help me."

Janiyah stopped her head from spinning in tandem with the rotating vibrator. "I'd love to."

Mrs. Driggers placed her hands on Janiyah's shoulders and squeezed. "Good. My slogan is: 'Let Lady Driggers show you how to be a lady in the street and a freak in the bed.'"

Janiyah spun in the chair to face her newly interesting neighbor. "What do you know about that?"

Mrs. Driggers laughed and picked up an anatomically correct red vibrator with what looked like bunny ears curved forward on the top. "Sweetheart, you don't bury a husband after forty years of marriage being a prude."

Janiyah grinned. "You're my new favorite client."

• • •

"Want to meet me for lunch?"

Janiyah turned off Harden Street onto Saluda Street in Columbia's Five Points area. After getting Mrs. Driggers set up that morning, she'd held off on doing work for some of her online clients to spend the rest of the morning cruising through the racks at her favorite consignment shop.

"I can't, I've got to get this project on my boss's desk before two. What have you been up to all day?" Liz's voice came through the speakers of her car via the Bluetooth.

"Playing with dildos."

"Too much information."

"Not playing with them for pleasure. Though it was kind of fun."

"Janiyah!"

"Just kidding. It was for a client. She's selling sex toys and needed help setting up a website."

"I'm going to need more of that story later."

"I'll have a lot more to tell. Too bad you can't meet me. I'm downtown, thought I'd try and meet up with you."

"What are you doing downtown?"

"Consignment shopping."

"Your favorite activity. Hey, I'm thinking of recommending my cousin for the administrative assistant job Fredrick has available. Do you think he'll interview her?"

She didn't immediately answer. Of course Freddy would interview Liz's cousin, someone he'd never met, just because of a recommendation from Liz. He'd known Janiyah his entire life and laughed off her suggestion that he consider her. She shifted in her seat as annoyance bubbled up. He of all people shouldn't have laughed. He'd helped her study for her final exams when she came home her senior year of college. He saw how dedicated she was to finishing projects for her business. If anything, he should have at least hesitated before turning her down.

"Janiyah, are you there?"

"Yeah, I'm here. Sure, he'll interview her. Maybe we'll interview on the same day."

"You're serious, aren't you?"

"Maybe not before, but I am now. I'm going to apply for his job." And just like that she had step three in her process to prove people wrong: get a desk job.

"I really can't imagine you working in Fredrick's office."

Janiyah pulled into a parking spot and jerked up her parking break. "So I can add you to the list of people who think I can't handle traditional responsibility."

"Don't get upset, but yes. And I don't mean that in a bad way. You're great at what you do, but tight routines are not your thing. In college you could organize your notes so well that people paid for copies, but getting you to a class on time was another story. You do things in your own time and in your own way. Forget the crazy looks Diana and Marlena gave you last night. You're great at what you do, and it works for you."

Janiyah sighed and leaned back into her seat. "It's not just that. Everyone looks at me as if I'm incapable of being a grown up. I'm honest enough with myself to know that on the surface it looks as if I don't have much order in my life. I'm not going to change who I am. I'm just going to, I don't know, give myself a bit of a makeover."

"Or drive yourself crazy. Do what you want, but I think you're perfect as you are. Besides, if you work all day, you'll be too tired to help me unwind from my stressful day."

Janiyah cringed, but laughed tightly. "I'm your go-to party friend. You wouldn't want to lose that. Hey look I'm here, so I'll call you later, okay?"

"Wait a second." There was a long pause. "One more thing about Fredrick."

"What about him?"

"I want to make sure you wouldn't care if I hooked him up with my boss, Missy."

Janiyah's hands fell from the steering wheel. Liz's boss was a petite, blonde haired, big-boobed bombshell. Even the starched suits she wore every time Janiyah saw her couldn't hide that. From what Liz told her, Missy had been promoted to head of her department after working for the company for only a year. And she'd done it all through hard work and tenacity. In other words, she was just the type of put-together woman Freddy would go for.

"You do mind, don't you?"

Janiyah shook her head to clear it. "Are you sure? I mean, he hasn't dated anyone seriously ... except that dental hygienist a few months ago."

"Desiree?"

Janiyah frowned. "You remember her name?"

"They were getting serious, until you broke them up."

She lifted her chin. "I did not. I only pointed out some of her less than stellar attributes." Liz's laughter filled her car. "Oh, come on. You know Desiree, or whatever her name was, was a serious buzz kill. She wasn't good for him."

"You scare away every woman he dates."

"I do the same thing with my brothers."

"He's not your brother."

Just because Freddy wasn't her brother didn't mean she couldn't look out for his best interests in the same way she did her older siblings. She wanted him happy. He just hadn't brought anyone around she thought would make him happy.

"Are you sure Missy would be interested?"

"Come on, Janiyah, Fredrick is good looking." Liz said it with a bit too much appreciation for Janiyah's liking.

"Yeah, but ... he's short."

"Five ten isn't short, and it's taller than her."

She frowned. "You know his exact height?"

"I asked."

"He's so ... staid."

"He's an accountant. One that owns his own business, I might add, and just landed a huge client."

"Yeah. I heard last night. What's up with that?"

"This deal with Nebulus is unprecedented for a firm as new as his. As soon as I saw the write up, I gave him a call to congratulate him. Didn't you two talk about it?"

"We did, I just didn't know everyone would go crazy over it."

She scratched the back of her head. Freddy rarely talked to her about his job. The second he started talking numbers her eyes glazed over. Most of the time she didn't mind their sparring matches about how disconnected she was from the real world, but the thought of him having those conversations with Liz—or Missy—made her queasy. It also made her want to shake Freddy for not making her listen to his good news.

"It's a really big deal. Nebulus is worth a lot, and now he's got a piece of that pie."

Money would buy a blonde bombshell. But Freddy would see right through that. "You know what, if you think your boss would consider spending evenings talking numbers with Freddy remotely fun, fine. It's no skin off my back."

"She will. We ran into him in on our lunch break the other day. She's interested."

Janiyah's stomach clenched. "Really?"

"Really. I'll call him after work."

Janiyah straightened from where she was slumped in her seat. "I can bring it up when I see him."

"No need," Liz said in a hurry. "You'd turn him off before they got a chance to go out. I'll handle it."

She sat in the car drumming her hands on the steering wheel for several minutes after hanging up with Liz. Lying to herself wasn't a habit, and she wouldn't start now. She was pissed that Freddy hadn't bothered to let her know his good news, but was willing to gab about it with Liz. It didn't matter that Liz called him, he should have told her. They were friends and went further back than he and Liz ever did.

And where did Liz get off wanting to hook Freddy up with her boss? They might make a cute couple, and sure they could probably talk about numbers until the end of time, but that didn't mean she would be good for Freddy. Freddy needed someone who would make him smile more, put down his books, and enjoy life. The same way she did. She and Freddy made a better couple than Freddy and Missy.

Holy crap, where did that come from?

She snatched up her purse and jumped out of the car. There was no reason to put her name, Freddy's name, and the word 'couple' in the same sentence.

Remembering that didn't get rid of her irritation. She couldn't waste her time thinking she'd have anything more with Freddy than the occasional lapse in good sense that made her jealous whenever he brought a new woman into his life.

CHAPTER 5

"Was there anything you wanted to review before we start our first interview, Mr. Jenkins?"

Fredrick looked away from the window in his office to his administrative assistant, Phyllis. She stood in the door holding a folder that he recognized held several of the résumés they'd received for the newly advertised accountant position.

"I'm sorry, can you repeat that?"

Phyllis smirked, her bright red lips standing out on her honey-toned skin. A tall, broad woman, with no patience for foolishness, Phyllis was the best assistant a man could have. She was the same age as his mother, but that's where the similarities ended. His mother was all about having fun, spending money, and ignoring reality. Phyllis was one of the most practical women he knew. She didn't play and was quick to let someone know that. The only people she seemed to tolerate were him and Janiyah on her occasional visits.

And there he went. Once again letting Janiyah hijack his thoughts.

"I knew something was wrong with you today. You've been distracted all morning. You know we've got four interviews today."

Fredrick rubbed the bridge of his nose. "Nothing is wrong with me." He glanced at the clock. "We've got an hour until the ten o'clock interview. I'm okay with the questions we came up with. Just check with Larry and make sure he's got the conference room set up."

Phyllis sucked her teeth. "I don't need Larry to check on the conference room. I've got it set up and ready. I'll make sure Larry knows what time to be there."

Fredrick shook his head. Two years and Phyllis still thought she could boss around the accountants. It would be annoying if she didn't keep all of them in line. She'd left his old firm to work for him when he walked out and started Jenkins Holdings, so he let her keep her sense of seniority.

"Do that. I'll be there in a few minutes."

"Are you sure you're okay? I can make you another cup of coffee." Her usually severe tone softened.

"I'm good, but thanks."

"Alright, but make sure you bring your game face to the interview. I don't need you not paying attention and hiring some idiot that's going to cause more work instead of help."

And just like that the severe tone returned. After Phyllis left, Fredrick turned to his computer to check emails. After opening one, he swung his chair back around to look out the window. He was tired. His head hurt, his eyes were dry, and his limbs were stiff from tossing and turning all night. He couldn't shake the edginess that came after waking up hot, sweaty, and rock hard thanks to an out-of-nowhere dream about Janiyah. He rubbed his temples and tried to will the images out of his head.

It didn't work. He was assaulted with the fantasy of having her in his arms. Wearing that red dress. Her soft breasts brushing against his chest. Her pouty lips kissing every inch of his body. The blissful sensation of having her tight, slick body surround him as he slid inside.

He slapped his forehead. Stop.

The dream evaporated, but the vision of her leaning against the bar in his kitchen wearing a lavender camisole with no bra, and black shorts with pink lips on them replaced it.

Too many emotions boiled inside whenever his subconscious decided to knee him in the balls and remind him that he was attracted to her. Guilt, for having those types of thoughts for his best friend's sister. He could only imagine how the Henderson men would crucify him if they knew he dreamed of Janiyah. For the most part, Aaron was laid back, but Fredrick never forgot how angry Aaron had been when they'd caught Janiyah kissing that boy years ago. Their friendship would be lost for certain. Embarrassment for harboring those feelings for someone he'd watched out for since they were kids joined the guilt. He was too old to be having wet dreams about a woman. But mostly he felt disappointment for straying from his life plan.

He spun back to his computer and opened the file where he'd actually written up his life plan. He'd first drafted it when he was fourteen. Updated it every year or so as he ticked off achievements. The major points: graduate from high school and college with honors. Done. Land a job with a top accounting firm. Check. Revise last point to read leave his job and start his own firm. Achieved with lots of hard work. He'd even exceeded it by landing a few high profile clients.

The cursor flashed over the next thing on his list: find a good, dependable woman to settle down with. As much as he might fantasize about Janiyah, she wasn't the type of woman he could see himself marrying. She was too unpredictable. Too unsettled. He didn't need that in a potential life partner.

It wasn't as if he could help being attracted to Janiyah. She was beautiful, flirty, and was at his apartment almost as much as hers. She had every man she knew wrapped around her pinky finger, including her brothers and dad. Only a blind man would be able to ignore the fact that Janiyah's smile brightened a room.

But he could control his reaction. He could remember that for all of her positive qualities, the fact remained she had other not so positive qualities. She didn't stick with anything long. Especially relationships. Every man who dated her ended up heartbroken and left behind. Getting involved with her would derail his plans.

His office phone rang and interrupted his thoughts. "Yes, Phyllis."

"Your dad is calling. Do you want me to transfer him through?"

He flinched. His dad didn't call this early unless something was wrong.

"I'll take the call."

"Are you sure? We've got a lot going on today. You need to be focused."

"I'm sure, Phyllis," he snapped.

"You're the boss."

It took long enough for her to remember that. A few seconds later his phone rang again. "Good morning, Dad."

"Hey, Fredrick, how's it going?" Christopher Jenkins's enthusiastic voice came through the phone.

"Going good. I've got a lot of interviews lined up today, so I can't talk long."

"Oh, this will only take a minute."

"Do you need anything?"

"How have things been going with you? How's Janiyah? Your mom ran into her the other week. We were thinking about calling up the Hendersons and getting together for dinner."

His father deflecting the question meant Fredrick was on to something. "That sounds like a good idea. So what do you need?"

"You know, I saw your write up in the Columbia Business Review. I was just telling your mom that I knew you'd turn out alright. You were always a worrier. Worrying about this and that. Remember that time when you were panicked we were about to lose the house?" His dad laughed. "You had your sister crying into her pillow for a week."

Fredrick took off his glasses and pinched the bridge of his nose. "A letter from the mortgage company saying we were three months behind and they were going to kick us out usually means you're about to lose the house."

Christopher laughed again. It was an easy laugh that brushed aside the tension in Fredrick's voice. "You worry too much, son. I told you I would find a way and I did. I always find a way."

Yeah, and lately Fredrick was the one helping them find a way. Since his dad wanted to stall, he tried another tactic to get to the point of this phone conversation. "How's business?"

"Oh, good, good. I finally got a meeting with that client I told you about. See, I know why you asked. You're worrying again. My business is going great, and once I land that account, it'll be even better. I won't even have to call you ... like this anymore."

His dad needed more than one new client to get his insurance firm out of the red. When Fredrick started Jenkins Holdings, his dad quickly offered to let him handle the books for his insurance firm, something Fredrick later realized was a way for Christopher to get free accounting. It wouldn't have bothered Fredrick so much if he didn't also discover just how much his dad was swimming in debt. It was a shock, even after growing up watching his dad throw away money in an effort to keep up appearances and please his mother. If there ever was a fool in love, Christopher Jenkins was him.

"I hope the meeting goes well."

"Why don't you come once we set the date? It'll go a long way to earn their trust if they realize you're my son." Meaning, Fredrick's recent success would go a long way to bolster his dad's reputation.

"I'll see what I can do."

"The meeting is going to be great and I do have a few other clients lined up. In fact, once I land this client, I'm going to buy your mom that set of skis she's been eyeing. Though she may be off skiing before then. Do you know the other day she came home talking about a boat?"

"You don't need a boat."

"Not a yacht or anything, just a small cruiser with a cabin. She went out with a few friends who take their boats down to Edisto. Now she's got it in her head about going deep sea fishing." Christopher chuckled. "That woman loves life."

"Yeah, too much."

"Ah, wait until you fall in love. You'll do whatever it takes to make your wife happy, too."

A prospect that scared the hell out of Fredrick, and was why he would marry someone dependable. "If you have friends with boats, get on one of theirs. You can't afford to buy a boat. Please make sure mom understands that."

"I don't like to trouble your mom with talks about money. If she wants a boat, I'll find a way. Like I said, don't worry. Things are looking up with this client and before you know it, I'll have a few more."

There was no getting through to his dad. "I've really got to go."

"Well, like I said, things are looking up. I know I've had to call on you in the past, but with this new client, that's all about to change. But for now, I need just a little help paying the note this month on your mom's car."

Fredrick suppressed a groan. The red Camaro his mom had gotten after seeing Janiyah in her yellow one was the same car he'd told his dad they didn't need. Never mind that his mom had never shown an interest in sports cars before. She saw it, she wanted it, and his dad took out a fourth mortgage to make sure she got it.

"And before you say I shouldn't have gotten the car, remember the look on your mom's face when I brought it home? I didn't get a full night's sleep for the next three weeks, and that was a good thing."

"There's more to life than making mom happy. Bills, responsibilities, making sure your business is a success. You can't make mom happy if you lose it all."

"I'm not going to lose it all. Quit getting upset about the way things are. I love your mom. She means everything to me. Would you really want to upset her by having her lose the car?"

He wanted to say yes. He wanted to teach his parents a lesson. Let them finally get crushed under the pile of debt hovering over their heads. But he wouldn't do it. As much as it upset him to constantly bail out his dad, it would hurt him more to see them destitute because he tried to prove a point.

"I'll transfer the money into your account today."

Christopher let out a huge sigh. "Thanks, son. I knew I could count on you. I'll let you go now. I know you've got a lot on your plate with your new clients. Looks like your business is growing by leaps and bounds. I'm proud of you."

Too bad he couldn't say the same. "I appreciate that. I'll talk with you soon."

He hung up, then leaned back in his chair to stare at the ceiling. His disappointment from having fantasies about Janiyah grew with each tick of the clock on his desk. For a second he allowed himself to imagine what it would be like to replace the dependable woman in his plan with Janiyah. Pictured the pleasure that would come from seeing her do that girly sigh when he walked in a room, or waking up to the smell of her vanilla perfume on his sheets. Then he countered that with him skipping meetings to take her out of town, or spending money on the latest hobby she picked up. Not too long ago he'd talked her out of buying a cello when she took a music appreciation class at the local community college. Her argument almost made him want to get it for her, and they weren't a couple.

Treat her like a sister. Acknowledge that she was beautiful then forget it. Despite the Hendersons' concerns, if he were really going to make it work with a woman he needed to consider moving. He was smart enough to know that Janiyah's presence in his life scared away women. He'd move and buy a house. His parents might need a place to stay in a few years.

He let out a humorless laugh. He hoped he married an understanding woman, because that last thought had a lot of truth in it.

"Are you okay?" Phyllis was back at the door. No doubt she'd been eyeing the light on her phone to know exactly when he got off.

"I'm alright, but thanks for asking."

"It's nine-thirty. The first person we're interviewing will be here soon. I'll get you a cup of coffee."

"Thanks," he said, letting her do something to ease her need to fix things.

She hurried out the door and returned a few minutes later with a steaming mug. She took a look at his computer screen and grunted. He'd pulled up his bank account and was already transferring the funds. Phyllis had overheard enough of his dad's phone calls and seen the reports on his father's business to know that Fredrick supplemented his parents' income. She never commented on it, but the frowns on her face and insistence that she could tell his dad that he wasn't available was proof that she disapproved.

He hit send and logged out. "Thanks for the coffee, Phyllis."

"You're welcome, Mr. Jenkins." She placed a hand on his shoulder and squeezed before turning and marching out.

Too bad she wasn't thirty years younger. A practical woman like Phyllis was who he should be fantasizing about. Not a woman who wore sexy red dresses to business functions.

• • •

At the end of the work day, after sitting through four interviews and spending the last fifteen minutes trying to figure out why the numbers in a spreadsheet didn't match the paperwork in front of him, when Fredrick's cell phone rang for the fourth time in an hour he snatched it up ready to tell Janiyah to forget dinner.

"I'm leaving in a minute."

"That's good to know," Aaron said with a laugh.

Fredrick sighed and shook his head. "My bad, your sister has called non-stop in the last hour pestering me to leave the office." He looked over the spreadsheet on his monitor then frowned. The damn formula wasn't correct in one of the cells. He could kick himself for not thinking to check that first.

"I'd guess why, but there could be multiple explanations about why she's pestering you."

"She says I need to eat." He corrected the formula and nodded when the numbers finally added up. "I've just finished what I was working on, so I guess I'll indulge her and leave the office now."

"How is Janiyah?"

"She's Janiyah." He saved his work and shut down the computer.

"No, I mean, if you saw her today, did she seem alright? My dad called one of his family meetings last night and she got upset when he gave her a hard time."

"She was alright at the mixer."

"That's good."

Fredrick thought about her moment of uncertainty when he said he wouldn't hire her. "She did have a second where she seemed upset when she came to my apartment last night."

"What did she come by your apartment for?"

He got up from his desk and stretched his free arm above his head. "She comes by almost every night for something."

A pause, then, "So, Janiyah hangs out at your apartment most nights?"

Ah, damn. The way Aaron said it made it sound a lot worse than it was. His earlier thought of being crucified by Aaron and his brothers if he so much as touched Janiyah crept back into his head. Along with the guilt for his dream the night before. "Not really, she just comes by to eat my food, or ask me to kill a bug or something. Nothing's going on."

"Who said anything was going on?"

"No one, I just want you to know that."

Aaron laughed. "Come on, Fred, I'm not worried about you and Janiyah. I just know how you like your privacy. I was concerned that maybe she was overstaying her welcome."

"No, she's fine. I don't mind her coming over." It was the truth. She might be exasperating at times, but he did enjoy their friendly back and forth. A vision of her legs in those pajama shorts popped into his mind. He pushed it aside. They were friends. That was all.

"Good. Was she really upset?"

Fredrick chuckled. "I've never seen Janiyah really upset. No, she just seemed a little annoyed about something and said she was tired of people viewing her as a joke."

"I figured as much. Normally she can brush it off when Dad gets all *Father Knows Best* on her, but last night was different. If I call she'll act like it was no big deal, but I figured she let you know how she was feeling."

"Why would you say that?"

"Come on, Fred, we both know you're the one she goes to when she needs advice about something. You practically tutored her long distance for every math class she took through high school and college, and can talk her out of most of her off-the-wall ideas. Just keep an eye out, alright?"

Fredrick slid his laptop bag onto his shoulder, but the weight of Aaron's words settled much heavier than the strap. The guilt from earlier revved up another notch. Here Aaron was, asking him to look out for his baby sister, and all day long Fredrick had had to stop himself from remembering his fantasy from the night before. If his dad's call earlier had been a wakeup call, Aaron's call was a bullhorn blaring that he needed to snap out of it.

Instead of responding, he changed the subject. "If you were there, it must mean you're in town. How long will you be around?"

"I'm going out tomorrow, but it's a quick haul up to Virginia. I'll be back in a week."

Fredrick turned the lights off in his office. His lobby was illuminated by the backup lights; the rest of the staff had left about forty minutes ago.

"Give me a shout when you're back in town. It's been a while."

"I'll do that," Aaron said. "And thanks, man."

"For what?"

"Looking out for Janiyah. I'm not home, and Dad, David, and Kareem aren't nearby. We appreciate it."

And with that, Fredrick's guilt kicked up way past a notch to catastrophic levels.

CHAPTER 6

Since she'd promised him dinner, Janiyah fussed, pleaded, and threatened to come to his office, until Freddy finally left and agreed to meet her somewhere. He'd chosen one of those fast casual places that prepared your food in front of you. She didn't have to insist on eating with Freddy, and he wouldn't have held her to her promise. Dinner served two purposes: she liked keeping the promises she made him, and it gave her an opportunity to convince him to accept her job application.

Freddy's late nights were becoming more frequent. He usually arrived home at six thirty—except during tax season. When she'd commented the week before about his late work hours, he'd said work was busy and she'd moved on. Guilt eased its way into her conscience for not asking what was happening at his job. He'd busted his butt to be this big success and hadn't shared it with her. Though she wanted to be mad she really couldn't.

Another check on her responsibility list: show an interest in her friends' lives.

She arrived before he did and waited in front of the restaurant. A few minutes later he pulled up. The top buttons of his shirt were undone, and his eyes were slightly red behind his glasses. They got that way when he rubbed them a lot—something he did whenever he was stressed.

"Did you wait long?"

She smiled; he was always considerate of keeping people waiting. "No, just got here. Your big new client keeping you busy?"

"Which one?" He opened the door for her and placed his hand on the small of her back to usher her in. The strong, steady pressure made her body tingle and once again forget they were incompatible.

She moved out of his grasp. "You mean there's more than one?"

He lifted a shoulder. "I've been busy."

"Apparently too busy to tell me everything that's going on."

"As if you care."

Ouch, that hurt. "I care."

"Since when?"

"Since good stuff starts happening to you. I mean really, Freddy, you're like a brother. You should tell me stuff like this."

"I'll be sure to let you know in the future ... little sister."

She frowned at the endearment. Before she could answer they were at the front of restaurant. They both ordered sandwiches and followed the guy down the line as he prepared their food. The guy making their sandwiches kept looking between her and Freddy. When he caught her eye he raised an eyebrow. She read the question, and shook her head no, though she felt wrong for it. Why, she didn't know, since she and Freddy weren't a couple.

When they got to the cashier and Janiyah paid, the guy pushed aside the woman who'd rung up their order to grin at Janiyah. "When are you going to finally give me your number?"

She glanced uneasily at Freddy. He cocked an eyebrow before turning to take their food to a table. A tiny hint of disappointment that he never cared when other men asked her out in front of him slumped her shoulders.

She turned to the guy. He was cute, always flirted when she came, and often gave her a free cookie. One phone call wouldn't hurt. "Five, five, five, six, seven, six, five." He grinned and jotted it down.

Once she sat in the chair across from Freddy he asked, "Do you give out your number everywhere you go?"

"Now you care?"

"I don't. But what about your dream lover from the mixer?" He took a bite of his sandwich, then licked his lips. A funny kinda vibration scattered across her skin.

"I'm still interested."

"And if this guy," he motioned with his head toward the guy, "calls, then what?"

She shrugged. "It's just a phone call." She wasn't here for another lecture on her dating habits. "Enough about me; how was your day?"

"Long."

That was helpful. "Hey, I asked you here for adult conversation. Not one word answers."

He raised an eyebrow, a teasing glint in his eye. "Adult conversation? I thought you were forcing me to eat, not looking for a partner to talk dirty with."

Crap, there her body went tingling again. "You wish."

"Not hardly," he said, taking a sip from his straw. "Okay. What do you mean by adult conversation?"

"Tell me about your job."

"What about it?"

"I don't know, how you got started, why suddenly you're so successful?"

"You sound surprised," he said after taking another bite and swallowing.

"I'm getting annoyed. Just answer the question."

His lips twitched and the dimple popped out briefly. "Let's see. I started my own accounting firm two years ago after working as an accountant for Hayworth and Boyd for five years."

"Why did you start your own firm?" She bit her sandwich.

"I wanted more control. Hayworth and Boyd is a good firm, but they didn't really care about their clients. It was more about landing the big deals to earn bigger fees. Their smaller clients that really needed help getting their books in order were being pushed to the side. This one mom and pop restaurant that had been a client with them since the early nineties was dumped to make room for an insurance firm. I was the staff accountant assigned to them, and I had to give them the bad news that their account was no longer *financially viable* to the firm."

"That's horrible."

"I know. I let them know on a Friday and the looks on their faces made my stomach hurt all weekend. On Monday I turned in my resignation. Started my own firm and took on that restaurant as my first client."

In her mind choirs sang. "Oh, Freddy, that's wonderful."

He shifted in his seat and took another sip of his drink. "Please don't look at me like that."

"Like what?"

He shook his head. "Never mind. Anyway, that was that and I've been in business ever since."

"How did you get more clients?"

"Pounding the pavement. First I approached the businesses Hayworth and Boyd dumped. And a few existing ones I knew were on the chopping block."

"Ruthless."

His cocky look gave him a definite sexy air. "All's fair in love and war, sweetheart. Most of them were familiar with my work. I was able to hire a few staff accountants and things have run smoothly."

"How did you land Nebulas? You beat out larger more established firms to get them."

He raised an eyebrow. "Talking to Liz, I see."

"Yes, since you refused to tell me the good news."

"If the ladies last night hadn't made a big deal out of it you wouldn't care."

That burned her stomach. She sat back and digested her guilt. He was right; if they'd said nothing about it last night neither he nor Liz would have brought it up. She thought he'd picked accounting just because he was a numbers freak. His job always seemed boring and ordinary whenever he mentioned it. Learning he brought compassion and caring for his clients softened her opinion of his chosen profession.

"You're right, but that doesn't mean I'm not enjoying myself." She smiled at his raised brow. "Go on, tell me about Nebulas."

"Nothing much to tell. They were on the lookout for a firm to handle their accounts. I'd landed the account of Congaree Family Practice—"

"That chain of doctors' offices. I didn't know that."

"There's a lot you don't know." He finished his sandwich then his soda. "Long story short, I went for it and won."

She silently chewed the remains of her sandwich. Freddy's business was bigger than she thought. She'd assumed from his small office and one secretary that he was doing the taxes of a few random homeowners, when in fact he was in charge of accounts for some of the largest businesses in Columbia.

"You're really successful."

"You can say that." No cockiness, no bragging. He said it like it wasn't a big deal.

"Why do you still live in that apartment? You could be anywhere but you're across the hall from me."

When he didn't answer, she looked up to find him staring at her. There was heat in his gaze that made her wish for one of those soap opera moments where he'd grab her hand and whisper, "You're the reason, Janiyah. I stay because of you." Her heart whacked against her ribcage as she was lost in memories of her old crush.

Finally, he cleared his throat. "Actually, I've thought about moving."

She sat forward. "What? You can't."

"I can. And I think I might. I can't be your handyman and random food supplier forever. I know that's the reason you want me to stay."

"Well, yeah, but there's more than that."

"I thought you'd be happy to be out of the watchful eye of a brother."

"You're not my brother."

He nailed her with a hot stare. "No, I'm not."

The way he said it, with an underlying hint of promise, made her struggle to take in a breath. Her body slowly warmed from the fire in his eyes. Her curiosity piqued. Too many times she'd suppressed fantasies about Freddy, about as many times as he said something to remind her that she wasn't what he was interested in. She didn't read great novels. She wasn't into the business scene as he was and wasn't nearly as structured as the women he typically dated. But just once she'd like to discover what was behind the sizzling looks he sometimes gave.

She leaned forward. "Freddy ... "

The sandwich guy came over. He dropped a napkin with a phone number scribbled on it in front of her. "I'll call you tomorrow."

Freddy balled up his sandwich paper and stood. "I'll meet you outside." He turned and strode out.

"Yeah ... sure." She gave the guy a weak smile before taking her food scraps to the trash can. This was just perfect. Instead of showing Freddy she could take an interest in his job, and give him a reason to accept her application, she'd given him a reason to doubt her. She knew he viewed her willingness to give her number to two different guys in twenty-four hours as a sign that she couldn't commit to anything. That was far from the truth; she just hadn't found anything worth committing to. Hell, she had more of a commitment with him than she'd ever had with anything else in her life.

She scratched the back of her head and left the restaurant. There she went again with the thoughts of her and Freddy in some form of a relationship.

He was already at his car. He had his cell phone out and was reading something on the screen.

"I thought about what you said last night," she said. He gave her a questioning look. "About proving people wrong. You're right, I do need to do that, but I think I need to also prove to myself that I can do it."

"You can do whatever you set your mind to."

"But that's the thing—I've never set my mind on anything."

"You have your business."

"That most people consider some hobby. I know I shouldn't care what people think, but I am tired of the pitiful looks and disregard of all my hard work. I want to prove to them that I can get up every morning, sit at a desk, and not only do a job, but do it well."

He rocked back on his heels and raised his eyebrows. "Good for you."

"That's why I'm applying for your administrative assistant position."

His panicked expression almost made her laugh. "Why me? Why not ask your dad for a job?"

"Because working for him makes it seem like I need my family to take care of me. I'm perfectly capable of taking care of myself." She saw the 'no' forming on his lips. She rushed forward and clasped his hands in hers. It was a dirty trick, but he never could resist her pleading. "Please, Freddy. It's just an interview. And if I completely suck, you can tell me what I did wrong. You know you'll love that."

He didn't immediately pull away. The warm spring air became hotter as something sparked between them. The moment only lasted a second. He swiftly slid his hand out of hers, but nodded. "Fine. We start interviewing for assistants on Monday."

"Thanks, Freddy!" She clapped her hands before throwing her arms around his neck. His strong arms automatically wrapped around her waist. His body was hard against hers, and it felt awesome.

He quickly pushed away. "Yeah ... well ... I've got to get home."

Her mind whirled from the sensations stirred up by their brief embrace. She wasn't ready for this to end. She wanted to explore this spark some more. "VH1 is counting down the top R&B hits of the nineties tonight. Want to watch it?"

"No, I've a long day tomorrow."

"I'll only watch an hour."

"I said no, little sister," he said in a rough voice. Immediately his face softened and, he gently nudged her chin with his knuckles. "I'll see you in the morning." He opened the door of his car.

He moved to get in the car then stopped. "Oh, by the way ... "

She leaned forward. "Yes?"

"Liz texted me about getting together with her boss. Has she said anything to you?"

Her elation tanked. "Yeah, but she's no fun at all."

"You and I have two different definitions of fun." He smiled, but she couldn't appreciate the appearance of the dimple. "I'll see you tomorrow."

He got in his car. She climbed into her Camaro and barely remembered the ride back home. She frowned the entire way as she tried to come to terms with why his interest in Liz's boss made her feel sick.

CHAPTER 7

"I'm getting cereal!"

Fredrick's hands slowed as he fastened his tie. It was the first time she'd come over in the week since they'd had dinner. Because of all the extra hours he pulled at the office, he only saw her in passing. Usually as he came in from work and she went out for the night. He should have known she'd pop in today. Her interview was that afternoon.

He finished with his tie and walked into the living room. Janiyah sat at the bar eating a bowl of cereal. He hadn't realized how much he'd missed seeing her there until just then. Her lime green cami and boy shorts didn't hurt. He looked away before he let those thoughts take hold. A week of no Janiyah also meant a week without that irritating attraction.

"Morning, Janiyah."

"Good morning. Not rushing this morning?"

"No, I've slept well the past few nights." He went into the kitchen to pour coffee into a travel mug. After adding sugar, he picked up the paper he'd dropped on the counter the night before. "I saw something in the paper you might be interested in."

"What paper?"

"The newspaper."

"You still read the newspaper?"

"Don't sound so surprised. They still hold useful information about what's happening in the world."

"Yeah, two days after it breaks on social media."

He dropped the paper in front of her and pointed to an advertisement. "There's a job fair at the convention center tomorrow. If you're still in the market for a job, that's a good place to start."

She picked up the paper and glanced at the ad. When she lowered it, her eyes sparkled with amusement. "I saw this online last night. But I don't have to go because after my interview, you're going to hire me."

"It's just an interview, Janiyah."

"I'm going to knock it out of the ball park, just you wait."

She dropped the paper and lifted her bowl of cereal to drink the milk. He couldn't help it—his eyes traveled down the smooth line of her neck to her chest in the lacy top. No bra. Desire kicked up inside him. Her small breasts thrust forward, drawing attention to her hard nipples pressed against the soft material.

He jerked his eyes away, and thought about the two different guys she'd given her number to last week. No telling how many others had asked for it over the past week. None of them had a chance of holding her for long. He was no different. She might enjoy coming over and teasing him, but she'd also stayed away for days. He was in the same boat as the other schmucks who were entranced with her.

He grabbed his keys and laptop. "Lock up after you leave."

"Any pointers for the interview?"

"Bring your résumé and try not to skip."

She laughed and hopped down from the bar seat. He turned away from the enticing bounce of her breasts.

"I think I already figured that out."

"Twelve o'clock."

"Are you sure? You need to eat lunch."

"I've skipped lunch before."

She shook her head. "I'll change that as your assistant. No more meetings through lunch."

"I've got to hire you first," he said with a half-smile.

She grinned and followed him to the door. He opened the door and stopped. Janiyah's brother, David, was standing at her door. He held a covered basket in his hand. He turned to Fredrick and frowned. "Do you know where Janiyah is?" David asked. "I knocked and got no answer."

"Here I am."

Janiyah ducked under Fredrick's arm into the hall. David's frown turned into a full blown scowl.

"You spent the night with him?" David's free hand balled into a fist.

"No," Fredrick answered. "She comes over to steal my cereal in the mornings."

David's eyes moved over his sister from head to toe. They narrowed before going back to Fredrick. Even though he'd done nothing wrong, Fredrick's face burned with guilt. First he admitted to Aaron she was over there most nights, now David caught her leaving in her pajamas. He definitely needed to move before her brothers began to guess that too many times he had non-sisterly feelings toward her.

"Quit, scowling, David. I just came over for cereal," she said with a laugh.

Fredrick hitched the strap of his laptop bag higher on his shoulder and glanced at his watch. "I've got to go."

"Bye, Freddy," Janiyah said.

He nodded at her, then David—who glared—and turned to march down the hall.

• • •

"What the hell are you thinking?" David said as soon as Freddy hit the stairs.

"What are you talking about? I ran out of cereal. Apparently a box only lasts a few days. I'll remember that the next time I go to the grocery store." She pushed her brother out of the way and opened the door to her apartment.

"You make it a habit to prance around his apartment in your pajamas? With no bra?"

Janiyah frowned, looked down at her pajamas, then back at her brother. "Freddy doesn't care about that. He probably doesn't even notice."

"He's a man. He notices. It's making me uncomfortable. You do this to him every day?"

Janiyah waved a hand. "I'm not doing anything to him. Like I said, he barely pays attention to me in the mornings."

"Not for your lack of trying."

She rolled her eyes and went down the hall to her bedroom. She grabbed her bathrobe off the bed and slipped it on. No need to make her brother *uncomfortable*. She paused on her way back. Did Freddy really notice? He never let on that it made him uncomfortable when she came over in her PJs.

She went back down the hall. David stood in the middle of her living room, the basket he'd carried on her cluttered coffee table.

"Are we done with the lecture?"

David crossed his arms, stretching the material of his tailored tan three-piece suit over his wide shoulders. "Is there something going on with you and Fredrick?"

"No, there's nothing *going on*. And before you get your boxers in a knot, calm down. I met a very handsome professor the other day and we're going out this weekend." Gerald Westlock had called her after three days like she'd expected. They'd had a few phone calls, nothing exciting, but interesting enough for her to agree to a date.

"You shouldn't date so much."

"Neither should you, but I don't see you stopping."

"It's different for a man."

"Oh, don't give me that crap. It's not like I'm sleeping with tons of guys." She plopped down on her couch.

"You shouldn't be sleeping with dozens of guys either."

"Oh, God, please save me that speech. Or better yet, give it to the women you sleep with."

David opened his mouth to reply, but a meow came from the basket. She pulled back the blanket covering it to find a small orange kitten.

"She's beautiful!" she said with a gasp.

"How do you know it's a girl?"

"I think of all cats as girls." She scratched the adorable ball of fur behind the ears.

"Well, you're right. She's for you."

She looked up at her brother. "You got me a cat?"

"You said you wanted one."

Janiyah laughed. "Yeah, six weeks ago. What gives?"

David uncrossed his arms and sank down onto the chair beside her. "I need you to work your magic on Pops and convince him not to sell the business."

"Why would he listen to me?"

"Because he always listens to you. Go over there and do your daddy's girl smile and tell him that the best way to make sure you're taken care of is if we keep Henderson Automotive."

"I can take care of myself."

"I see how. You walk around Fredrick's apartment half-dressed and he gives you everything you want."

She frowned and gently put the cat back in the basket. Otherwise she'd throw her at David's face. David's request was more proof that her family thought of her as a kid. *Pops won't listen to reason, well let's send in the eyelash batting, smiling baby girl.*

"Are you saying the only way for me to help is by going over there and acting like a five-year-old? That it wouldn't work for me to talk with him like an adult?" Her irritation came through with each word.

David gave her a look that said that was exactly what he meant. "Don't get mad at me. You've played the daddy's girl for years; now you're upset because I'm calling you on it?"

"For your information, I won't be playing that anymore. I have an interview today. For a," she made air quotes with her fingers, "*real job*. I'm working on my budget to start a portfolio and I'm planning for the future."

"Interview where, and why? You can always work for Henderson Automotive."

"Because you and the rest of the family think I'm a toddler instead of a grown woman. I don't need a reason to look for a job. Nor do I need one handed to me. There's more in my head than you all give me credit for."

"Hey, look, I'm sorry." He took her hand between his and gave her the same sad eyes she'd perfected. "I'm the worst brother in the world, and you have every right to refuse to help me convince Pops from selling something so crucial to the family."

She shook her head and smiled. "Please don't tell me this tired reverse psychology thing works on women?"

"Let's see, are you going to help me?" His face became serious. "All jokes aside. If asking you to do the daddy's girl thing upset you, I'm sorry. I know Pops gives you a hard time, but I respect what you do." His face twisted with a frown. "Except for the no bra thing around Fredrick."

She dropped his hand. "You can go now, David," she said with a chuckle that he joined in on.

"C'mon, sis, will you help me with Pops?" David said.

She studied him. Behind the smile, there was actual worry in his voice. He really didn't want the company to go. "I thought you'd be happy not working there."

His jaw hardened and determination filled his eyes. "I didn't dedicate my life to growing Henderson Automotive only to watch him sell it on a whim. I'm going to fight to keep the business."

Janiyah placed a hand on David's clenched fist. Out of her three brothers, she worried about him the most. Kareem, with all his faults, could take care of himself. Aaron might not be able to nail himself to one location, but he knew what he wanted in life and pursued it. David, on the other hand, had spent too much of his life trying to live their father's dream.

"I'll help you. Daddy may not want it or think I can run it, but that doesn't mean I want him to sell it."

He flipped his hand and gave hers a squeeze. "Thanks, Janiyah."

He stood and she did as well. She picked up the basket and gave it to him. "But you can keep the cat."

Something like panic came across his face. "I don't want the cat. It's for you."

"I've got a lot going on, and Freddy made a good point when I first brought up wanting one. I can barely remember to feed myself; why try to feed an animal?"

"I'll take it back to the shelter."

Janiyah grabbed his arm. "No, that would be cruel. Look, she already thinks of you as her daddy. You picked her out and took her away from that cruel shelter."

"I paid one hundred dollars for this cat and it was living in a padded cage. It wasn't a cruel shelter."

"Still, it's wrong. Keep her, you need companionship." She pushed her brother toward the door.

"I have plenty of female companionship."

"Well, you need someone that'll love you unconditionally. Tammy will do that."

"Who's Tammy?"

"Your cat." She opened the door.

"I'm not keeping the cat."

She pouted and turned pleading eyes on her brother. "Please, Davie, don't send her back. I'll come visit and she'll be so upset if you take her back. Think of what all the other cats will say."

"Janiayah ... "

"I'm pulling the baby sister routine on this. Promise me you'll keep Tammy." She gave the smile that always got her what she wanted.

David grunted. "Promise to wear a bra every time you visit Fredrick."

"I promise." She leaned up to kiss his cheek. "All bets are off if he comes to my apartment."

She pushed him out and shut the door before he could reply, but the angry way he growled her name on the other side of the door said enough.

CHAPTER 8

Janiyah wiped her hands on her dress, then cursed and smoothed over the material. She'd picked this outfit with the sole purpose of proving to Freddy that she would make a great administrative assistant—until the lady who interviewed before her walked out in a fitted black pant suit and perfectly cut hair looking exactly like what Freddy would want. Janiyah's black pencil dress with red trim was supposed to give her a fifties secretary flair, while taking a jab at Freddy for teasing her about her red dress. Maybe it wasn't the best way to prove she was the right person for the job.

Phyllis came out of the conference room. She didn't smile as she approached Janiyah. "Mr. Jenkins told me you were applying."

Janiyah stood and forced herself not to use her dress as a towel for her sweaty palms.

"I'm sure he said it with a scowl."

"Not at all." Phyllis straightened her shoulders and lifted her chin. "If I would have known you were looking for a permanent position I would have recommended you myself. You were a life saver when you helped me organize my family reunion last year."

Janiyah's shoulders nearly sagged with relief. Phyllis was a critic of everyone. Janiyah had only offered her minimal help with getting the reunion together. And Phyllis had complained about all the details that needed to be thought of the entire time. Yet, when it was all said and done, she stopped barking at Janiyah when she called the office and even threw her a compliment on her clothes the last time she saw her.

"Well, that makes me feel a lot better."

"Yes, well, you still have to do good in there. We aren't just handing out jobs to anyone." And just like that, Phyllis was back to being a hard ass.

Freddy came to the door of the conference room. He looked at Phyllis, then her, before checking his watch. "Are we ready?"

Phyllis tugged on the jacket of her suit. "We are, Mr. Jenkins. Coming now."

They both walked to the conference room. Freddy gave her a sweeping gaze from head to toe. His expression didn't change.

She smiled. "Hi."

He stepped back so she could enter the room. "Nice to see you, Ms. Henderson. Please have a seat."

Ooohkay. Did this mean she had to call him Mr. Jenkins or—*cringe*—Fredrick? Her smile tightened as she passed him and went further into the small conference room. She recognized the other guy in the room as one of the accountants who worked at the firm. She couldn't remember his name.

Phyllis indicated the single seat on one side of the table. Freddy took the seat between Phyllis and the accountant on the other side. When his serious gaze landed on her, it was as if someone capped off the passage to her lungs. Never in her life had Freddy intimidated her, but seeing him on the other side of the table with his suit, serious eyes behind his glasses, and a packet of papers that must be the interview questions in front of her did. This was her chance to prove herself. The first step to showing her family that she was more than a pretty girl who needed taking care of.

She straightened her shoulders and took a deep breath. Then Freddy gave her a smile. Not full blown dimple, but enough to make her stomach quiver and send warmth up her cheeks. An affection she'd felt for Freddy since she was nine years old overwhelmed her. No matter what happened, by giving her this interview he proved he believed she was capable.

• • •

Janiyah wanted to find the nearest couch to fall on when she left the interview. Instead she drove to her parents' house. If she didn't keep her promise to David while it was fresh in her mind, she'd forget all together.

Her brain hurt after thinking so hard to answer the interview questions. She had no clue if she'd done well or not. Freddy's face remained impassive during the entire interview. Phyllis and the other accountant, Larry, had given her one or two smiles and nods of encouragement. That was nice, but Freddy gave her nothing. She couldn't have done too badly. She gave detailed answers, was fluent in many of the software programs they used, and had experience with web design—something she casually mentioned when pointing out that the Jenkins Holdings website could stand a few updates.

She cringed and clutched the steering wheel. She shouldn't have said that. No one wanted to hire someone who criticized their business ... even if it was constructive, nicely given criticism. Freddy's lip did quirk when she said it, but she wasn't sure if that was in approval or disapproval. Probably the latter.

When she pulled up to her parents' house, the garage was up. Her dad was inside moving boxes off a shelf. He'd officially retired from actively running Henderson Automotive six months ago to give full control to David. He still served as chairman of the board, and president of the foundation he'd started that provided scholarships to students. But she knew that the extra free time was driving him crazy. Her dad was never one to sit around idle.

"Hey, Daddy," she said, after getting out of the car and sauntering over.

Even messing around with boxes in a garage her dad wore an old pair of slacks and a polo shirt.

Roger smiled at her and put the box in his arms on the pile by the door. "Hey, baby girl. What brings you by?"

"Just stopping in to check on you and Mom."

"You're really dressed up just to visit me and your mom," he said, eyeing her dress.

She smiled and brushed down the sides. "I had a job interview this morning."

"And you didn't wear a suit?"

She forced herself to not roll her eyes. "No, I didn't wear a suit."

"Well, things are different nowadays." He went back to the shelf with the rest of the boxes.

"What are you doing?"

"Getting rid of some of this stuff," he said. "I'm tired of the clutter. It's time to get things in order."

He reached for another box then stopped. He rubbed his chest. Sweat beaded on his brow and he took a few deep breaths.

Concern made her hurry across the garage to her dad. "Are you okay?"

"Yeah, just winded." He patted her hand on his arm and nodded. "That's another thing I need to start doing, working out. I've got all this spare time on my hands. Might as well do something useful other than reorganizing the garage."

He took a deep breath and stepped away. He reached for a box on the shelf.

Still feeling shaky, Janiyah took off her shoes and decided to help. He might just be winded, but the strain on his face had scared her. "You know the guys could have done this." She took the last box off the shelf. It was heavy, but she managed to carry it to the pile he started and set it down with the others.

"If I wanted it done in a year I would have asked them," he said, a teasing glint in his eye.

Janiyah laughed and dusted off her hands. "You're probably right."

"Now your dress is dusty. You didn't have to help, I could have gotten it."

"Well, you looked about ready to keel over so I figured I had to help." Her voice held some of the worry from earlier.

Roger grimaced. "Sometimes I feel like I'm going to keel over."

Her humor died. Even though she was annoyed with him from the other day, she couldn't stand thinking of her dad being sick. "Daddy, are you okay?"

He met her eye and smiled, any traces of the grimace gone. "I'm perfectly fine. Why don't you tell me about this job interview?"

She took in his tired expression and frowned. "Only if we go inside and you forget these boxes for the rest of today. I'll call Kareem and see if he can finish moving them."

For a second she thought he would argue before he nodded and headed for the door leading into the house. Once he was settled at the kitchen table, she went to the fridge and got both of them a bottle of water.

"So, where did you interview? If you wanted a job, you could have easily come and work for Henderson Automotive."

Her scoff of disbelief was out before she knew it. "You're seriously telling me that I could work there, when just last week you said I couldn't handle it."

"I said you couldn't handle running it, not that you couldn't handle working there."

"Why can't I handle running it? Because I don't wear suits to interviews? Or because I was foolish enough to take the money you put into my account every month, or maybe it's because I'm just a silly little girl and my head can't handle the information."

"You're overreacting again. Just like you did the other night. This is why you can't run the business. You're too impulsive. Too quick to go with the first thing that comes into your head instead of thinking things through."

"I know what I want and I'm not afraid to go after it or to try new things. In what world is that a bad thing?"

The bottle of water in his hand hit the table with a clunk as he gave her a hard stare. "In the business world being impulsive can cost you everything."

"And sitting around waiting for things to happen means opportunity will pass you by."

Her dad threw up his hands. He stood and shook his head. "You kids are going to give me a heart attack. Every time I try and give you advice, all you do is argue."

Janiyah jumped up from the chair and paced back and forth. "And every time we try and talk to you, all you do is brush aside whatever we say."

"I don't brush you aside," he said as if she were being ridiculous.

"You're doing it now. That's the point of your family meetings, right? To tell us all the things we're doing wrong?"

"The point of those meetings," he said, straightening his shoulders, "is to find out what's going on with my kids. You don't tell me anything if I don't ask."

"Because if we tell you, you'll just turn around and tell us the right way, also known as your way, to do things."

Before Roger could answer, her mom hurried into the kitchen. "What's going on in here? I can hear you arguing down the hall." She looked between the two.

Janiyah took a deep breath. "I came over to ask Daddy to reconsider selling the business; instead I get another round of why Janiyah is too dumb to run the company."

"No one said you were dumb," Roger said in an exasperated tone. "I just said you weren't cut out for it."

"It's the same thing."

Loretta came over and placed a hand on Janiyah's arm. "Sweetheart, please. Can't we just sit down and discuss this rationally?"

"Fine, okay, Daddy." She crossed her arms. "Tell me rationally why I can't run the business."

Roger took a breath then met her eye. "Because I don't want you to."

If he would have taken her high heel and slammed it into her heart it wouldn't have hurt worse. She'd hoped she had overreacted. That her dad didn't really think she was too flighty to take over the business. But he'd just confirmed it. She wasn't good enough.

Janiyah was beyond talking rationally. Her heart pumped adrenaline to every tight muscle in her body. She wanted to hit something, or scream out her frustration. Something snapped inside of her. Annoyance with them, but also with herself for not recognizing the way they'd seen her for so long. She wasn't a kid that needed coddling. She could excel at any job she took. And dammit, she would. She'd give them hard proof that they'd seriously underestimated her.

A part of her wondered if it was worth all the trouble. She didn't really want to run Henderson Automotive, so why fight so hard to show them that she could? It wasn't as if getting the administrative assistant position at Freddy's office would prove she could run a large organization.

But it would prove that she wasn't as helpless and silly as they thought. No, it wasn't the job of a lifetime, and it wouldn't earn her acclaim, but it was a step in the right direction. It would get her started in the business world, maybe help her think of a way to expand her work as a virtual assistant—something she tossed around in the back of her mind but never really thought out.

She squared her shoulders and looked at her mom. "No, we can't talk about this rationally, because I'm done talking." She turned to her dad. "If you sell Henderson Automotive, it'll break your heart, and hurt David far more than you realize."

She turned to the door.

"Janiyah, wait," her dad called.

She spun around, but not for whatever excuse he would try and give. "And starting immediately, you can cancel the deposits into my account."

"There's no need for that," Roger said.

"Cancel them, or else I'll change my bank account. I make enough money to support myself."

CHAPTER 9

Janiyah looked through the peephole of her apartment, then turned away with a heavy sigh when she saw nothing, and paced the length of her living room. She checked the clock—it was nearly nine-thirty. Wringing her hands, she fell onto her couch. Where was Freddy?

She picked up one of the many magazines on the coffee table, flipped the pages, and then dropped it to jump up again. He had been working late the past few nights, and there was no reason he needed to hurry home today. Just because he said they were ending interviews the day before and would make a decision by the end of the week didn't mean he would rush home to tell her. Though it made absolutely no sense for him to work so late on a Friday.

She froze in her pacing. Unless he was avoiding her. She chewed on her pinky fingernail. He wasn't going to hire her. They'd gone for that starched, black suit wearing woman who'd interviewed before her. She knew that black and red dress was a bad idea. Cute, but a bad idea.

Her mom called this morning. At first, she'd barely paid attention to the conversation, she was so busy making dildo flyers for Mrs. Driggers. After her mom kept probing, she confessed that her job interview was with Freddy. Loretta seemed excited for her, which annoyed the crap out of Janiyah. She couldn't remember anything close to that much excitement from her mom when she'd mentioned getting a huge bonus because a presentation she'd put together for one of her clients was such a success—because of her, he'd gotten a raise and a promotion. No, only praise on a damn performance evaluation would count with her parents. Even if Freddy didn't give her the job, she'd just try again somewhere else.

The thought of competing with people far more used to the business world than she was, wasn't her idea of fun. She wasn't into the suit and tie life, but if it got her family off her back, she'd make herself fit.

What should have been a bright spot earlier in the day was her conversation with Gerald Westlock confirming their date the next day. Her enthusiasm about getting back out there and dating again had vanished. Getting her life in order, proving that she wasn't the joke her ex-boyfriend accused her of being, seemed more important than finding a new guy to get involved with, her starving libido be damned.

She went back to the door to check the peephole. Just as she was about to pull away, Freddy came down the hall.

She hopped up and down then ran her fingers through her hair. She probably looked a mess in the same Hello Kitty pajamas he'd teased her about a week ago. She'd gone for curls again and they were falling flat. Maybe she should wait until he was in and settled. That way she wouldn't look as if she'd desperately stalked her peephole all day. She stopped bouncing and drummed her fingers on the door. She'd give him five, maybe ten minutes to get in and get comfortable before she confronted him.

She looked out the peephole again. Freddy turned to her door.

"I know you're watching," he said. "I can see the shadow of your feet beneath the door."

With a relieved sigh she snatched open her door. "I didn't want to disturb you."

"That's a first." He unlocked his door and walked in.

She hurried over and closed his door behind her.

"Already in pajamas? No plans for tonight?"

She glanced down. Remembering her promise to David, she had put on a bra.

"I felt like staying in." She'd turned down several party invitations in order to wait on Freddy.

He dropped his laptop bag on one of the barstools and walked into the kitchen. She trailed behind him, wondering how long to wait before asking about the position.

"Want any ice cream?" He opened the freezer and took out a small carton of vanilla.

"No, you go ahead."

He raised an eyebrow. "No lecture on not eating ice cream this late?"

"It's Friday. And ... you know ... you can't argue with the boss."

"I'm not your boss."

She sagged against the counter and watched him dig out a spoon. So that was it. He wasn't hiring her.

"No, I guess not."

He turned to face her, and leaned a hip against the counter. He ate a couple spoonfuls of ice cream before meeting her gaze.

"At least not until Monday. Congratulations, both Phyllis and Larry thought you were the best person for the job."

Elation burst within her. She jumped up and clapped. Then his words settled in. "But you didn't think I was the best one."

"I thought you were one of the best."

That didn't do a lot to soothe her.

He finally smiled, full on dimple. "But I couldn't give you my highest vote since I'd already done you a favor with the interview."

She threw her arms around his neck. "Oh, Freddy, you're wonderful!" She buried her nose in his neck, letting that old admiration swell inside as she breathed in his cologne. It didn't take long for her body to heat up from another sensation. Even with her bra on, the feel of his muscled chest hardened her nipples.

As usual when she hugged him, he automatically slipped an arm around her waist. They fit together, chest, stomach, hips, legs, him solid and strong where she was soft. He felt good against her. So good that she snuggled closer, rubbing her body against his.

He tensed, but didn't jerk away. That was a first. She lifted her head. His eyes burned bright with something she'd seen numerous times from other men. Desire.

The box in her heart with her warm and fuzzy feelings for Freddy rattled. Those feelings strained to be let out, sending vibrations through her chest with their escape attempt.

She had two choices. One, do the smart thing—pull away, and pretend she didn't see it. Or, two, go with the electricity simmering between them and see what happened. The second thought pushed her forward. Her dad was right about one thing—she was impulsive.

She leaned in and gave him a soft kiss. Heat sparked across her nerve endings. He didn't lean in, but he didn't let her go either. His lackluster response challenged her. She could do better than that. She pushed her hips forward to brush against him.

Holy crap, that was an erection! Heady excitement coursed through her as the lock on her emotions released. He wanted her. Freddy actually desired her. He might not want to, and he might deny it forever, but the proof was right there.

She leaned in to kiss him again. Freddy jerked away. His nostrils flared with his rough breaths. Her disappointment couldn't put her feelings back inside. She ran her hands through her hair, then tugged and pulled at her clothes. She didn't know what to do with them. They wanted to grab him and pull him back against her. She didn't bother to look away. She wanted him to see her desire. He blinked and lowered his eyes. When he glanced back at her, his emotions were hidden.

"Um ... you're welcome. But it wasn't me. You did well during the interview." His eyebrows met over his glasses. "You were very meticulous about your answers, and gave good examples of how you've assisted others. I even called your references and got nothing but glowing reviews. Apparently, virtual assistants can save many people in tight situations."

"I told you it was a real job." Her breathless voice wouldn't cooperate with his attempt to ignore what just happened.

"That you did." His eyes dropped to her chest, then jerked away. He turned and took a bite of his ice cream.

"So, what's my first assignment?" That came out a little more normal.

"Can't that wait until Monday?"

"Just trying to be proactive."

The smile he gave her brought out his dimple, and kicked up her internal body temperature several notches. "I'm working on a proposal for Satterfield's. The restaurant chain is considering outsourcing their books and I want to be the one they choose. So be prepared to work hard on that."

She raised an eyebrow and gave him a once-over. "Oh, I'm ready to work hard for you." Crap, she didn't mean to make the double meaning so obvious.

Freddy cleared his throat. "That's good to know." He ate a heaping spoonful of ice cream.

He didn't sound very excited, and he didn't take the bait. As if he'd ever take the bait. "You know what, I think I'll go home and celebrate."

He swung around. "You're not hanging out here tonight?"

He wanted her to stay. That at least made her feel a little better about him ignoring what just happened.

"No, I think I'll let you chill. You've had a long week." She reached out and wiped a smear of ice cream off the corner of his lip, hoping he would grab her, toss her on the counter, and give her libido some much needed attention.

He stepped back. "I think that's a good idea. I may turn in early."

She hid her disappointment behind a smile. "Yeah, I should rest too. You know, I'm having coffee with the professor tomorrow."

"You don't like coffee."

"Yeah, well, he asked me out. I'd break it if something better came along."

Her voice held all of the invitation he should need. She waited for something in his expression. Jealousy, anger, some clue that the desire wasn't just a fleeting moment. She got nothing. If anything, his face became more impassive.

"Well, have a good time. Let me know how it goes."

"I'll do that."

With a frown, she turned and walked to the door. She glanced at him over her shoulder. He raised an eyebrow and gave her a wave goodbye. Still frowning, and feeling slightly foolish, she left.

CHAPTER 10

"Hey, Freddy, I have a question."

Freddy didn't turn away from his computer. Janiyah had had tons of questions since she started. "Okay, shoot."

"Congress is out of session, right? So what tax issues will they have to pick up when they return?"

Freddy looked away from the audit report to stare, most likely dumbly, at Janiyah.

"Come again?"

She sashayed into his office and plopped into the chair across from his desk. If her question threw him off, then her outfit struck him speechless. It wasn't a bad outfit, just so ... Janiyah. White camisole, pink blazer and powder blue skirt. She reminded him of a cupcake: his favorite dessert. The mental image, her vanilla perfume, and the way it clung to her curves gave him a bad case of desire. More like worsened it. He'd been plagued with wanting her ever since that kiss in his kitchen.

He thought about it constantly: the invitation in her pretty eyes, the soft touch that wasn't enough when her lips brushed his, and how perfectly her warm body molded to his. He'd considered calling Liz to ask about her boss just to get his mind off Janiyah. He needed to do something, because having her in his office every day wasn't going to make it go away.

She'd been busy her first two weeks while she learned their office procedures from Phyllis. This week Phyllis released Janiyah from her assertive grip and let her take over handling the admin assistant duties on her own. She'd spent the week bouncing around the office chatting to everyone. He didn't know what was more distracting—her surprisingly insightful observations to make their office more efficient, or the sexy way she sashayed through the hall.

Regardless, she had too much free time. Which would be annoying if it weren't because she'd quickly completed the items he needed for the Satterfield proposal in an afternoon. The woman finished work almost as soon as he gave it to her and better than he'd expected.

She crossed one leg over the other, giving him a generous view of the soft skin of her thighs.

"You heard me. What tax items will Congress take up when they're back in session?"

Thanks to that glorious glimpse of thigh, he'd almost forgotten what they were talking about. "Several on the individual and business tax side. Not to mention the tax extenders they should have voted on last session."

"Such as?"

He leaned forward and rested his arms on his desk. "Why do you want to know?"

"For the blog."

"You're not supposed to blog at work."

She laughed and sat back in her chair, and her ponytail swung from side to side. She looked so carefree, and sexy, it made his body tighten.

"As if I'd blog about that. No, this is for your website. It's boring and dated. I know that you can't do much to make accounting fun ... but you can at least provide useful information."

He rubbed his nose beneath his glasses. "My website has useful information."

"No, your website says who you are, what services you provide, and who works here. You need to provide some type of insight on what your company is about. You said yourself you started it to help out small businesses. Well, your site doesn't say that. You need a page for small business, a page for individuals, and maybe one for non-profits since you do work with them. And a blog and newsletter—"

"Newsletter?"

"Yes, sending a newsletter with updates on tax law shows that you're savvy."

"I'm not trying to be savvy."

She shook her head. "I really don't understand how you landed Nebulas with that attitude."

"I did it without a blog and a *newsletter.*"

"Just email me the stuff, and I'll update the website. Once that's going, I'll work on the social media links." She stood.

"We don't need social media."

"Yes we do. Even Phyllis agrees." She turned away and sashayed back to the door.

Damn his eyes for following the sway of her hips.

"Oh, and another thing."

He jerked his attention to her face when she swung around. "What other thing?"

"I brought in some of my receipts, invoices, and stuff from that other little side job I had before. Do you mind staying late and helping me work on my budget? Pretty please? You promised weeks ago."

She batted her lashes and gave him that playful pout that got her whatever she wanted. He should be angry at her for coming in here and telling him his website was crap. For pushing him into the realm of social media when he vowed to avoid it like a sugar free diet. But her argument was sound. Once again, she surprised him. He'd half expected her to sit at her desk, on the phone, filing her nails, and sighing about how boring it was to work here. Instead, she'd had Phyllis gabbing like a high school girl in the break room, brought his staff doughnuts on Friday, and searched for ways to make his office better without being off-putting about the way things used to run. Not an easy task when Phyllis was the previous administrative assistant.

His only complaint was her tendency to arrive for work five to ten minutes late. He'd put his foot down on carpooling. He needed some time without the Janiyah temptation. Seeing this side of her was making it hard to remember she was the type of woman he stayed away from.

"So, will you?"

"Fine, Janiyah. I'll stay late and help you."

She grinned. His heart thudded.

He watched the door for several seconds after she left, before cursing himself for being a fool, and returning his attention to the audit report.

• • •

The corner of Fredrick's mouth twitched as he listened to Janiyah talk fashion with Phyllis outside his office. Phyllis's taste in clothing was severe to say the least, but she always tried some way to liven it up. Usually with clashing results. Now that Janiyah worked here, his stiff employee was growing increasingly excited about being more eccentric with her wardrobe.

Janiyah's laughter flitted through the air, sending an unwelcome thrill through his body. He jumped up from his seat and went to the door. The faster they got through this budget session the better.

They didn't notice him when he stopped at the door. Janiyah stood next to Phyllis, her lips pursed prettily while they both gazed at a catalogue. He let his gaze quickly rove over her blue and pink outfit and licked his lips. He'd buy cupcakes on the way home tonight.

"Don't worry about what your husband says. I think that dress is fantastic and appropriate. You definitely should buy it." Janiyah tapped the catalogue with her finger.

"That's what I said. Just because I'm over fifty doesn't mean I can't pull it off."

Janiyah grinned. "Exactly."

When they slapped hands and giggled Fredrick's jaw dropped. Never in his life had he heard Phyllis giggle. He didn't even want to see what they were discussing. The last thing he needed was a mental image of her in any type of dress that could be described as inappropriate.

He cleared his throat. They both looked up from the catalogue. Janiyah's smile softened at the edges, sending another shot through his body. She'd wanted him to kiss her the other night. Now, whenever she smiled like that, all sweet and happy, it made him want to do just that. Forget the reasons why he was fighting this attraction, and make her smile like that all the time. So he broke eye contact and looked at his watch.

"Are we going to work on your budget, or am I interrupting fashion hour?"

Phyllis closed the catalogue and shoved it under her arm. "You're not funny."

"That's exactly what I tell him," Janiyah said.

He cocked a brow. "I'm ready to get to work. Going through your finances might take all night."

Janiyah sucked her teeth. She hitched the strap of her denim bag on her shoulder. "My finances are not that bad."

"I'd be surprised, considering you've never created a budget before." He waved her over.

Janiyah rolled her eyes at Phyllis. "The man lives to torment me."

Phyllis smiled at Janiyah, then gave him the evil eye. He returned her glare with a *so what* look of his own. She finally turned away and left.

Janiyah pulled off her blazer and tossed it over her arm. The tops of her breasts pushed above the white lace camisole, and his mouth watered.

"You have that all wrong," he said, snatching his eyes way from the enticing view of her cleavage. "It's you who lives to torment me."

She reached up and patted his cheek. "Oh, Freddy, if only."

Adrenaline surged within him from the simple touch. He stepped back into his office. "Let's get started."

He sat at the conference table beside the windows. When she didn't follow, he glanced at her. She stood by the door, the corner of her mouth twisting as she studied him.

He pushed out the seat next to him. "You coming?"

She sighed then closed the door. The intimacy of the simple action caused a tightening in his pants.

He shifted in his seat. "Why close the door?"

Her shoulder lifted in an unassuming shrug. "As of now, I'm a client, not a friend."

"Since when did we become friends?"

She plopped down into the chair next to him. The sweet smell of her vanilla perfume drifted over. She smelled like a cupcake. The discomfort between his legs increased.

"Ahh, Freddy, don't be that way."

"One day I'm going to make you call me Fredrick." He could think of a lot of ways he'd make her call his full name. Ways she wouldn't expect a "good guy" like him to do.

Her full lips lifted into a playful smile. "I'd like to see you try." She leaned forward, bringing her scent and a view of her breasts with her.

"I don't think you do." He would turn her around. Hit it from the back as she screamed his full name.

The teasing glint in her eye turned to something more threatening to his good sense. "Oh, I do."

Damn, his dick got hard. This was going down the wrong path. He leaned back. "Interesting outfit choice today."

Her eyes called him a coward for pulling away, but she leaned back. "Do you like it?"

"It's colorful."

She bumped him with her shoulder. "It's cute and you know it."

"You look like a cupcake."

"You love cupcakes, so I take that as a compliment."

Double damn. The woman knew too much about him. "I like eating cupcakes, not looking at them."

She raised an eyebrow and leaned forward again. "Hmmm, that's interesting."

His heart beat triple time. His erection pulsed painfully with each beat. This conversation was beyond going down the wrong path and over into dangerous territory. He was reading too much into it. Another unfortunate side effect of the almost-kiss: he saw innuendo and flirtation in everything she did.

"Where's your paperwork?"

She pulled the bag off her shoulder. "All my bills, income statements, and the other stuff I could think of."

His eyebrows drew together as she pulled handfuls of paper from the bag. After three grabs, there was a pile in front of him. He looked from the pile to her.

"This is in no kind of order."

She shrugged. "I usually stuff everything in a drawer. This is the entire contents of that drawer."

He lifted several sheets of paper. "How do you keep up with everything?"

"I pay as it comes. Or if it's not important, put it off until I can."

With a shake of his head he continued to riffle through the stack. "This is crazy. I'm going to need my laptop."

"For what?"

"To put your expenses, earnings, and savings into our budget management software. We've got to get a handle on this before we can create a roadmap for the future."

She pushed the chair back. "Okay, sounds good. I'll go home and when you finish, you can stop by my apartment and let me know what you came up with."

When she tried to stand he grabbed her hand. "No, ma'am. You're sitting here with me, and we're going through this together."

She groaned and rolled her head in a circle. Her ponytail brushed the back of her neck, drawing his eye to the softness of her skin there. "I figured you would say something like that. Come on, Freddy, do it for me, please." Her thick lashes batted and her lower lip poked out temptingly.

He shook his head and turned away. "No. You want to become more responsible with your money. You've got to do this with me."

She sighed. "Fine, but you owe me."

"I can't possibly see how I owe you for doing *you* a favor."

"You know I hate math. You owe me for making me do math."

He let go of her hand. "How do you make money as a virtual assistant when you balk at the idea of getting your stuff in order?"

She frowned. "I don't get paid to put my stuff in order. I'm better at getting everyone else's stuff in order. Mine works itself out."

With a shake of his head he turned to the mess on the table. "Just get my laptop off my desk."

Two hours later it was past nine and they'd finally gotten through the pile of material she'd dumped on the table. The papers were separated into neat piles corresponding to bills and expenses and further broken down into necessities and extraneous purchases. Her knees were tucked under her in the chair, and her elbows rested on the table as she leaned forward to look at what he input on the screen. He should be used to the smell of her perfume by now, and the warmth of her body next to his, but he wasn't. He was easily distracted whenever she shifted next to him. His body hummed with tension, and he was more than ready to finish her budget and get out of the office.

She leaned forward to point at the computer screen. Her plump little breasts nearly spilled from the top of her camisole. His mouth went dry and he licked his lips. Definitely buying cupcakes tonight.

"No, Freddy, that should be $350 not $450," she said. Her voice was low, her exhaustion from going over numbers for two hours apparent. Still, his mind imagined it as the way she'd sound first thing in the morning after a long night of lovemaking.

He shook his head in a vain attempt to clear it. "My bad. I'm getting ... tired."

She blew air between her lips. "You're tired. I'm exhausted. Are we finished?"

He nodded. "Almost." He corrected his mistake and frowned. "Janiyah, your budget works out ... miraculously." She hit his shoulder but he continued. "But you're spending way too much money on clothes. You almost didn't meet your budget last month." She leaned closer to the screen. "What? I buy from consignment shops and online. I don't shop in fancy department stores. You're looking at something wrong."

He shook his head. "No, you spent nearly twenty-five hundred dollars just on eBay last month. If your dad hadn't given you that money for your birthday, you would have been short." He turned to her. "Do you spend that much regularly?"

"No, there were just a lot of good deals last month. And it was my birthday. Nothing was that expensive," she said, still examining the spreadsheet as if the numbers would change. "Twenty-five hundred isn't much. And now that I'm working here, I'm making more and it should cover my spending."

"Maybe while your dad is supplementing your income, but it won't be if you stop accepting his money."

"I've already stopped accepting his money."

She said it with a little bit of an *F-you* in her voice that he couldn't help but admire. "All the more reason to use your salary here for your everyday expenses and put the money from your virtual assisting clients into a high yield account. But to do that, you can't afford to spend that much on clothes. You've got to slow down with the consignment shopping."

"Okay, fine."

With a sigh, she pulled her hair out of the ponytail. She massaged her scalp and moaned, then pushed the thick strands behind her ear. He stared at the pulse at the base of her neck. Never had he had a vampire fetish in his life, but he wanted to lean in and softly suck on that spot with a vengeance. His fingers flexed on the keyboard before slowly running across the keys, the smooth surface a meager substitute for her skin.

When she turned back to him he quickly looked at the screen.

"Are you okay? You look kinda flushed."

He nodded stiffly. "I'm good. Overall, your budget isn't bad. You could manage to pay all your bills just off your virtual assisting job. But I still recommend less clothes shopping. And maybe cut back on purchasing items on a whim, like the violin you bought a few months ago."

She hmphed and sat back. "You know why I bought that."

His desire cooled a notch. He kinked his brow. "And that relationship lasted how long?"

She waved a hand. "I developed an appreciation for music."

"And he developed an appreciation for ... "

She narrowed her eyes. "We're not talking about him."

Lifting a shoulder, he said, "Fine. Just limit your purchases and you should be able to start saving. I know someone who can help you with a retirement savings plan."

"Retirement? Goodness, Freddy, you're killing me." She stretched her hands over her head and yawned.

His eyes zeroed in on her breasts pressed against the shirt. He might have been able to speak if her nipples weren't pebble hard beneath the flimsy fabric. His lips parted, breathing became difficult, and heat burned inside. Uninhibited visions of pulling the top down and watching the dark tips pop free of her shirt projected in his mind. He'd grab them gently. Squeeze them just enough to cause them to protrude even more before slowly running his tongue across them. His teeth would tease them, she'd pant his full name before he finally took them into his mouth. Would her skin be as soft as cake? Would she melt against his tongue and moan deeply?

"Freddy?"

Her voice snapped him back. Embarrassment heated his face. Instead of meeting her eyes, he looked at the computer screen. He was making a fool of himself. Janiyah Henderson was not the woman for him. She stretched and he was ready to forget that and have sex on a table.

"We're through here. I've got some other stuff to wrap up before leaving the office."

"But it's late and you've been staring at reports all day. Let's grab something to eat then go home."

He shook his head. "No, you go. I'll pick up something later."

She touched his shoulder. The warmth from her small hand only increased his arousal.

He jerked out of reach. "Look, I've gotten behind doing this. We can finish up another day."

"Are you mad at me?"

The hurt in her voice almost weakened him, but he ignored it. Bruising her feelings now prevented him from making a fool of himself later.

"I'm not mad at you. I've just spent too much time on this." He glanced in her direction. Her shoulders slumped. A real pout pursed her full lips. He softened his tone. "We're done. Go home."

The corner of her mouth lifted in a sad smile. "For what it's worth, thanks."

She leaned forward to press a kiss to his cheek. Without thinking, he turned his head so that their lips brushed. She gasped, her soft breath caressing his lips. His body prepped to go in and take her mouth the way he wanted. Explore every soft crevice before ripping that damn scrap of a shirt off and reliving his fantasy.

He stopped himself. He had a plan. She wouldn't fit in that plan. If he forgot how she twisted every man she knew into agreeing to everything she wanted, he could kiss all of his hard work goodbye. No longer would he be the smart businessman who opened his own accounting firm and made it one of the most successful in the area in two years. He'd be the guy who sleeps with his assistants. Possibly lose his best friend. Be the latest schmuck to fall in love with Janiyah. And the fool who tossed aside his well laid plans because of a woman who lost interest in him after a few weeks.

He leaned back. "I'll see you tomorrow."

She frowned, confusion and disappointment clear in her eyes. When she slid back in her chair he mentally relaxed, but didn't trust himself enough to relax his body. Otherwise he might reach toward her again.

"Sure. Have a good night," she said softly.

His tension didn't go away until the door opened and closed behind her. With a sigh, he did the one thing that would snap him back to reality after being tempted by Janiyah. He called his dad, knowing there would be some new drama with his parents that would quickly remind him why he should continue to ignore this desire.

CHAPTER 11

Fredrick slid the key in his door at the same time Janiyah's door flew open.

"Thank God you're home," she said.

He turned toward her with a sigh. After his reaction to her earlier in the week, he'd spent an extra hour at the gym two nights in a row taking out his frustration on the weight bench. The last thing he needed was to further tax his muscles moving a piece of furniture she'd found at a consignment store. The extra workouts helped. But not as much as the call to his parents. Instead of being excited about possibly luring a client that would help save his fledging insurance company, his father had told him about the new cooking classes his mom signed up for. He had at least gotten his dad to nail down a day for the meeting with the client by agreeing to come.

Janiyah hopped from one foot to the other. Her silky hair, which hung straight today, bounced around her face with the movement. Her workout shorts and Atlanta Falcons t-shirt meant she wasn't going out tonight.

"Too much sugar?" he asked.

She rushed over and pushed him out of the way. "There's a spider camping out in my bathroom and I can't go in there." She opened his door and flew inside. "I'm gonna use yours until you kill it," she said over her shoulder.

He pulled the key out of the door. "This is why I'm moving," he said to himself. If he was going to work with her he definitely couldn't continue living beside her.

He set down his gym bag and sat on the couch with a groan. He stretched his right leg out in front of him, placed his foot on the coffee table, and rubbed the dull ache in his knee. He'd hurt it a year ago playing in a flag football tournament. It always bothered him after a strenuous workout. Usually he paced himself, but physical taxation was worth it. If he was exhausted, he wouldn't stay up half the night dreaming about her.

He rested his head along the back of the couch with his eyes closed when she came out of the bathroom. He sensed her beside him before the scent of her perfume wafted over him. He probably smelled worse than his gym bag.

"Freddy, what's wrong?" she said, her voice soft.

He kept his head back and eyes closed. "Nothing."

Cold fingers moved his hand out of the way and massaged his knee. His head popped up, and he pushed her hand away. "What are you doing?"

"You were rubbing it like it was bothering you."

"You're bothering me. And your hands are cold."

She cocked her head to the side and smiled before moving closer.

"I wanted to thank you, but you're being such an ass I might say forget it." She rubbed her hands together before blowing in them.

"Thank me? You? I don't believe it."

"I'm serious. For showing confidence in my abilities, and not treating me like I'm a joke. I appreciate you giving me the job."

"I only gave you the interview; you got the job on your own. I could have easily been overridden on the hiring decision."

"I know, but the fact that you even trusted me enough to not screw up the interview. I appreciate that. I loved being a virtual assistant. Still do, but it was easier for me to work for people I didn't know than those I did."

He shifted to face her fully. "Why?"

"No one viewed my work seriously, so I kept that part of my life to myself. This job has been good. It's teaching me to not be afraid to show everyone that I'm more than just the spoiled daughter of a rich daddy. I wouldn't have believed I was capable of joining the ranks of the suit and tie club if it weren't for you and this job."

She finished warming up her hands and went back to rubbing his knee. Her small fingers gently rolled around the joint, relieving the ache there but causing another one higher.

He didn't push her away this time. He liked her hand on his knee more than he should, and he was floored by her confession. He'd seen her red-eyed and groggy the morning after she stayed up late working, and listened to her when she gushed about a project that had turned out even better than she expected. He'd assumed she shared that with everyone. To know that she'd only had with him brought home what Aaron said. She trusted him enough to reveal a part of her life that others brushed off. Shame filled him for the doubt he'd harbored about how well she'd work in his office. He'd seen the evidence himself that she was a hard worker.

"You're doing a great job. I know you're not turned on by numbers and figures."

"I'm learning to appreciate them." She met his eye, her hand slowing its massage on his knee.

"I'm should go take a shower."

She scrunched her nose. "You are kinda musty."

"I thought women liked a man's musk," he said, lifting his shirt to sniff.

"Only to a certain extent."

He relaxed when they slipped back into friendly teasing. "You're the one who got on me for eating too much ice cream. I'm going to the gym so you'll hush, so get used to the aftereffects."

She scooted closer and ran her fingers along the side of his neck. "I like it that you go to the gym, Freddy."

His blood heated and settled thickly in his crotch. The look in Janiyah's eyes was killing his willpower. He cleared his throat.

She lifted her head. Their faces were close enough it wouldn't take much to kiss her. Her coffee colored eyes lowered to his lips. The pink tip of her tongue poked out to run lightly across her own tempting bottom lip. His body tensed in anticipation. His mind screamed to do it. Her shallow breaths and parted lips were as much an invitation as her saying "Kiss me, Freddy." And his hard dick screamed for the precursor to the ultimate goal, sliding into the slick spot between her soft thighs.

"I like your muscles very much," she whispered.

If he kissed her now, the way he wanted to, she'd no longer view him as the boring best friend of her brother. He'd give her the excitement she craved in a relationship. The excitement he sometimes craved. But the next day she'd have to work with him. He'd have to pretend as if there was nothing between them in order to avoid rumors and risk his friendship with Aaron. It would almost be worth it to erase that teasing smile off her face and show her how a real man, not those fools she dated, could satisfy her.

He jumped up from the couch. The thought was too tempting. "I'm getting in the shower." He lumbered across the living room toward the hall.

"But ... but ... " she stammered.

He turned and took some delight at the bewildered look on her face. He raised a brow and she sat back with a huff.

"What about the spider?" she finished lamely.

And they were back to normal.

"I'll get it after I've showered," he said, turning away.

"Okay, I'll wait."

The sound of his television coming on followed him down the hall.

CHAPTER 12

When the bathroom door closed and the shower came on, Janiyah collapsed against the back of the couch with a hand against her forehead. She took several deep breaths to calm her racing heart. The strong ache and wetness between her legs pulsed with the beat. She would be using the new vibrator she'd bought from Mrs. Driggers later. She twisted in the seat and squeezed her legs together.

Why hadn't he kissed her? The timing was perfect. She'd practically begged him with her eyes; her body language screamed *come and get it*. Hell, she'd almost grabbed his head and pulled it forward. Was he really that uninterested in her that he could turn down a perfectly innocent kiss?

Okay, there was nothing innocent about what would have happened if he had kissed her, but still.

Twice Freddy had let his guard down. He wanted her, and it was more than just a small interest. She'd seen the struggle, and finally the decision to pull away, in his eyes. The last time he'd done that, in the year before she went to college, she'd let him push her away. She'd believed that because they were too different, and he was too much like a brother, they should just be friends. She'd done her best and tried to move on. She'd dated other men, pretended as if Freddy was like a brother, and ignored the fluttering of her heart when he threw her the random hot glance. She was tired of ignoring the obvious. She couldn't push Freddy out of her mind.

Her heart pumped a mixture of anxiety, excitement, and adrenaline through her system. It was the closest thing she'd ever come to being high, a surge that made her feel like she could do anything. Which meant one thing: a rash decision was on the horizon. There was no way of knowing if it would be fantastic or disastrous until afterward.

If things didn't work out, she couldn't cut Freddy out of her life like other boyfriends. If he later felt like her asshole ex, and thought of her as more of a fun pastime, it would hurt a hell of a lot more. Her brothers might throw in their objections, but since they all liked Freddy, she could easily overcome that. She hoped, anyway. Working together would make things complicated, but they wouldn't be the first people who worked together and slept together. All of the reasons not to go with her impulse didn't change anything.

Her heart wanted Freddy. And if Freddy wanted her, he could have her.

Tonight.

On the damn couch for all she cared.

The VH1 countdown on television went to a commercial. Then another. He was still in the shower. More than ten minutes passed. Very unFreddy like. He was a stickler on conserving water.

Reckless energy pushed her off the couch. She had to investigate. Something could be wrong. He could be sprawled helpless at the bottom of the shower.

The cocktail of anticipation and giddiness pumping in her veins drove her actions. It was unlikely she'd find Freddy lying helpless in the shower. But she might get a glimpse of him naked. That thought was so clear she would swear a mini Janiyah with devil horns had whispered it in her ear.

She gently pried open the bathroom door and peeked around.

"Freddy?" she said softly. He wouldn't have heard her even if the shower were off.

She sucked in a shallow breath before breathing became nearly impossible. He definitely wasn't hurt.

Desire rushed through her, focusing its intensity in the tips of her breasts and the juncture of her thighs. Freddy faced her, his back against the shower wall, his eyes closed, his muscled legs spread wide as his right hand slid up and down his erection.

His long, thick erection.

Based on the bulge in his pants she'd pretended to ignore, she'd guessed his size was impressive, but nothing was like seeing it elongated and rock hard in all its glory.

Her need soaked her panties. Her nipples beaded longingly within her lace bra. She clenched the slick muscles of her sex in tandem with each stroke of his hand. Dragging her gaze up, she took in the intensity of his expression. His bottom lip clenched between his teeth, and the grove between his eyebrows was so thick, if she didn't know he was masturbating, she'd assume he was scowling. He was magnificent and incredibly sexy.

Unable to keep her gaze away, she looked back at his impressive dick and licked her lips as soap suds ran down his wide chest, swollen from his workout, across taut abdominal muscles, and dripped off the wide, blunt head. Her fingers flexed with the urge to replace his hand with hers.

Her chest burned. First from desire, then from a lack of oxygen. She took in a stuttering breath. This was private; she shouldn't be here. Yet, she stood frozen. His movements became jerky, less controlled. She swallowed hard as her desire increased with his. She sensed his release; her wet sex throbbed for its own.

He groaned. "Janiyah." Her name burst from his lips with as much force as the first stream of frothy ejaculate.

It shocked her out of her trance. She quickly jumped back and softly pulled the door closed. She hoped his orgasm masked the sound as she ran into the living room.

She tried to sit on the couch and pretend as if that hadn't happened, but it had. He'd jacked off in the shower. And called her name when he came.

That box holding her emotions exploded. There was no containing what she felt, what she wanted. She was more turned on now than she'd ever been. No man did that and called the name of a woman he wasn't interested in. Her mind was made up. It was about to go down.

He looked normal when he came out of the bathroom a few minutes later wearing a pair of pajama bottoms and a red t-shirt. She couldn't prevent her gaze from dropping to the front of his pants. Her fingers itched to discover if he'd put on underwear. If she hadn't seen with her own eyes what he'd done she would never know. This wasn't the first time he'd showered when she was there. Maybe it wasn't the first time he'd done that. Her body trembled with a new rush of desire.

She sat up and grinned at him. To hell with the consequences, she was riding this high and seeing where it led.

He raised an eyebrow when their eyes met. "Are you okay?"

"Great, but I'm about to be better."

"Oookay," he said slowly. He headed toward the kitchen. "Did you get more information from Liz about her boss? I don't have plans for this weekend, and I may call and ask her out."

Her passion cooled like an Antarctic breeze. "You're thinking about her?"

He grabbed a Ziploc bag out of the cabinet and opened the freezer. "Why wouldn't I? I said she was cute. I'm sure you have a date this weekend with your professor. We can compare notes." He winked at her from over his shoulder. "Unless one of us gets lucky. No sex stories, remember." He tossed some ice into the freezer bag.

She was speechless as she watched him come over to the couch, prop his foot on the coffee table, and settle the ice on his knee.

"Can I turn this?" he said, picking up the remote.

"You almost kissed me. Now you're thinking about her." It was out before she could think.

He shook his head. "I didn't almost kiss you."

"Yes you did. We both felt it."

"No, I saw you doing your flirty thing and I left instead of following you up." He didn't look at her as he spoke. He flipped through the channels before stopping on PBS.

She was too frustrated to argue about his choice.

"You punked out. Then you go in there and ... " She let her voice trail off. No need admitting to her invasion of his privacy.

He glared at her. "I go take a shower then come out and try to have a normal conversation. I can't believe you even care that I didn't kiss you. Come on, Janiyah, we both know you're a flirt."

"Not with you."

"Especially with me. Now can we move on?"

She stood up and paced in front of him. "How can you go from ... thinking of me to asking about a date with her?"

"I don't understand where this is coming from. You've had several dates with Mr. Wonderful, hounded me about getting back in the dating game, and now you're suddenly having a fit because I didn't fall into your little trap. That's a little low, even for you."

She sucked in a breath and placed her hand over her heart. "Now you're accusing me of playing dirty. You're the one playing dirty." It was overdramatic, but she was past caring.

He threw down the remote. "What the hell is wrong with you?"

"You're what's wrong with me."

He scowled and she stomped her foot. A part of her brain registered that to him she was making no sense. Yet her mind swirled with memories of how he'd turned her away years ago. Here she was again, horny and frustrated for Freddy, and he didn't want her. Except now it was ten times worse because the pain was magnified with knowing he could go from calling her name during an orgasm to asking about another woman.

"You know what?" she said. "I'm out of here."

He sighed and pulled the ice off his knee. "What about the spider?"

"Forget the damn spider. I'll kill it myself," she said as she ran out.

Slamming his door behind her, she rushed into her apartment and slammed that door for good measure. She hated spiders, so right now would be a good time to take out her anger by killing the annoying creature.

Her two bedroom apartment was set up like his, but was nowhere near as orderly. Where Freddy had tasteful, heavy wood and leather furniture, her furniture was a mixture of thrift store and yard sale finds. Remnants of hobbies she'd picked up and dropped were scattered throughout. The sewing machine from her brief interest in fashion design, a telescope she'd bought while dating a guy who was really into astrology, an old violin.

Her throat burned. The violin hurt the worst, a reminder of her relationship with the asshole that crashed and burned. *You were a fun lay, but it's time to move on. I need someone serious, and let's face it, you're a joke, Janiyah.* She hadn't admitted to Freddy how far that went. He'd warned her against going out with the asshole from the beginning. But he'd been with that damn dental hygienist. She'd let her jealousy cloud the fact that she was getting close to a creep.

Her apartment was a testament to how much of a joke she was. She could get a nine to five job, but even that was a struggle. She was already running out of things to keep her busy, and the monotony of answering calls for the same things at Freddy's office was forcing her to look for new things to do. If Freddy knew that, he would take her even less seriously. No wonder her dad didn't think she could handle running the business. If she kept up with this lack of direction, she would end up a helpless hoarder drowning under a stack of crap she'd picked up after dating random guys.

Her vision blurred with tears. She hastily wiped them away, snatched up a magazine from the stack against the wall, and marched toward her bathroom. To hell with how boring the job was—and to the pit of hell with her ex-boyfriend. She wasn't a joke. She might not love her job, but it proved she could hold her own in the corporate world. She'd prove to everyone that she was just as capable as those starched, suit-wearing women at the mixers.

Starting with killing the damn spider in her bathroom.

She threw open the door to the bathroom. That's where her bravado ended. She took a hesitant step across the threshold. It was still there on the wall right above the toilet: brown, hairy, and looking ten times larger than it had earlier.

A shiver went down her spine and she cringed. *You can do this,* she thought. With a deep breath she took a small step forward and raised the magazine above her head.

The spider twitched. She screeched.

She spun around and ran out of the bathroom only to slam into Freddy's wide chest. She screamed again and hit him with the magazine.

He jerked the magazine out of her hand and tossed it to the floor. "What was that for?" Taking her shoulders in his grasp he pushed her back.

"You scared the crap out of me. And that spider tried to attack me."

The tension left his body. His eyes filled with laughter and he smiled. Full on dimple. Her heart melted. "It didn't attack you."

"You don't know that." Her panic subsided. She was being silly again.

His thumbs gently brushed back and forth against her shoulders, fanning the waning flames of her desire. The humor in his eyes shifted to a look very similar to what she'd seen in his shower. Electricity thrummed between them. Her skin prickled with anticipation.

He smelled good. His body was hot next to hers. And she would die if he didn't kiss her.

The seconds ticked by. Any other man would do it, but he wouldn't. She lowered her gaze and tried to step away. He didn't let her go. Her eyes lifted to his and she seriously forgot to breathe. Hunger blazed fiercely from him. Without a word, he pulled her against the hardness of his chest and brought his mouth down on hers.

In all her fantasies Freddy's kisses were slow, hesitant, easy, but this wasn't. It was fast, straightforward, and demanding. His fingers cupped the back of her head and angled it to the side in sync with his tongue thrusting past her lips. She moaned when his other hand squeezed her butt before trailing down to the back of her thigh. Lifting her leg, he pushed her against the wall. He boldly drove his considerable erection into the trembling juncture of her thighs. Her breasts, heavy and aching for his touch, were crushed against the unyielding muscles of his chest.

Her body burned from the inside out. She wrapped her arms around his neck. But it wasn't enough. She needed to touch him. Her hand lowered to the hem of his shirt. He grabbed her wrist and pinned her hand over her head against the wall.

Excitement raced down her spine. She moved her other hand. He jerked that one above her head as well. Her leg around his waist tightened, pulling him closer. She gyrated her hips against him. Holy crap, his dick was big.

He took both of her hands in one of his. The other trailed lightly down past her cheek and neck to softly palm the swell of her breast. His caress was hesitant compared to the direct nature of his kiss. She moaned against the fullness of his lips. He was driving her crazy: caressing but not quite gripping the weight of her breast, slightly rubbing her beaded nipple, but holding back from giving it the full attention she craved.

Just as quickly as it started he ended it. He jerked his head up to stare into her eyes. His hand fell away from her breast.

Their ragged breathing mingled as they stood entwined. Her pulse pounded where his thumb pressed against her wrist.

She stared at him with wonder. Guys like Freddy didn't kiss like that. They didn't overwhelm you and make you want to tear their clothes off and have sex against a wall.

"There. I've kissed you," he said in a desire thickened voice.

He released her hands and methodically removed her leg from around his waist. She continued to lean against the wall for support. She didn't move from her spot as he walked into the bathroom and came out a few seconds later with a handful of balled up paper towels.

"The spider is dead." He cocked an eyebrow. "Have a good night, Janiyah."

Her eyes followed him as he walked away and out of her apartment. When the door shut quietly behind him she slowly sank to the floor. Leaning her head against the smooth surface, she replayed the kiss over and over. Definitely a new vibrator initiation night. But compared to Freddy, she'd need to upsize.

CHAPTER 13

Janiyah smiled at Gerald Westlock sitting across from her in a booth at Panera Bread. Her cheeks burned from the effort to keep the smile on her face while he talked about a new project he'd given his students. She guessed that's what he was still talking about. She'd tuned out about fifteen minutes ago.

She was trying to enjoy this date. Trying not to sneak a look at her phone to see if Liz posted any updates about her date with the architect she'd met the week before. She would not think about only having one more day—ugh—before returning to an office job. And, above all else, she would not think about the way Freddy kissed her the night before then acted as if he couldn't care less when she reminded him she had a date with the professor today.

She clenched the cup in her hand. *Have a good time.* That's what he'd said.

Gerald's tone of voice changed and she focused on him. So much for not thinking about Freddy. She smiled and nodded as Gerald talked, without really paying attention to what he said. Feigning interest in subjects she wasn't interested in wasn't usually this hard. She used to do it when Freddy talked about his work. She'd tune out, but enjoy watching his eyes light up with excitement. It was usually full on dimple mode from his smiles when she let him go on about a subject. Something about having all of his attention focused on her would send her heart clamoring like a horde of shopaholics at a shoe sale.

She tilted her head to the side and watched Gerald. He was just as enthusiastic about his subject. No doubt his smile took him from 'handsome' to '*dayum* he's fine', but no clamoring.

Damn Freddy for kissing her! He should seriously be worried about her falling for this guy. Instead he'd told her to have a good time. What was up with that?

Oh wait, Gerald had stopped talking. His eyebrows were raised, an expectant look in his eye. Crap, he must have asked a question.

"Can you repeat that?"

His smile was slightly patronizing as if he were dealing with a hopeless child. "What books are you reading?"

"Books ... like more than one?"

"Yes, you nodded when I mentioned the importance of reading. You're not one of those 'I don't read' people?" He laughed with the comment, but she sensed the awaiting censure.

"Of course not. I love to read."

Magazines, online articles, and the occasional newspaper piece Freddy insisted she look at, that was the extent of her reading. She got that some people loved reading, but spending hours inside with her nose in a book wasn't appealing. Why couldn't she get points for living life instead of reading about other people's experiences?

"So, what books are you reading? I just finished *A Nation of Wusses*. Have you read it?"

She thought about the entertainment magazine on her coffee table. She thought the pop star on the cover was a wuss for admitting she was afraid to have a relationship with Hollywood's newest heartthrob, but that probably wasn't what he had in mind.

"Um ... no, I'm between books actually."

"What was the last book you read?"

An image of President Obama's face on Freddy's coffee table zapped her brain. "Uh ... *The Audacity of Hope.*"

Gerald frowned. Great, he didn't like the president.

"You're just now reading that?"

"Oh, you know, it was so good I had to read it again."

He grinned and leaned forward on the table. "That's how I feel about the biography of Fredrick Douglass. You've read that, right?"

She filtered through the books she'd read in a history class in college. That had to have been one of them. "Mmmhmm."

"It's so inspiring. I read it at least once a year. What is it about *The Audacity of Hope* that makes you read it over and over?"

She lifted her cup and sucked down the raspberry green tea to stall. No more smiling and nodding when talking to people. That's how she ended up in awkward conversations like this.

When there was no more tea left in the cup she said, "The entire thing is just so ... *hopeful*, you know? I can't help but feel ... quite hopeful after reading it."

His smile deepened and he reached over to put a hand over hers. "Isn't that the best part about reading? Non-fiction especially? To get inspired from a true story. Now don't get me wrong, fiction has its place, literary fiction, I mean. But real life stories of tragedy, triumph, and perseverance are the things that really matter. You know?"

"Sure do."

He started talking again, and she considered the last book she read. About a year ago, Liz had gotten caught up in some vampire erotica that everyone was reading and insisted Janiyah try it. It had been an interesting novel, though the idea of having elongated canines biting and sucking blood from her nether regions wasn't as titillating as Liz and a few other women said it would be.

Now, having Freddy's crooked canine biting and sucking those areas ... That held some promise. Those areas tingled in agreement.

There she went thinking about *him* again.

And Gerald wasn't talking again. Dang, Janiyah, focus.

"I see what you mean," she said. You couldn't go wrong with that phrase.

"Exactly, I don't understand how someone could say they don't read. Those people are jokes."

She flinched. He'd looked at the family passing by their table and didn't notice. A vision of Gerald one day sneering at her and calling her a joke the same way *the asshole* had done came to mind.

Reading, that was the next thing to add to her responsibility list, and not blood sucking vampire erotica. Something about the way Gerald gushed about non-fiction made her doubt he'd view that as prime reading material, although Freddy hadn't teased her about reading it. He'd said reading what you liked was what made the activity enjoyable.

His lips had looked nice that day. He'd been putting on Chapstick while talking. Her head leaned to the side. They'd looked soft. Soft enough to trail slowly up the side of her leg and gently bite on her—

Stop! There she went again.

Gerald chuckled at something he said and she giggled in return. When he dabbed at his eye she snuck a glance at her phone. They'd been here long enough to call it to an end.

"So, Gerald, I'm sure you're busy," she said as soon as his laughter died down. "I promised my mom I'd stop by this afternoon so I've got to go."

Disappointment replaced the laughter in his eyes. He cocked his head to the side, his lips curling into a small frown. The man did get bonus points for looks. Chocolate skin, coal black eyes, and a body shown off to perfection beneath his oxford shirt and khakis.

"So soon? I've really enjoyed myself."

"Yeah, me too. Call me later."

She slid out of the booth, her sandwich barely touched on the table. She'd been too distracted to eat, and he'd been too busy talking to notice. He stood with her. Her gaze traveled up his six foot two inch frame appreciatively. He would've been nice to date for a while longer. But today proved she needed a serious Freddy detox before moving along with anyone else.

They walked out together to their cars. She held out her hand, which was engulfed by his larger one. "Talk with you soon, okay?"

He leaned over to kiss her cheek. "I look forward to it."

He did smell good. Not as good as Freddy.

Again, she wanted to kick herself for the Freddy comparison.

Things could possibly work out with Gerald later. She'd made the monumental mistake once of assuming Freddy would fall under her spell if they kissed, and like before he'd proved he could move on without caring.

Have a good time. The jerk.

Why was she always left craving more from him than he wanted to give?

She needed a diversion. But her mom had called a family meeting. She hadn't been to her parents' house since fighting with her dad. Having Loretta call the meeting meant Janiyah had to declare a ceasefire in her parental boycott.

Her cell phone rang after she was in the car. Without checking to see who the caller was, she activated the Bluetooth device through her radio.

"So how was the date?"

Freddy's smooth voice filled the interior of the car. Her stomach clenched. Her foot pressed the gas. The traffic light turned red, and she quickly slammed her foot onto the brake.

"Why do you care?" she said. Her voice trembled.

"Are you okay? Did he bother you?"

She sighed. "No. I almost ran a red light."

"You should pay attention to the road."

"I was paying attention until you called."

"Just because your phone rings doesn't mean you need to answer the phone. We can talk later."

She rolled her eyes even though he couldn't see it. "Oh please, Freddy. I'm talking to you on the Bluetooth. It was one red light."

The light turned green and she eased ahead with traffic. Freddy's sigh echoed through her vehicle. "Okay, so tell me about the date."

"You really want to know?"

"Why wouldn't I want to know?" His voice was calm and collected.

She gripped the steering wheel, allowing a small fantasy that it was his neck. He shouldn't want to know what her date was like. He should not have told her to *have a good time* after laying a kiss on her like that. He damn sure shouldn't be interested in how the date went after jacking off and calling her name in the shower!

She took a calming breath. "The date went well."

"I've heard that tone before. The guy doesn't stand a chance."

She scoffed. "Well, that's where you're wrong. I think things could go far."

"Really? I would have expected you to grow bored with the professor."

"He's very interesting. He talked about some project his students were doing."

"What was the project?"

"Why do you want to know?" She turned off Killian Road to hit the interstate.

He chuckled and her heart did a crazy flutter at the sound. "I'm curious if you tuned him out the same way you do me."

Freddy knew her too well. She couldn't help but smile. "I will admit it is more fun tuning you out. At least I can enjoy watching you get all excited about your work."

"He isn't excited about his work? I would expect a college professor to ooze enthusiasm."

"Yeah, just like an accountant."

He chuckled. She wondered if it was full on dimple or not. "Touché. Alright, well I've got to give Liz a call."

Her foot slipped off the gas. The car behind her blew the horn and whizzed around. With a silent curse she paid attention to the road. "Why are you calling Liz?"

"She texted for me to call."

"I'm sure it's nothing important." A buxom, blonde bombshell hooking up with Freddy wasn't important in her book.

"Well, I'll find out when I talk to her."

"I could call her for you."

"I don't think that's necessary. You just pay attention to the road," he said. "I'll talk with you later."

He ended the call. A pain she'd never thought to feel again stuttered in her chest. Freddy may have kissed her, but it was pretty obvious he didn't want to want her.

• • •

Fredrick dropped his phone on the counter. He shouldn't have called. More importantly, he shouldn't have kissed her. He'd known she was egging him on to do it. And like a fool he'd followed her up. Another example of why he couldn't trust himself when it came to Janiyah.

Obviously, she'd quickly forgotten about their kiss. The way she breezed into his apartment this morning all giddy with excitement, constantly emphasizing that she was meeting the professor today was proof of that.

That didn't surprise him. How much it upset him did. He'd wanted to grab her and kiss her again until she forgot all about going anywhere with that damn professor. It was nearly impossible to pretend as if he didn't care. His dreams the night before had been filled with the memory of her soft body merged with his. But dreams were unfulfilling. No matter how good his mind was at recalling the kiss, it was nothing compared to actually having Janiyah in his arms.

He picked his phone back up and called Liz. He'd put off asking about her boss long enough. It was time to start dating again and get back to his plan before he forgot Janiyah wasn't the woman for him.

"Hey, Liz, how's it going?" he asked when she answered.

"Going good, Fredrick. How's business?"

"Good, things are leveling out ever since I've hired new staff. Now I can focus my efforts on Nebulus."

"How are things working out with Janiyah?"

"Pretty good. She's come up with ideas for our website and caught on quickly. It's kind of surprising."

"I'm not surprised. Janiyah is great at getting other people's affairs in order. It's focusing on hers that's the problem. I guess it's easy to be that way when your family is always insisting on doing things for you."

Fredrick walked across the room and sat on his couch. "It's not as if she has a problem with that."

"For someone so close to her, you don't see a lot."

"What's that supposed to mean?"

"The baby treatment does get to her. She doesn't let it show too often, but it's there. She goes from being mad as hell they treat her like a child, to being afraid her dad's going to pressure her to take an active role in Henderson Automotive. I think she's afraid of trying and failing, so she just lets everyone else handle things."

"Is that the reason why she was so intent on working with me?"

"I think it's one of the reasons. But you know, with Janiyah, you never get the entire story."

She was right about that. "Well, I didn't call to talk about Janiyah."

"Really?"

"Don't sound surprised. I called to ask about your boss." He cleared his throat. "The one I met a few weeks ago. You said she was interested in me giving her a call."

Liz didn't answer immediately. "I figured you weren't interested."

"I was. I am. I've just been busy."

"Does Janiyah know you're calling?"

Fredrick gripped the phone to keep from tossing it to the floor. "Janiyah is on a date with a college professor, and therefore doesn't care about who I go out with."

Liz laughed. "Oh, that guy. I don't think she's serious about him."

"The way she carried on tells a different story. He's interesting."

"Sounds like you have a problem with that."

"I don't. Janiyah's like a sister. I just want to make sure she doesn't get hurt."

"Okay, you two are always insisting you're like siblings, but you're not."

As if he didn't know that. It was all this close proximity to her, first living near her, now working with her. It's why he left his real estate agent a message right after leaving Janiyah's apartment.

"Liz, are you going to give me the scoop on your boss or not?"

A sigh and a pause, then, "Yes, I'm going to give you her number."

Freddy's shoulders relaxed. This was good. Exactly what he needed to do. Get back on the dating scene. Get his mind off of the woman across the hall playing havoc with his good sense.

CHAPTER 14

When Janiyah arrived at her parents' home, their two cars and all three of her brothers' vehicles blocked access to the garage. She parked beside Kareem's motorcycle. The garage door was up so she walked through to enter in the kitchen. The sound of male voices came from the direction of the den. Janiyah followed the sound to where her three brothers were sprawled out much like they'd been the last time she was here, except now all were focused on some investigative show on television. Her parents weren't in the room.

"So what's the news this time?" she said. "After Daddy sells the business you're going to offer up a dowry and get me married off?"

Her parents came in right at the end of her statement. "Now that we've gotten the drama out of the way," Loretta said, completely ignoring Janiyah's comment, "we can get down to business."

They walked into the room and Roger sat in his recliner. Loretta sat on the arm of the chair beside him. They clasped hands and exchanged looks. Janiyah's stomach sank; that wasn't a "this is going to be good news" look.

"What's going on?" Aaron asked.

Roger lifted his head. "I had a stress test yesterday and the doctor found blockages. Next week I'm having triple bypass surgery. It's routine and nothing you all should worry about."

Janiyah sank into the couch next to Kareem. Her dad's words and visions of him rubbing his chest, out of breath, and sweating from the day he'd moved the boxes whirled around her head like a tornado. Blockages. Surgery. Doctors. She should have seen the signs that something was wrong. He could have had a heart attack right then and there. Right in the middle of their argument. The thought made her stomach queasy.

Her brothers each wore different expressions of disbelief mixed with fear. They started firing questions, but it was a muffled sound to Janiyah.

"Calm down," Roger said, silencing his sons. "They wanted to rush me straight into surgery, but I refused. For this very reason. I don't need the four of you overreacting. This is a wake-up call and proof that it's time for me to get my things in order."

"You're not going to die," Janiyah said.

"Maybe not today, but one day I am. That's why I called you all here the other day and asked about your plans. The chest pains made me realize I need to make sure you're taken care of."

"Come on, Dad, you don't need to be thinking like that," Aaron said.

Roger held up his hand. "Yes, I do. Your mom and I worked hard to build the business and support you. You think it was easy to go from selling cars in a gravel lot to owning four dealerships? I'm not going to die knowing you three will let it all fall through the cracks. I'd rather sell it now than let that happen."

David sat up. "Come on, Pops. You know I won't let that happen."

"You've sacrificed yourself enough. You kids don't give a damn about keeping it."

Kareem stiffened beside Janiyah. "We care."

Roger turned to Kareem, a sad look on his face. "I've put too much pressure on all of you and in return you all made choices you normally wouldn't have. Now I'm going to make things right." He stood. "This conversation is over. All I ask is that you keep my surgery to yourselves. I don't need sympathy in the form of get well cards, useless flowers, or a bunch of visitors."

"What day is the surgery?" Aaron asked.

"I'll call you the morning of." When they began to protest, Roger cut them off. "I'm not having my kids treat me like a baby. I'm still the parent. You worry about how you're going to use the money from the sale."

David stood. "Dad, you can't—"

"End of discussion," Roger said in a sharp tone. He looked at the four of them, his eyes softening when they landed on Janiyah. The love in his eyes after fighting with him the last time they were together made her feel like the head of Bad Daughters Are Us. "Don't look so sad. Everything will be okay. Selling the business is for the best. You'll understand that later." He took Loretta's hand and went into the sunroom.

An uncomfortable silence remained. Her dad was ... sick. He needed surgery. And bypass surgery wasn't something you just jumped out of bed after. What if something went wrong? She couldn't fathom a world where he wasn't there.

She shook her head. No, she couldn't think like that.

But with ice cold clarity she realized her daddy wouldn't always be there. She cringed when she remembered saying he looked like he was about to keel over. Those words were closer to the truth than she'd like to admit. That could have been the last time they talked.

She thought of Henderson Automotive. She didn't want to run it, and he didn't want her to, but David said he would fight to keep it. Aaron and Kareem wouldn't let it go either. There might come a day when she would need to help out. No wonder her dad was so worried about his kids' disinterest. He was facing a real threat to his life and had no comfort that his kids could carry on his legacy.

What if she couldn't? It was already a struggle to stay interested in her first corporate job. The monotony. The set schedule. The repeated stories from co-workers. It was tedious at its best. If she couldn't get used to being an assistant, how in the hell would she help run Henderson Automotive?

What if, at the end of all this, she only realized she really was just a big joke?

"Janiyah, are you okay?" Kareem asked.

She looked at her brother, and smiled to try and erase the worry on his face.

"I'm fine. Dad's right. We need to get our lives in order. He ... he won't always be here."

Kareem flinched and looked away. David and Aaron both shifted uncomfortably.

The weight of a future she wasn't sure about caused a frantic beat of her heart. She couldn't stay here. "I've got to go. I'll see you all later."

She jumped up from the couch and rushed out of the house before they could answer. She wanted to feel better. Wanted to think about something other than her dad being sick, and a life she wasn't sure she could manage.

She'd find Freddy. A few hours with him would do it. His calm, focused demeanor always prevented her from a meltdown.

Suddenly she understood David's sacrifice to the business. Because she'd do whatever it took to ease any worry her Daddy carried. He'd done so much for her; she had to do the same for him.

CHAPTER 15

Fredrick was leaving his apartment for an afternoon at his favorite used bookstore when Janiyah came up the stairs. Her smile lit up her entire face when she saw him. A twist of longing tightened in his gut. In her seventies-inspired outfit, wide leg jeans and flowered blouse with the ends tied beneath her breasts, her curves brought to mind the Commodores song "Brick House."

"Where are you going?"

He turned his back on her enticing image to lock his door. "Out."

"Out where? Maybe I can tag along."

He turned around and leaned against the doorframe. "I doubt you'll want to come with me. I'm going to the bookstore."

"Good, I need to read more. Let's go."

"You can't be serious."

She cocked an eyebrow and propped one hand on her hip. All she needed was an afro instead of the sleek bob to look like a diva from one of those Blaxploitation movies.

"Is there some reason why I can't read, Freddy?"

"I have no problem with reading. You're the one who always searches for a reason not to."

"I know how to read."

"No one said you didn't."

"Well you're acting like it's unheard of for me to read."

He pushed away from the door. "You wanting to go to a bookstore is unheard of." He made a move to walk around her but stopped. Moisture glistened in her eyes. She blinked and turned away.

"Fine, have fun."

He gently took her elbow in his hand and turned her to face him. She avoided eye contact and visibly struggled to keep the tears from falling. "Are you okay? Why the tears?"

"It's nothing ... just ... I'm tired of being considered a joke."

"You're not a joke. I've never considered you a joke."

Her lip trembled and something snapped. The need to save her swelled up. It made him want to stop her from crying ever again and make sure she only smiled that beautiful smile that drove him crazy.

"That's sweet of you to say, but we both know you don't take me seriously."

"If I didn't take you seriously, I wouldn't have agreed to interview you in the first place, and I definitely wouldn't have given you the job. I wouldn't listen to your ideas about how to improve things in the office."

"You don't listen to me when it comes to clothes."

She tugged on the collar of his shirt. It was a plain blue oxford shirt that he hadn't tucked into his khaki shorts. Her actions pulled him close enough for him to catch a whiff of her vanilla fragrance.

"If it'll stop you from crying today, I might start listening to your fashion advice." And if her body continued to brush against him he would let her pick out his clothes for the rest of the week. His blood heated with the memory of their kiss. Her eyes darkened with the same inviting look she'd had the night before.

"Sometimes I think you listen to me just to make me happy. Or get me to shut up."

"Mostly to make you happy." The words slipped out. Her lips parted, then spread with a satisfied smile.

Sanity slammed into him. He blinked, and stepped away. He was falling into her trap again—becoming a carbon copy of his dad and making decisions just to make a woman happy.

"It's the least I can do," he said. "I wouldn't want Aaron and the rest of your family angry because I upset you."

The glow dimmed in her eyes, and her shoulders slumped. "I guess not."

The guilt for adding to her upset prompted him to say, "If you really want to come, then that's fine."

"Sure, it'll give me something to talk to Gerald about."

And just like that, the last vestiges of Janiyah's spell wore off. This was all about impressing a guy—a guy that wasn't him.

He gripped the keys in his hand, though he wanted to throw them. "Let's go."

● ● ●

Janiyah was quiet on the ride to The Book Dispensary, and only raised an eyebrow when they got out to go inside the white brick building located on the frontage road off Interstate 26.

"You buy from a used bookstore?" she said as they entered the store. "I know you can afford new books."

Something his mom would say, though there was no judgment in Janiyah's voice. "I can, but I prefer the atmosphere here. Not so many people hanging out and buying lattes like at the chain stores."

"Hey, Fredrick, good to see you," the man behind the counter said.

"Hey, Bob, how's it going today?" Fred walked over and shook his hand.

Bob shrugged. "Not too bad. Quiet for a Saturday."

Janiyah walked over and cleared her throat. Fredrick pulled her closer to the counter. "Bob, this is Janiyah."

Bob raised an eyebrow. "Hello, Janiyah. Nice to meet you."

"Same here." Janiyah flashed her smile and Bob's smile turned into a love-struck grin. Another man turned silly by a glance from Janiyah.

"Any new arrivals?" Fred asked.

Bob looked back at Fredrick, but he darted glances at Janiyah. "We got some new biographies traded in this week. I think you'll find some that you like."

Fred nodded. "Sounds good." He looked at Janiyah. "What are you interested in?"

She looked around at the crowded shelves and wrinkled her nose. "I'm not sure."

"We have a great selection," Bob said. "We get a lot of people trading in fairly new books."

"I don't know what I'm looking for."

"Well, I'm happy to help." Bob made a move to come around the counter.

Fredrick held up his hand, then placed it possessively on Janiyah's back. "We'll figure it out."

Bob looked between the two and turned red. "Yes, Fredrick knows his way around. You're in good hands."

Janiyah leaned in close. "I couldn't be in better hands."

He ignored her suggestive tone, and the way his body wanted to react to it. He pulled her away from the counter, then dropped his hand. "Look around. You might find something you like."

He went to the biography shelves. Janiyah followed and skimmed through some of the books beside him. She pulled out a few to read the first few pages, but eventually put them back. After a few minutes she strolled away to check other shelves.

Before long he was engrossed in looking. When he finally checked his watch, forty-five minutes had passed. He looked up, but didn't see Janiyah anywhere. He looked to the front, where Bob pointed to the room in back.

With a sigh and a suppressed smile, he headed to the room where the romance novels were stocked. He shouldn't be surprised. The last book she'd read was some type of romance, though the appeal of sex with the undead he couldn't understand.

She turned to him and grinned from the stepstool she was sitting on when he walked in.

"It was my intention to find something serious, but these seem pretty good."

He walked over and picked up one of the books in her lap. "Seem good or look good? There's a man with no shirt on the front."

She snatched the book away. "Don't judge a book by its cover."

"Point taken. I don't care what you read. The joy of reading is getting lost in a story that appeals to you."

"So you don't think it's silly to read romance? Or that I'm foolish for not automatically gravitating to the non-fiction section?"

"As long as you're reading and enjoying the book, it's not my business what you read."

Her head tilted to the side. "Don't you think reading true stories of perseverance and triumph are better than made up ones? Or that if I'm going to read fiction it should be some great literary work of art?"

"That would be hypocritical of me, considering I'm a fan of mystery novels. I admit I read non-fiction more than I do genre fiction, but sometimes it's fun to get caught up in a story just for the sake of the story."

She got up to lean against the bookshelf. "It's kind of how I felt about that book Liz gave me. I never would have thought I'd get into romance, but besides all of the sex, there was a good story. I can see the appeal."

"Then read what you like."

Her face lit up like he'd told her she won fifty million dollars. "I love that you're not pretentious. You're smart, but you don't flaunt it in people's faces."

"I'm not trying to impress anyone. Pretentious people often are."

"So what did you pick?" She straightened and pulled one of the books out of his hand. "A biography of Clarence Thomas." She scowled. "Didn't he sexually harass some woman back in the day?"

"He was accused of sexual harassment, but that doesn't mean I can't read his biography. He is one of the few black Supreme Court justices this country has seen."

"I wouldn't want to read it."

He held up another of his books. "You don't have to like a person to learn about what they accomplished." He held up the biography of Condolezza Rice. "Try this one."

"Are you serious?"

"Yes. You might like it."

The look she gave him said she doubted it.

"You're worried about people seeing you as a joke; well, I guarantee she's not viewed as a joke. She was the first black female Secretary of State, served as President Bush's national security advisor, and taught political science at Stanford. You might find it inspiring."

"I know who she is, that doesn't mean I want to read her life story." Janiyah took the book out of his hand and eyed the picture on the cover with a raised eyebrow. "Her hairstyle isn't inspiring."

"Just give it a try."

A wicked twinkle came to her eye. "Alright, but I think you should step out of your comfort zone, too. She pulled out a book from her stack. "I'll read the biography, if you read this for me."

He looked at the cover and groaned. The chest and abs of a man who probably lived in a gym were on the glossy cover. "You can't be serious."

She leaned in. Her vanilla perfume made his mouth water as she pressed a kiss to the side of his mouth. Her soft body sank into his and just as quickly she pulled away, a cute pout on her lips. "Please."

It was just a book. No real harm done if he did her this one favor.

Spoken like the son of Christopher Jenkins.

He took the book from her hand and squeezed it tightly in his. The cover bent from the pressure. He was hopeless. "Fine."

CHAPTER 16

On Monday morning, Janiyah sat at her desk searching for something to do. She wasn't succeeding very well, and the work she had wouldn't take long, so she was pushing it off until after lunch. She'd filled an hour checking on her dad. There'd been no call from her parents. She wouldn't be surprised if her dad didn't call until after the surgery. So she'd called the local hospitals to see if any had him as a patient. They didn't, and calls to Aaron and David, who'd both gone by their parents' house, confirmed their dad's heart wasn't being operated on just yet. Without that to worry about, her day was truly going down as the most boring day in history.

The monotony was broken when her cell phone rang. Liz's face from one of their wine and art outings lit up the screen. She ignored the call on her cell, but picked up her desk phone to call her back.

"Still staying off the cell phone at work?" Liz asked.

"Yeah, got a few side eyes last week."

Freddy hadn't said anything about her talking on her cell, but one of the newly hired accountants always gave her annoyed looks. Stupid really, considering she quickly completed all of the work she was being paid for. It wasn't as if it took eight hours of day to type letters, review spreadsheets, and take messages.

"You didn't call over the weekend. How did the date go with Gerald?"

Oh yeah. She hadn't thought about him again since her dad's announcement and her bookstore date with Freddy.

"It was okay. He's kind of conceited. I don't think it'll go anywhere."

"I told Fredrick you weren't interested in that guy."

Janiyah sat up in her seat. "When did you talk to Freddy?"

"On Saturday when he called for Missy's phone number."

"What?" She stood and paced back and forth behind her desk as far as the phone cord would let her. "Why didn't you tell me this?"

"Because he said you were out on a date and wouldn't care." There was a pause. "Do you care?"

Janiyah leaned her hip against the desk. "I don't know. It's complicated."

"I knew it! You two are making this complicated. Just do something before he calls Missy. I'm not trying to lose my job over your love triangle."

"There is no love triangle."

Someone cleared their throat behind her. She spun and caught the side eye from Evan, the new accountant who didn't like her.

"Look, Liz, I've got to go."

"Alright, keep me in the loop of what's going on with you two."

Janiyah hung up without answering. How the heck was she supposed to keep Liz in the loop when she didn't know what was up with her and Freddy? They still hadn't mentioned *the kiss*. He'd hurried out of the bookstore, dropped her at her apartment, and left without another word the other night, not returning until close to ten. He was already on his way out the door by the time she got up, and he hadn't been in the office all morning.

Evan cleared his throat again.

"Can I help you with something?"

He looked from her to the phone. "Another personal call?"

"Unless you need something, let's not go through this."

"Being the boss's pet only allows a certain amount of leeway."

"Once again, Evan, we're not going there. Now what do you want?"

Evan huffed and clenched his teeth. So what if he was frustrated? Unless Freddy had a problem with her work she wasn't going to let this guy who was just as new as her try and ruffle her feathers.

"Fredrick called. The Association of CPAs day of service is today, and he's volunteering to serve lunch at Conversions homeless shelter. Two people from our staff are supposed to help, but everyone is tied up with clients. I'm on my way. He suggested I bring you." The last part came with a scowl.

Janiyah didn't care if Evan was pissed. Something different to do today was worth a few minutes in a car with the angry accountant.

"Who's going to cover the front desk?"

"Phyllis agreed to answer any calls."

A few minutes later, Phyllis had routed calls to her desk and Janiyah and Evan were on their way.

The Conversions shelter opened two years ago. It provided long and short term arrangements for the city's homeless, while also working with local health clinics and job readiness organizations to provide assistance in helping people go from homeless and unemployed to working and in permanent housing.

Janiyah had volunteered there once during the week she'd dated one of the shelter's counselors. His passion for trying to help people had thrilled her, his enthusiasm for natural personal hygiene products not so much. It was a fun week, and he did open her eyes to the joys of helping others, but she ended it with the promise to be friends. He did switch to regular deodorant as a way to make her stay. Too little, too late.

Evan barely got the car in park before she popped off her seatbelt and got out. She hoped she wasn't forced to spoon out corn standing next to him.

She went in through the visitor's entrance. Fluorescent lights gleamed off the white linoleum floors, green plastic furniture, and framed motivational messages on the wall. Freddy stood with a group by the receptionist sitting at a desk behind a clear plastic barrier. When he saw her he lifted his chin in greeting then motioned for her to join him.

His eyes didn't light up. Not even a hint of the dimple when she walked over. Just a casual greeting as he quickly introduced her to the five other people in the group. The three men and two women were all members of the committee Freddy chaired with the Association. Evan joined them a few minutes later.

"So you're Fredrick's new assistant?" One of the members Freddy introduced as William asked. He was a tall guy with killer green eyes and a smile she was sure melted many female hearts.

"I am. Have you heard good things about me?" she asked.

"Very good things. If he doesn't treat you right give me a call. I could use a good assistant."

Freddy placed his hand on her back. "You have a good assistant."

William looked at the hand on her back then raised an eyebrow. "Just teasing."

Janiyah stepped out of Freddy's grasp. He'd done the same thing at the bookstore. He wasn't going to stake a claim on her without backing it up. Failure to discuss their kiss meant she was still swimming in the *just like a sister* zone.

"I like the teasing, William," she said, giving him her flirty smile. "Though I am happy with my new position."

A light went off in William's eye. "Well, maybe I can tease you some other time."

Habit almost made her rattle off her phone number. "We'll see," she said instead. Freddy's expression hardened. Guilt for flirting in front of him tried to rise up, but she ignored it. If he planned on kissing her senseless then pretend it didn't happen, he'd just have to deal with it.

Further conversation ceased when they were told the tour would start. She turned at the familiar voice calling them over.

"Hey, Joey!" she said.

Joey grinned in her direction. "Janiyah, long time no see."

They embraced, and she noted he smelled fresh. When they stepped back he got the puppy love look in his eyes that attracted her in the first place. The old attraction wasn't there, but she was happy to see him.

"You're our tour guide?"

"That's right. I'm head counselor now and in charge of volunteer groups. You're an accountant?"

The humor in his voice nearly wiped the smile off her face. Mr. All Natural found the idea of her working a nine to five humorous.

"Not quite. I'm working at Jenkins Holdings. You remember Freddy."

By now Freddy's jaw was clenched. Her suppressed guilt converted to dread. An ex-boyfriend and an easy flirtation with a new guy probably weren't going to convince him that they should talk about what that kiss meant. She'd never considered that her unstable dating life might be the reason he insisted on treating her like a sister.

Freddy and Joey greeted each other stiffly and then the tour began. She'd heard this before and tuned out Joey's spill about the goal of Conversions. A few times she caught Freddy's eye and smiled, only to watch his lips tighten. By the time they'd put on their plastic aprons, gloves, and hairnets to serve the food, her annoyance was alive and kicking.

What the hell was his problem anyway? It wasn't as if she'd invited William to flirt with her. And was it her fault Freddy had chosen to volunteer here? If he had a problem with her dating habits then he could easily rectify it. She was not throwing herself at Freddy. He'd pushed aside anything between them every time it tried to surface.

She passed out bread, while William dished out coleslaw to her right and another female accountant handed out the full plates to her left. The equally grumpy Freddy and Evan dished out meat and potatoes at the start of the line. William kept up the flirty routine throughout serving, while Joey came behind the line to make sure she was okay every few minutes.

Despite Freddy's heated looks, she enjoyed talking to the people in line and laughing with William.

"So, are you going to let me tease you another day? Maybe over dinner?" William asked after lunch was over and they were all back in the kitchen taking off their aprons and gloves.

Janiyah laughed. He was cute and persistent, attributes she liked in a man. Still, she wasn't going to follow this up.

"I can't believe you're asking me out when I'm wearing a hairnet." She pulled the hair net off and ran her fingers through her hair.

"You're pretty cute in a hairnet."

"And you probably tell that to all the women you meet in hairnets."

"You got me. I can't resist a woman in a hairnet. You won't believe the crush I had on my high school lunch lady."

Cute, persistent, and funny. He might be a good choice for Liz if things didn't work out with that architect.

Joey interrupted her and William. "So, Janiyah, it was good seeing you again."

"It was good seeing you too, Joey."

"Maybe we can catch up later. Has your number changed?" Joey puffed out his chest and moved in close to her. The look he shot William was a definite back off signal if she ever saw one.

It would be cute if it weren't completely inappropriate. "I'm kind of seeing someone right now."

Both Joey and William's shoulders drooped. Joey recovered first.

"I don't see a ring, so what's the harm in drinks with an old friend?"

"Or a new one," William chimed in.

Oh crap, this was awkward. She edged back, trying to think of a way to nicely let both of them down when a warm hand settled on her back. She immediately leaned into Freddy.

"Are you ready? We can ride back together."

"Yes. Let's go." She waved at Joey and William. "Bye, guys."

Freddy didn't move his hand. He didn't look at her or speak as they exited into the warm spring air, just walked stiffly beside her. She couldn't think of normal conversation thanks to his thumb rubbing back and forth across the small of her back. The friction of the movement against her silk blouse heated her faster than the warming plates and plastic apron had in the kitchen.

He'd parked two blocks away from the shelter. It was less crowded this late after lunch. His car was the only one on the side of the road, shaded by a large live oak tree.

When they reached his car, his simple touch had escalated to all of his fingers gliding back and forth against her lower back. Each movement slowly pulled her blouse up until the edges of his short nails lightly scratched her skin. She gasped, her nipples tightened, and moisture blossomed between her thighs.

"Get in." He opened the door and waited for her to slide in.

He slammed it shut then marched around to his side of the vehicle. She sweated, not from the heat of the car. Apparently, Freddy was upset. And apparently, it was making her horny as hell.

He sat in the driver's seat, turned on the ignition, and switched the air conditioner to blast. The cool air ruffled the hair around her face and she pushed it behind her ears.

"They fall for you quickly."

"It's never the one I want to fall."

His hands gripped the steering wheel, tension radiating from his body. "I shouldn't care."

"I want you to care."

"We work together."

"It has nothing to do with this."

Desire popped across her skin like corn kernels in a skillet. Her core was wet, and her breasts hummed for the feel of his mouth on them. Denying this was stupid. There was something between them and they couldn't ignore it any longer.

"Freddy— "

He spun in the seat and silenced her with a kiss. His tongue thrust past her lips at the same time as her arms shot around his neck. If he intended to make her forget any other man he'd succeeded. This was different from the last kiss. He kissed her thoroughly, barely giving her time to catch her breath or think. Her body went on autopilot, savoring his skillful lips, masculine smell, and hard body instead of wondering what it all meant.

She pressed against him, wanting to get closer, to have more of him against her. One of his hands cradled the back of her head, the other gripped her thigh. The heat of his palm burned against the material of her skirt. With eager hands, she reached down to pull it up, then gasped when his hot palm made contact with her skin. His deft fingers firmly caressed her thighs, easing their way upward to where she yearned for him to go. She parted her legs and his fingers flexed. He groaned, and his kiss switched from urgent to erotic as his tongue played against hers. His hand neared the aching spot at the juncture of her thighs, only to work its way back down. She whimpered, spread her legs farther, and pushed her hips forward.

He broke off their kiss to softly suck on the hollow of her throat. Then he was there. Kissing her spot. The tender place along her neck that made her tremble and pant for more.

"I shouldn't care, but damn, Janiyah, I do." His warm breath against her neck sent a delicious tremor through her.

Once again he kissed and licked along her neck. His hand made its way back up her thigh. When his fingers grazed the edge of her underwear she clutched the front of his shirt. The blunt tips of his fingers pushed aside the wet fabric of her panties to boldly caress her slick heat. He didn't hesitate to part her swollen folds and caressed her inner walls and the sides of her clit with his fingers.

She cried out. "Oh, my, Freddy!"

"Open wider," he said in a demanding voice.

She did by propping one foot against the door. His hand massaged her entire mons before he slipped one long finger into her. He repeated the motion again and again until her hips were twisting and her eyes watered from the pleasure. She buried her face in his neck, and his sweat mingled with hers as she whimpered in his arms. He trailed light kisses up her neck to gently suck on the outer lobe of her ear.

"Tell me you want me."

His thumb ran slippery circles across her clit. Her thighs shook as she struggled to breathe.

"I want you," she gasped.

His thumb alternated between quick flicks and slow rotations across the throbbing heart of her desire. "Not them, just me."

She moaned before saying, "Always you, Freddy."

He eased two thick fingers inside then bent them directly into her G-spot. "Good. Now come for me, baby."

Pinpricks of pleasure became a rush of shattered ecstasy across her skin. She cried out. He murmured against her head as the trembles went through her, useless words that made no sense in her muddled brain.

She finally lifted her head to stare at him. His light brown eyes were bright like fire. He looked both ready to pounce on her and shocked that they'd gone so far. His surprise was nothing compared to hers. Freddy, of all people, had made her come from a hand job. No guy had done that since high school.

She opened her mouth. Then closed it. A flush appeared beneath his tan skin and he looked away. With tentative movements, he slid his hand from beneath her skirt. A delicious tremble went through her.

"Freddy ... we should ...."

He reached into the glove box and pulled out a few napkins. After wiping his hands he gripped the wheel, avoiding eye contact with her the entire time.

"I know." His voice was filled with regret.

Suddenly embarrassed, she pulled her skirt down and tried to smooth her hair back in place. They rode in silence. She was too nervous to talk after Freddy got her off in the front seat of a car. Eventually they'd have to talk—maybe not now while they were at work, but soon.

His jaw remained clenched the entire time. When they arrived back at the office, he shifted the gear to park, but didn't cut the engine.

He took a deep breath and faced her. "I shouldn't have done that and I'm sorry. I know we're not together, but I behaved as if we were. It won't happen again."

"But ... " Her voice trailed off as he shook his head.

"It won't happen again," he said with a determination that nearly broke her heart. "I've got to get to a meeting." He turned away to stare out the windshield.

Screw his meeting; this needed to be worked out. Her mind raced without fully grasping what had just happened. This couldn't possibly be ignored. How could they go back to before after the way he'd touched her? She'd never be able to look at his hands without remembering them sliding and flexing inside of her. But his rigid expression and tense shoulders said now wasn't the time to push.

She slowly got out of the car. He gave her one last glance that swam with regret. She watched in anguish as he backed his car out of the parking space and hurried off.

CHAPTER 17

Janiyah skimmed through the slim pickings in her brother Aaron's fridge. Only he would have a more pitiful assortment of food than she. At least she had essentials such as milk and eggs. Often very close to their expiration dates, but still they were essentials. The only offerings in his fridge were a moldy lump of cheese, a few bottles of beer that looked the same as when she visited him a month ago, and a hard slice of pizza still in the box.

She'd left the office at exactly five to go home and then escape to Aaron's apartment. She'd chosen to hide rather than possibly face Freddy after what happened at lunch today. Even her not easily broken heart couldn't handle seeing the rejection in his eyes this evening.

"You're such a man," she called out over her shoulder.

"What?" he yelled from his den.

"I said you're such a man. There's no food in here," she called back.

His laughter was the only response. With a shrug, she grabbed two of the beers and joined him on the couch. Aaron's downtown apartment was sparsely furnished, but comfortable with a large couch, two recliners, and plenty of throw pillows for lounging. It served him perfectly since he only spent time there in between trucking jobs.

She handed him a beer. He held the bottle up to the light, examining it through narrowed eyes. "How old is this?"

"You tell me, it's your fridge." She found the date and her eyes widened. "Hey, only expired by three weeks. Drink up."

He shrugged and popped the top. "So, why are you raiding my fridge tonight?"

"Can't I just spend time with my brother?"

"Not unless you want something. And since I know it's not the old beer in my fridge, it has to be something else."

She avoided his direct stare by flipping through the channels on his television. "You're in town, so I thought I'd hang out. I don't see you often," she said.

"You'll see me a lot more soon. I've hired some new drivers who can handle the routes while Dad goes through this."

"Did you find out when he's having surgery?"

"Yeah, Mom finally caved. It's Thursday. That stubborn old man, he refused to have it until he got his business affairs in order."

Tears burned her eyes. "It's routine, right? He wouldn't really die from this, would he?"

He rubbed his eyes, a heavy sigh coming from his lips. "He'll be fine. You know Dad, he's a fighter. He'll probably wake up in the middle of surgery to tell the surgeon he's doing it wrong."

Janiyah laughed. Her dad was the strongest man she knew. Not just physically, but in every aspect of his life. She'd never seen him show fear.

Aaron reached over and squeezed her shoulder. "Don't worry. Everything will be okay."

"What about Henderson Automotive?"

"We won't let him sell it."

The conviction in Aaron's voice made her smile. One thing her dad hadn't taken into consideration was that his kids were just as stubborn as he was.

He patted her shoulder. "Okay, let's change the subject. We can't be all sad when Fred gets here."

"Freddy's coming over?" She frantically wiped the tears from her eyes. "Why didn't you say so?"

"I didn't think it would matter. You've always hung out with the two of us before."

"Yeah, well, I wanted to just spend time with you tonight." And avoid facing Freddy and memories of what he'd done with a few strokes of his finger.

"Hey, he called me earlier to see if I was in town and wanted to hang. You've seen the state of my fridge so I offered to come to him, but he insisted on coming here." He leaned back in the chair, his eyebrows raised. "Seems like I'm pretty popular tonight. Both of you trying to escape something?"

She shook her head and took a swallow from the stale beer. "What would I need to escape?"

Aaron laughed. "Answering a question with a question. Must be something going on."

She scoffed and flipped channels again. "Please. There's nothing going on. Freddy's dry as toast." But saturated with passion. She took another sip and shifted in her seat.

"Fred's not as dry as you think. He's more fun than you give him credit for."

"He's too stiff. He won't just go with things."

Aaron shook his head. "He's structured, and I don't blame him. You know how his parents are."

"I like his parents. His mom's a hoot."

"You would think so."

"What's that supposed to mean?"

"Nothing. She is fun, I will admit to that. But she drives Freddy crazy. And the way his dad flips from one idea to another without thought of consequences. It was bound to make Freddy either crazy irresponsible or very principled."

"Fine, it's great to have structure in your life. I'm learning that. But what about letting loose, having fun, and going with impulse?"

Aaron gave her a sly look. "That woman he dated a few months ago thought he was pretty fun."

Janiyah thought of the dental hygienist with her sensible shoes and plain hairstyle and waved her hand. "That isn't surprising. She was as straight laced as he is."

Aaron propped his feet on the coffee table. "I wouldn't say that. Fred really liked her. And don't let their outward appearance fool you. From what he said, they made some pretty good sparks together."

Janiyah dropped her beer. The cold liquid soaked through her Pac Man t-shirt. She quickly snatched up the bottle and placed it on the coffee table, while Aaron laughed.

"Freddy talks to you about sex?" she asked, holding her wet t-shirt away from her body.

"Hey, we're guys, what do you expect?"

"But she was so ... "

Aaron shook his head. "The right guy can bring out the freak in any woman."

"I don't make a habit of discussing Freddy's bedroom goings on with his girlfriends. Besides, Freddy's like a ... " She couldn't say brother. Not with the very un-brotherly thoughts going through her head. "You know," she finished weakly.

"Like family? Sure." He said it like he was responding to a lie he'd heard too often.

Her eyebrows snapped together. "What's that supposed to mean?"

There was a knock on the door and Aaron stood. "Remember, Fred is not your brother."

She frowned; her brothers would normally shit a brick when she started dating a new guy. A part of her assumed they would put up some type of fuss, even if it was Freddy. She'd always assumed Aaron would be the one most upset, but his tone implied differently.

"Hey, Fred, what's up, man?" Aaron said after opening the door.

He and Freddy gave each other a fist pound. "Working hard, that's all. I'm glad we finally caught up. You're always driving."

"Hey, business is good, so I can't complain. But, I'll be around more."

"I don't know. It's not like you to stay in one place for long."

Aaron shrugged. "I can afford to send others out right now, so I'm chilling."

Janiyah smiled sadly. Aaron did hate staying in one place long. Only concern about their dad would make him farm out his work.

Freddy held up a pizza box. "I figured you had no food, so I brought my own."

Aaron laughed. "You sound like Janiyah. She was just trying to raid my fridge."

Freddy froze. His eyes flew from Aaron to where she sat on the couch. Her stomach clenched. His muscular body, the grey button up shirt, and tan slacks excited her more than winning a bid on eBay. He'd lost the tie and jacket from work. The memory of earlier that day hit with a vengeance that made her lick her lips in a vain attempt to relive the taste of him.

"Hi, Freddy," she said in an airy voice. Thank goodness none of her inner trembling came through.

"What's up, Janiyah. When you didn't knock on my door to watch the Fashion channel, I thought you were hanging with Liz or something." He came over and placed the pizza box on the coffee table.

"So you remembered tonight's Fashion Police night?" she teased. She could at least pretend everything was normal in front of Aaron.

His lips quirked, but no dimple. "After two years of you forcing your way in to watch it, how can I forget?"

"Ha, ha. You love my company."

"As much as I love a head cold."

She stuck out her tongue and he gave her a relieved, partial dimple, smile. He didn't have to worry; Aaron might have hinted around that he wouldn't be upset about her and Freddy, but she wouldn't dare push it by bringing up what happened in the car.

Freddy turned to Aaron who'd followed him over. "You got anything to drink?"

Aaron cringed. "Just some old beer."

Janiyah held her empty bottle up. "It's not too bad."

Aaron laughed. "I think you dropped it on purpose so you wouldn't have to drink it."

"It was kinda stale." She stood. Her t-shirt stuck to her stomach where most of the beer had spilled. "You got a shirt I can change into?"

Aaron nodded. "Sure, get one out of my drawer. I'll run to the store and grab something to drink. Anything in particular?"

"I'm good with anything," she said. She looked at Freddy, who was scowling at the front of her shirt. "Why is your face all screwed up?"

He blinked and his expression cleared. "Did you pour the beer on your shirt?"

"You're such an idiot. No, I dropped it."

Freddy lifted a brow, but thankfully turned to Aaron. "Whatever you pick up works for me, man."

"Cool. I'll be right back." Aaron grabbed his keys off the nail beside his door. "You two make yourself at home."

They stood staring at each other after Aaron left. She'd never had trouble talking to or teasing Freddy before. Now her tongue might as well be lead.

"Are we okay?" he asked.

She crossed her arms, only to quickly uncross them due to the cold wetness of her shirt. "I don't know, are we?"

A solemn look came to his face. "I hope what happened won't ruin our friendship. I'm sorry I took things too far."

He looked so genuinely concerned that her wish he would take back what he said was dashed. "I get kissed by guys all the time."

He scowled. "Thanks for the reminder, but I did more than kiss you."

Heat ran up her face. "I know ... but you're the one saying it was nothing."

He took a step toward her. His eyes blazed behind his glasses, sending a shiver down her spine that had nothing to do with her wet shirt. "It can't be more."

She gulped. "Do you really want that?"

His nearness sent her heart into overdrive. Her gaze lowered to his lips and her body heated. It took everything in her not to squirm. His features relaxed and he took a step back. "I think forgetting it would make the most sense." His eyes lowered to her shirt. "You smell like beer."

Going with impulse, she lifted the edges of her shirt and whipped it over her head. His nostrils flared as his searing gaze traveled over her body. Her nipples beaded beneath her bra, the flimsy fabric doing nothing to hide them.

"I can fix that."

His face became impartial, the desire there earlier quickly hidden by a bland look. "Go get a shirt, *little sister*."

So that's how he wanted to play this. "Will do, *big brother*." Her fingers lightly brushed his chest on her way and she took some satisfaction that his body trembled.

CHAPTER 18

Do not follow her. Do not follow her.

Maybe repeating it would help it sink in. Fredrick clenched his fists. Closing his eyes, he tried to ignore the lust that roared to life at seeing her without a shirt. It was useless. The memory of her body pressed against his and her silky wetness on his fingers flaunted itself. Torturing, tempting, and tearing through all the reasons why he should forget that she made sanity fly out of his head.

As much as he wanted to regret what he'd done to her in the car, he didn't. She'd been so responsive. So damn wet. When she came around his fingers, he'd nearly ruined his pants and joined her.

That was the problem. They'd been in public. Anyone could have seen. Most women he dated would have kissed him back and said they should save it for when they were in private. The women he dated would have gently reminded him they were responsible adults, and as such, did not have sex in public. Janiyah hadn't shied away. She hadn't cared where they were.

She made him forget everything except her. Touching, kissing, and bringing her pleasure. And now she wanted him. The look she'd given him when he first arrived didn't help either. As much as he wished he didn't like it, he was turned on by the hot look in her eye. For once, Janiyah wasn't looking at him like the boring boy next door, but as a man.

He sat on the couch and drummed his fingers on his knees. Blowing air through his lips, he leaned back. He could ignore this.

Running his hands over his face, he laughed softly to himself. Even here in her brother's apartment, the last place where he should be overwhelmed with the need to have her, he still couldn't force her out of his mind.

"I'm pathetic."

"No, you're not."

He opened his fingers to look at Janiyah through the cracks. His heart crashed like the 1929 stock market. Instead of wearing one of Aaron's oversize t-shirts, she wore a black t-shirt that revealed an enticing expanse of her flat stomach with the word *Cocks* emblazoned across her chest.

He swallowed repeatedly before lowering his hands and speaking. "Tell me that's not your brother's shirt?"

She grinned before gliding over and hopping onto the chair next to him. "I was just as surprised as you when I saw it."

"Is there something Aaron needs to tell me?"

She shook her head and turned around. The University of South Carolina's Gamecock logo was on the back. "I thought the same thing until I saw the back. I think one of his girlfriends must have left it here," she said, turning back. "It's a woman's tee."

He took in the way the cotton material squeezed her breasts. "More like a child's t-shirt."

Her head fell to the side. "What child would walk around with *Cocks* on their shirt?"

"What woman would?"

Her eyebrow lifted. "One that wanted attention."

"You don't need to take such extremes to get attention."

"Really?" She leaned forward. "I like your reaction when I get too much attention."

"Stop it, Janiyah. I thought we settled this."

"No, you settled this. Why, Freddy? Why do you keep pushing me away?"

She was close enough for her delicious smell to tempt him. Need made his breathing haggard.

He slid away. "Because, it wouldn't work. There are too many things that make us incompatible, starting with the fact that you work for me. Let's remain friends. It's better that way."

"After what happened today, we can't just go back to being friends."

"We can and we will."

"Ugh, you're so stubborn. You make me want to ... " She balled her fists and scowled.

She looked so frustrated and adorable. He chuckled, then laughed, at her baffled expression.

"You think this is funny?"

"You looking like you want to hit me? Yes, it's humorous."

"You asked for it." She grabbed the pillow off the couch and hit the side of his head.

He sat stunned for a few seconds while she giggled. When he turned to face her she tried to suppress her laughter. He reached out to grab her, but she squealed, jumped from the couch, and ran. He quickly gave chase and followed her into the dining area. She used the table as a shield. Her shoulders shook with amusement as she avoided him by running to the opposite side whenever he moved to get her.

"You can't hide behind the table all night."

"I can hide here until Aaron comes home and makes you stop."

"Your brother's got nothing to do with this." He dashed around the table. She shrieked and ran down the hall, but he was on her in an instant.

One arm held fast around her waist. He got his revenge by tickling her ribs. She laughed and squirmed against him in her efforts to escape.

"Are you going to hit me again?" he asked, not relenting.

"Yes ... " She laughed. He increased his efforts. "Okay ... no ... no."

He stopped, but didn't let her go as they both laughed. She always did this to him. Whenever he tried to be serious she found a way to make him laugh. She always made things he thought were insurmountable seem insignificant.

His amusement gradually gave way as he became acutely aware of their position. In the back of his mind he'd known chasing her might lead them here. And honestly, he wanted another taste of her lips, another touch of her body. Her heavy breathing shortened while her heart pounded against his arm wrapped beneath her breasts. Her vanilla perfume danced around him, killing the remnants of his humor and breathing life into his desire.

Her laughter stopped, her body stiffened. He should let her go now. He didn't. He was pumped up on adrenaline and the vestiges of lust. She relaxed, her head tilting back just enough to make her neck available to him. With a shuddered breath, his arm around her waist relaxed and slowly slid back until his hand splayed against her flat stomach. She quivered, a soft whimper igniting a primal need within him. Hesitantly, only because some dim part of his brain acknowledged if he did this it was a point of no return, his hand moved up to cradle her soft breast in his palm. Her nipple hardened, burning his hand like a branding iron. A tremble went through his body. He pressed his dick against her butt and she gasped.

The front door opened. "Hey, I got the drinks!" Aaron called.

Fredrick snatched away from her. She spun, the small amount of light from the living area illuminating the rapid rise and fall of her chest. Her eyes were soft and inviting. He had to get away before he pulled her back into his arms and Aaron rightly punched his lights out.

"Excuse me," he said, rushing past her into the bathroom.

He stayed in there until his erection finally died down and his breathing returned to normal. He couldn't do this. He would fall in love. He'd watched enough men fall in love with Janiyah and end up heartbroken. Or worse, she'd love him back and he'd do anything to make her happy.

He finally left the bathroom. Aaron and Janiyah sat on the couch watching a reality show about men hunting alligators in the swamp. Aaron looked from the television and frowned.

"Damn, man, did you blow up my bathroom?"

Janiyah glanced at him and just as quickly diverted her eyes.

"Uhhh, something like that. I'm not feeling too well, I'm gonna bounce."

"You just got here. You haven't even eaten the pizza," Aaron said, holding up the pizza box.

Fredrick shook his head. "You keep it. I'll give you a call tomorrow. You'll still be in town, right?"

Aaron nodded. "Yeah, I'll be around for a while."

"Cool. Have a good night, man." He looked at Janiyah. "You too, Janiyah."

"Alright, Freddy, feel better." She gave him a weak smile then snatched the pizza box from Aaron.

Aaron looked between the two with a questioning look on his face. He raised a brow at Fredrick. With a shake of his head, Fredrick turned and left.

CHAPTER 19

Fredrick needed a wakeup call, so he went straight to his parents' house. They lived close to the Hendersons. He used to walk the short distance between their houses when he was younger and needed to escape the flights of fancy his mom often went through. There had been a time when he didn't understand how his dad could risk so much for the love of a woman. The last thing he had wanted was to end up like that. But wasn't he playing the fool for Janiyah? He gave her free run of his apartment, agreed to interview her for the job, then gave it to her knowing she'd wreak havoc on his good sense. And if that weren't enough, he'd seriously considered making love to her in a parked car in the middle of the day. He had to face it: Janiyah had him whipped and he wasn't even dating her.

Lights shined from every window of his parents' two story home. His dad answered the door. Similar to him in height, but larger in build, Christopher Jenkins smiled broadly.

"Fredrick, what brings you here?"

Fredrick followed his dad into the house. Smoke and the smell of something burning filled the air.

"Is the house on fire?"

Christopher chuckled. "No, your mom is making ... scratch that ... is trying to make cookies. The first batch didn't come out so well, but the second is edible."

"Mom's making cookies? Where did that come from?" Fredrick asked as they walked through the house toward the kitchen. His mom barely boiled water; the family had eaten in restaurants constantly when he was younger—another expense they could have avoided.

"She signed up for those cooking classes Janiyah recommended. Now she's trying to make cookies."

Fredrick suppressed a groan, but clenched his jaw. Even here he couldn't escape a conversation about Janiyah.

The haze in the kitchen was thicker. Smoke and noise greeted them when they entered the spacious area. The vent over the stove blasted, along with the ceiling fan and a floor fan propped in front of the open sliding door to the patio. His mom hummed happily as she pulled a pan of dark brown cookies out of the oven. When they entered, her brown eyes lit up. His dad beamed back at her. He'd never seen his dad look at his mom without resembling a lovesick fool.

"Oh, Fredrick, you're here. Just in time to try one of my cookies." Even in a smoke filled, hot kitchen Viola Jenkins was beautiful. Taller than his dad by two inches, her mocha skin didn't show a hint of her real age, thanks to the dermatologist and personal trainer his dad paid for.

He went over to the bar where she laid the cookies and kissed the cheek she held up for him. "What kind of cookies are they?"

"Peanut butter," she said, scooping the hot cookies off the pan.

Fredrick cringed. "Not my favorite. Aren't you supposed to wait for them to cool?" he asked, when half of the last cookie fell off the spatula onto the plate.

She lifted a slim shoulder. "Your dad likes them hot." She grinned at Christopher. "Don't you, sweetie?"

"You know it, honey," Christopher agreed, taking the broken cookie and stuffing it into his mouth.

Fredrick shook his head. They were sickening. "So, Dad tells me you've taken up baking because of Janiyah?"

His mom propped a hand on her hip and leveled him with a stare. "Fredrick, I don't know why you don't just marry that girl and make us all happy."

Fredrick held up his hands. "Whoa, where did that come from? Janiyah and I aren't even dating."

His mom tsked. "I know. Such a shame, too. I ran into her a few weeks ago and we just started gabbing about this and that when I mentioned how upsetting it was that I couldn't bake your dad's favorite cookie. Then she told me about this fantastic cooking class she took." She leaned across the bar and put a hand to the side of her mouth. "And the good looking instructor."

"You know Dad can hear you?"

His dad shrugged. "Window shopping never hurts. It helps when she comes home to me."

His parents both laughed, and Fredrick shook his head. "Janiyah dated the cooking instructor."

His mom frowned. "I know, and while I agree the man is gorgeous, I can see why she dumped him. All that knowledge of spices and the man has no flavor." She shook her head as if it were a shame.

"Mom, in case you forgot, I'm an accountant. I have even less flavor than a chef."

His mom waved the spatula at him. "Oh hush, you're full of flavor. And fire, according to your last girlfriend."

"Mmmhmmm," his dad added and stuffed another cookie in his mouth.

Fredrick's eyes darted between the two. "Excuse me?"

"Oh, please, Fredrick, I wanted to make sure my son knew how to please the ladies. So I discreetly ask all your girlfriends." She winked at him. "You're definitely your father's son in that department."

"I can't believe this," Fredrick moaned, placing his face in his hands.

"Don't be ashamed, son," his dad said with a laugh. "We may only brush on the door of six foot, but we more than make up for it in the bedroom."

Fred raised his head. "Please tell me you're joking."

His mom waved a hand. "If it makes you feel better to believe that, then suit yourself. I'm just saying if you grabbed Janiyah and ... " She looked at his dad. "How do you say it, sweetie?"

"Put it on her," his dad said, lifting another cookie.

"That's right. Once you put it on her and show her what you're blessed with, she'll come around."

Fredrick frowned. "What if I don't want to do that? Have you ever stopped to consider that Janiyah isn't my type?"

"Take it from me, Fredrick," his dad said. "Janiyah is just what you need. She's like your mother, beautiful and full of life. Have you ever seen me unhappy?"

Fredrick didn't answer. He'd seen his dad frowning over a mountain of bills. Working extra hours and hustling for new clients just to pay for the latest thing his mom wanted. Telling Fredrick there wasn't enough money to pay for college, but still insisting that he go to Duke because it would look good and make his mom happy. His dad didn't remember any of that. It all disappeared whenever his wife smiled at him.

He nodded. "You're living the life you want."

"And I love it. Janiyah will make you happy," his dad said.

Or drive me insane, he thought. She drove him crazy now. But even when she was annoying she made him smile. The way she fussed whenever he ate ice cream was cute. She always teased him about being stuffy, but never tried to change him. Except for his wardrobe. And he couldn't deny how much she drove his body crazy. She'd done that since he'd come home from college that summer and she'd forever altered their relationship. After looking at her finances, he had to concede she was better with money than his mom. He could tell it was killing her to work behind a desk, but she was doing an excellent job.

But those good traits didn't change the fact that keeping up with what she wanted was akin to riding a rollercoaster. Her mood changed so much. Not to mention she'd break off their relationship in a heartbeat when someone more interesting came along. His parents, no matter how dysfunctional, loved each other. He hadn't seen Janiyah put up with someone who wasn't related to her for longer than a few weeks, much less love. The closest was the damn violin instructor, and she'd dumped him.

"Can we drop this subject? I'm not interested in Janiyah. She's not interested in me. In fact, she's dating some college professor now."

His mom raised an eyebrow. "So you're watching who she dates."

"She's right across the hall from me and barges in whenever she pleases. I can't help but notice." He took a deep breath. "It's a good thing I'm moving."

His mom dropped the spatula and put a hand to her heart. "Where? You can't leave me, Fredrick, I'd just die."

He shook his head. "You won't die, Mom. You said the same thing when Debra and I went to college."

"I nearly cried every night," she said, wiping an imaginary tear from her eye.

"No you didn't, because Dad took you on vacations."

"Only to stop the crying," his dad said.

"I'm not moving out of town, just looking at getting my own home. My business is growing, and I'm tired of living in the apartment."

"What will Janiyah do?" his mom asked, her crying over before it started.

"Live. She's got a dad, three older brothers, and any man she bats an eyelash at who can help kill her spiders and buy her bananas. My moving doesn't concern her."

His mom scowled, but didn't say anything.

Fredrick stood. He'd gotten his reality check. "I just came by to see how you two were doing. I'll leave you to your baking and call later this week."

His dad held up a hand. "Don't bother; your mom wants to visit her sister. We're going in a few days."

"But Aunt Melena lives in California. Don't you have an important meeting with that potential new client next week?"

"I moved the date." Christopher wrapped an arm around his wife's waist. "Gotta keep your mom happy."

"And you do daily, sweetie," his mom gushed, kissing his dad's forehead.

Fredrick rubbed the bridge of his nose. "You've already postponed that meeting three times. How do you expect to get their business?"

"See, there you go worrying again," Christopher said, shaking his head and darting his eyes at his wife. "Everything is under control."

"You always handle things, sweetie." His mom wrapped her arms around his dad's shoulders.

Why waste his breath with a lecture? His dad never listened. "Call me when you get back."

They didn't answer and he knew they were wrapped up in an embrace. He should be grateful to have two parents still together that obviously loved each other. But watching his dad ignore the basic responsibilities of adulthood to make his wife happy, and the way his mom treated any aspect of reliable behavior as a chore, put a sour taste in his mouth for that type of love. No matter how much his body wanted Janiyah, he feared his heart would take over and override his good sense. He refused to risk everything he'd achieved just to have her.

CHAPTER 20

It surprised Fredrick to see Janiyah's yellow Camaro parked at her parents' house on Thursday afternoon. She'd called in sick without saying what was wrong. She hadn't come by his apartment that morning. That wasn't too surprising. They'd been avoiding each other outside of work since the lunch incident three days ago. He hated to admit how much he missed her presence in his apartment.

He grabbed the folder with the information Roger had requested about Henderson Automotive's assets and got out of the car. He was further surprised when Aaron answered the door with a tired look on his face.

"Fred, what are you doing here?" Aaron smiled, but it didn't reach his eyes.

"I'm dropping off some papers your dad asked for. Hey, man, are you okay?"

Aaron looked over his shoulder before coming out to stand on the porch. "I'm fine. It's was a rough day."

"What's going on?"

Aaron rubbed the back of his neck. He avoided eye contact, unusual for him. "It's no big deal."

"I doubt that, you can barely look me in the eye. If something's wrong you can tell me."

"My dad doesn't want us to make a big deal out of it."

"Out of what?"

Aaron finally made eye contact. Fredrick couldn't hide his surprise when he noticed the red rims around his friend's eyes. "Aaron, man, what is it?"

Aaron sat in one of the large wicker chairs on the porch.

"Might as well tell you. You're like family. Dad had bypass surgery today. He made it, but for a moment ... they thought his heart wouldn't start again."

Fredrick dropped into the chair next to Aaron. His relief that Roger was okay was overshadowed by the fear that he almost hadn't made it. How could Janiyah not say anything to him about this? How had she gotten through the day?

Aaron sighed and pulled the twists on his head. Fredrick cleared his head to focus on his friend. "Damn, man, how's he doing? What are you doing here? Do you need anything?"

Aaron shook his head. "No, he's okay now. That's the only reason we left to get Mom's overnight bag. She forgot it in the rush this morning." Aaron paused and frowned. "It was scary when they told us about his heart. Then seeing him in ICU. He looked so ... weak. My dad's always been larger than life, you know? It hit me that he almost didn't make it."

"He made it," Fredrick said automatically. He couldn't imagine Roger Henderson weak. The man personified everything a real man should be: strong, loved his family, successful, and always kind.

"I know, but he's talking about dying and getting his affairs in order. He wants to sell Henderson Automotive. Can you believe that?"

Fredrick looked at the packet of paperwork in his hand. He hadn't questioned why Roger wanted it, but now it made sense. "Do you think he's serious?"

"I'd hoped he would change his mind, but after the complication, there's no telling what he'll do," he said, shaking his head.

Aaron dropped his head into his hands and Fredrick fell back in his chair. He empathized with Aaron's fear. Roger Henderson was the male role model he'd strived to be like. More stable than his own father, Roger was the one who'd given him advice on starting and running a business. He'd treated him like another son, which added fuel to the flames of guilt whenever Fredrick thought about how much he wanted Janiyah.

Why hadn't Janiyah confided in him? Instead, she'd avoided him and called in sick with no explanation. He'd had to listen to Evan complain about her and even Phyllis disapproved that she'd called in. All of that could have been avoided if she'd let him know what was going on.

Or had his actions already ruined their friendship?

Fredrick sat up and placed his hand on Aaron's shoulder. "I can't say it'll be okay, because no one can guarantee it. But what I can say is that your dad is a fighter. I've never seen that man give up or let anything beat him. As for Henderson Automotive, it's too much a part of this family for him to sell. Let him get through recovery, then see what he says."

Aaron lifted his head. "You're right. I know it, it's just hard, ya know?"

Fredrick shook his head. "I can only imagine. I'm here for you. Just let me know if you need anything, and I'll do my damnedest to get it."

"I know you will." Aaron tapped Fredrick's hand on his shoulder. "Hell, you're practically family."

Fredrick thought about the way he'd touched Janiyah earlier in the week and dropped his hand. "Not quite."

"You're right, but if Janiyah had her way you would be." Aaron gave him a knowing look.

Fredrick struggled for something to say. "Aaron, look, I promise there's nothing going on there." It sounded like a lie even to himself.

"Believe it or not, I'd prefer her with you than some of the other idiots she's dated."

Fredrick was speechless. A glimmer of something ... excitement maybe ... sparked in his chest. If Aaron really meant that, then one of his reasons for staying away from Janiyah vanished. He shook his head to clear it. There were several other reasons to stick to his plan—his dad skipping the meeting he was supposed to have today in response to his mother's whim, being the biggest of all.

As if summoned, Janiyah came onto the porch. Fredrick's breath caught in his throat. Her hair was curly today and pulled back in a loose knot. She wore a green tank top with the Mellow Yellow logo on the front and knee length shorts that clung to her shapely thighs. He shifted in the seat in a useless attempt to relieve the sudden tightness in his pants.

When their eyes met, electric heat shot through him.

She gave him a tentative smile. "Oh, hey, Freddy. Sorry about calling in."

"It's alright. Aaron told me what was going on."

She glanced at Aaron, who shrugged. "Might as well let Fred know."

"I'm glad you told me." He threw an accusing look at Janiyah.

"What are you doing here?" she asked.

He held up the envelope. "Dropping off paperwork for your dad."

"Oh." She clasped her hands in front of her while twisting one foot back and forth.

"Are you two okay?" Aaron asked, looking between the two.

"We're fine. Just like friends who're as close as siblings should be. Right, Freddy?"

"Perfect. I won't stay. Just give this to your dad." He shoved the envelope at Aaron.

"Alright, man," Aaron said.

Fredrick stood and Janiyah blocked his way.

"Have a good night, Janiyah." He went around her and headed for his car.

• • •

"Freddy," Janiyah called.

She rushed off the porch and followed him. She felt bad for calling in, but hadn't known what else to do since her dad didn't want them to say anything. If she'd known Aaron would cave she would have told Freddy.

He stopped but waited several seconds before facing her. "Yes?"

She didn't know what to say, so she went with repeating herself. "I'm sorry about calling in."

"I wish you would have trusted me enough to say something, but I guess I understand."

She walked over and placed her hand on his arm. His muscles hardened as he stiffened from her touch. "No, you don't understand. After what happened earlier this week, I wasn't sure what to say to you."

He shifted his stance so that her hand fell away. "That's what I was afraid of. I knew it would change things between us."

"Is that really so bad?"

"I don't what things to change. I value our friendship, Janiyah, and I regret that I let my actions threaten that."

"We both want—"

"No, we don't. We should remain friends. Nothing more."

She didn't believe him. "Are you afraid of what's between us?"

"No, I'm realistic."

"What's that supposed to mean?"

"That we don't make sense as anything more than friends. I care about you."

"And you want me."

He hesitated. She waited on the denial, the lie, but to her surprise, he nodded.

"Yes, I do. But I'd rather do what's right than do what I want and screw everything up. And let's face it, Janiyah. We'd screw things up."

Without another word, he turned and went to his car. Janiyah watched him pull away from the curb. He threw his hand up in goodbye to Aaron, but didn't spare her a glance. It was the last straw. The last squeeze she didn't need on an emotional day. Tears burned the back of her eyes. She wanted to cry for her dad, for Freddy's denial, and for herself because she still wanted him after he firmly said nothing more would happen. She blinked several times to stop herself from giving in to her emotions. She might want to cry, but she wouldn't. Freddy she'd figure out later. Something was holding him back, and she'd find a way to get past that. Right now she had to survive this family emergency.

With a deep breath, she slowly went back up the stairs onto the porch.

Aaron touched her arm when she tried to brush past him. "What was that all about?"

She pulled out of his grasp. She loved her brother, but now wasn't the time for his advice. "Freddy's being difficult."

"Fred is never difficult. Is there something going on between you two?"

She raised her chin. "Does it matter?"

Aaron held up his hands. "Not to me, I've been expecting it for years."

"You can't be serious. You guys are always threatening to kill any guy who looks at me too long."

"What are we supposed to do, offer you up on a platter? Just because I'm protective of you doesn't mean I'm unreasonable. I have always seen the potential between you two." Aaron leaned down to meet her eye. "Just answer one question. Do you really like him, or is this a game?"

She met her brother's stare head on. "I love him."

Holy crap, she did. She waited for the regret, or doubt about saying it out loud to Aaron. It didn't come. How long had she loved him? She tried to remember a time when she didn't love Freddy. From the moment he'd walked through the door after playing basketball with Aaron when they were ten and she was five she'd liked him. And over time it had changed into something deeper, a love that she let out once only to lock away when he tossed it back. That was the reason why she'd never admitted to loving Freddy before, because she knew how painful it was to love him and not have him feel the same. But now he wanted her. He'd admitted it, and she didn't turn away from second chances.

"Janiyah ... " Aaron said.

"I do. I always have, I just never thought I'd have a chance. Now I've got to figure out what to do about it."

Aaron stared for a few minutes before nodding. "You'll figure it out." He came over and draped his arm around her shoulder. "Come on, let's go in and get the rest of Mom's things and go."

The memory of her dad in the hospital bed earlier came back. Once again tears threatened. "I can't believe he almost didn't ... "

He squeezed her shoulder. "He made it, and before long he'll be back here ordering us around."

She let out a wobbly laugh. "Maybe he'll order me to marry Freddy. Then everything will work out."

"Joking about Dad ordering you to marry and there's no derision in your voice. You must really like Fred."

Yeah, but what good was that if he didn't love her back?

CHAPTER 21

"Janiyah, did you get a good picture of the Ben Wa Balls?"

Janiyah shook her head to clear it and turned to Mrs. Driggers. "Sorry, what?"

Mrs. Driggers crossed the room to place a hand on Janiyah's shoulder. "I asked three times if you got a picture of the Ben Wa Balls."

"Oh, sorry, Mrs. Driggers. I'm not much help today."

She was no help at all today. Too many distractions in her brain. Her dad was back home after eight days in the hospital. As Aaron predicted he was ordering them all to quit fussing over him, but she saw the happiness in his face when he thought no one was looking. His release was a blessing after the touch and go moment during surgery.

Now that her dad was recovering at home, she couldn't help but stress about the situation with Freddy, how stiff they were around each other at work. She hated the way she had to pretend it didn't bother her when Liz called to say he'd contacted Missy, and her boss was smitten. Or how she continued to ignore Gerald's calls in a vain wish that Freddy would snap out of it and realize they should be together.

"What's on your mind?" The plastic cover on Mrs. Driggers's couch squeaked as she sat down.

"It's nothing."

"Is it between you and Fredrick? Don't look so surprised. I've noticed you haven't gone over there much."

"We see each other enough. I work with him now ... "

"Excuses. I'm too old to pussyfoot around. You're crazy about that man, and he's crazy about you. He just needs a kick in the head to realize it."

Thank you. Here was validation that she wasn't the only one who saw it. "I've tried, Mrs. Driggers, and he turned me away. He doesn't want us to be more than friends."

"Foolishness. Quit sitting over here pretending to work when you should be over there making love to that man." Mrs. Driggers leaned in and raised her eyebrows. "And from what I hear through the walls, he's good at that."

"Mrs. Driggers!"

Though she wasn't that surprised by the lady's forward speaking. After the success of her website, Janiyah convinced Mrs. Driggers to try a Facebook page. At first Mrs. Driggers hesitated, but once Janiyah convinced her that she could hold discussions about her products she'd agreed. Now the woman posted a sex question of the day, held relationship discussions on the weekend, and posted man candy pictures every Monday. Mrs. Driggers's sexy advice was a hit.

"If you'd overheard what I have, you'd already be over there." Mrs. Driggers stood and picked up her purse. "If it'll ease your discomfort, I'll go out for the afternoon so you don't have to worry about me eavesdropping. Time I paid Jessie Lyles a visit and get my freak on." She opened the door and stood waiting. "Go on, girl, go get him."

Janiyah jumped up from the chair and followed Mrs. Driggers out. Her neighbor gave her a pat on the back before going down the stairs.

She hesitated outside of Freddy's door. How many times was she going to throw herself at him only to have him push her away?

She spun and faced her door. But what about the way he made her feel? How one look sent her heart into damn near cardiac arrest? Or how her day was perfect if she made that dimple appear.

She turned back to his door. Would they really screw everything up if they got together? Were they really compatible?

Perfect compatibility was overrated. She wanted someone who would challenge her, someone she could laugh with, a person who made her see and think about things in a different way. He might have been content with that dental hygienist, but for all of their "serious" discussions, Janiyah had never once seen him give her full on dimple. Freddy was hers. He'd always been her friend, the one constant man in her life. Was she really *not* going to fight for that?

The familiar heady mixture of excitement and recklessness made her skin prickle. Maybe he didn't want to see her. She'd deliberately given him his space. But, darn it, on top of everything else she missed talking to him.

She rushed into her apartment and picked up the biography he'd convinced her to buy at the bookstore. That way it wouldn't be so obvious that her goal was to end up in bed with him. With a deep breath and mental pep talk, she knocked on his door.

It swung open a few seconds later. He stared at her over the top of his glasses. "Yes?"

She was supposed to play things cool, but it was difficult if he insisted on looking so positively delicious in pajama bottoms and a tank top.

"Want some company?" she said in a forced breezy tone.

Surprise flashed in his light brown eyes. Then he smiled, not full dimple, but it was enough to melt her heart. "Since when have you asked? You usually push me aside and come in." He opened the door wider and let her in.

Instead of entering, she frowned. "Am I really that rude and inconsiderate?"

He reached out and pulled her in. "You do tend to think the world revolves around you, but you're not intentionally rude or inconsiderate."

She stood close to him and tugged on the edge of his shirt when he tried to pull back. "Is that why you never asked me out?"

"I never asked you out," he said slowly, "because we're friends."

"Friends go out."

"Not when the female has placed the male so far in the friend zone she asks him to buy tampons."

She cringed and let go of his shirt. "Okay, that was one time. And you said no."

He chuckled, full on dimple. Yes!

"Damn right I said no. I can only take so much."

He closed the door and walked to the couch. His television was muted, the stack of books he'd purchased on the coffee table. Surprisingly, the romance novel was the one open on the table.

"You're reading that?" She sat beside him.

"Correction—I'm trying to read it."

"That bad?"

"No, it's pretty good." He picked up the book and studied the couple wrapped in an embrace on the inside cover. "I can see the appeal."

She curled her feet underneath her and leaned her head on her hand. "But ... "

"But ... I'm anxious to read the biography I bought. I can't concentrate on this."

She rolled her eyes. "Leave it to you to find someone's life story more interesting than a steamy romance."

"I like a good romance."

Oh, his voice made her skin tingle. She couldn't do this anymore. "I miss you."

He blinked. Once, twice, then cleared his throat. "You see me every day."

"You know what I mean. Ever since ... we haven't talked, and I miss you."

He let out a heavy breath and rubbed the bridge of his nose. "That's why I didn't want to go there. I didn't want things to change."

"I do. You already told me that you want me. Well now it's my turn, and Freddy, I want you so bad."

Something flashed in his eyes, and it wasn't regret. "We work together," he said.

"No one will know but us."

He stared at her so intensely for what felt like hours. His eyes projected all of the uncertainty going through his mind. She unbuttoned the top two buttons of the old sundress she had on. His fiery gaze lowered to where she lightly rubbed her chest above her breasts.

Quickly his eyes focused on her face. The passion in his eyes made her suck in a breath. In an instant he went from the boy-next-door to irresistible temptation. Desire aimed at her, and shining so bright, it sent heat between her thighs and made her breasts ache for his touch.

"This isn't a game," he said. "I don't just fall into bed with someone lightly."

"You're only making me want you more."

He licked his lips; she bit hers to fight the urge to retrace its path. "I can give you a lot more," he said.

She moved closer, until only the barest space separated their faces. His cologne intoxicated her, his warm breath caressed her chin, and the coiled sexual tension in his body inflamed her senses. He was cocked and ready to pounce ... on her.

"How much more, Freddy? Don't be afraid to give it to me, because I'm not afraid to take it." She leaned in to kiss the side of his mouth. His body trembled. When she pulled back she couldn't suppress the smile on her face. After today, he wouldn't dare try to brush aside what they had.

She moved to get on her knees, but his hand shot out to seize her arm. "I'm going to fuck that cocky smile right off your face."

Her eyes widened as excitement sent a rush of desire straight to her center. "Do it."

Within an instant his mouth was on hers. This time she was ready for Freddy's demanding kiss. Craved it. She fed off his hunger, anxious to bring him to his knees and tear down any barriers he tried to put between them. His thick arm wrapped around her waist as he swiftly lifted her from the couch. She yelped with excitement, thrilled by his strength.

"You're gonna do a lot more yelling," he said in a gravelly voice.

"Make me scream."

Heat flashed in his eyes. His arm tightened around her waist before he kissed her again. His tongue was urgent as it plunged past her lips. Janiyah was vaguely aware of them leaving the living room and going into the bedroom. He unceremoniously dropped her on the bed. She leaned back on her elbows and waited in anticipation. He jerked up the hem of her dress.

"Spread your legs."

The demand was soft, but the power was undeniable. Her thighs parted, her wet flesh throbbing. He slid his hands up her legs and tugged her underwear down, before he pushed her knees farther apart. Slowly, the tips of his fingers glided across the sensitive skin of her inner thigh. The feather light touch sent trembles through her overheated body. Her back arched. With each agonizing inch his fingers made toward the juncture of her thighs her legs spread further.

His teasing fingers drifted along the crease between her thigh and her sex. A gasp rushed past her lips as she bit her lip in anticipation for his touch. She yearned for him to touch her there again. Instead, he retraced his route. His withdrawal made her ache for his touch even more.

"Freddy," she gasped.

He lightly slapped the inside of her thigh. The sting, coupled with the vibration so close to her core sent another tremble through her.

"Fredrick." His eyes were dark, his voice low.

She grinned. "Freddy."

Cocking a brow, he took another trip up her thigh, this time lightly brushing the wet curls of her sex. Her body tensed, but like before he pulled away.

Taking her hand, he tugged her into a sitting position. In a swift motion he unbuttoned the rest of her dress and pushed it off. Again those torturous fingertips wreaked havoc on her as he traced the edges of her bra, lightly brushing her nipples protruding beneath the satin cups.

"Take it off."

"I want you to take it off."

His eyes narrowed. With the speed of a professional, he unfastened the clips and tossed it across the room. She couldn't hide her gasp of surprise, but it was short lived as he filled his hands with her breasts. A low moan escaped as he expertly massaged the slight weight before gently pinching the sensitive tips.

His head came down and she lifted hers for a kiss, but he swerved and latched onto her neck. When his teeth gently nipped, her head fell back to give him unblocked access.

Her hands shot to his waistband. She struggled to push down his pants and get to the thick erection she'd fantasized about since seeing it.

Freddy pushed aside her fumbling attempts and stepped back. He took off his clothes with the same efficiency as he'd removed hers. She couldn't speak when he stood, naked, before her. His thick, muscled, and compact body was beautiful in all its glory.

"On your knees. On the bed. Facing me."

She scrambled to comply. As she did as he'd ordered, he put on a condom from the nightstand. His arm snatched around her waist as he pulled her against him. At the same time his mouth took hers in a kiss. His hot skin burned into hers, his erection pressed against her belly. It was heaven, perfection, and so where she wanted to be. In his arms, wrapped up in Freddy.

In a blink, she was on her back. He bent her knees, spread her legs, and without preamble slid two fingers past her honeyed lower lips.

Her eyes rolled to the back of her head. "Freddy," she sighed.

"Fredrick." He pulled out his fingers, replacing them with a strong thrust of his hard dick.

It was magnificent. "Freddy!"

Spreading her knees farther apart, he pushed in and out, fast and hard with no denial of who was in control. Soft moans slipped past her lips; her fingers dug into his tight biceps as he claimed her body. Her moans grew louder, becoming cries of pleasure that made her thankful Mrs. Driggers had decided to leave. This was Freddy, completely possessing her, making her scream. It brought her close to the edge. Her body began to tremble.

"Fredrick," he said through clenched teeth.

She shook her head, and rolled her hips. He was her Freddy, always would be. She wouldn't let this change it, wouldn't let him take the one thing she clung to. He was her friend, her support system, the man she loved.

He pulled out, and she shouted her disbelief. Not when she was so close. His mouth replaced his length, engulfing her clit as he sucked deeply. His stiff tongue swirled around the erect nub, lavished in the creases between her swollen outer lips and plunged within her before his entire mouth covered her quivering flesh yet again.

"Oh, God, yes! Freddy!"

His head lifted. "Fredrick."

He flipped her over and entered her from behind in a long, sure stroke. One arm hugged her waist, the other hand grabbed her shoulder.

"Fredrick," he ground out.

"Fre..." She couldn't speak. Only shout in ecstasy as he stroked her from behind.

The hand around her waist moved to spread her legs. Without missing a beat, two of his fingers surrounded her clit. He gently squeezed; she bucked.

"Fredrick." His voice was rough, almost a growl.

He squeezed again, continuing to pound within her. This was not Freddy. This was a guy who was completely turning her out!

He slapped her behind. Her body shook as her climaxed neared.

"Fredrick," she cried out.

He squeezed her clit. Her vision blurred, her toes curled, and her breathing stopped as her body bucked from an earth-shattering orgasm. His hand moved to lock onto her hips and his pace hurried. He slapped her butt again. Her body clenched around him. Another wave of wetness rushed over his hard flesh, brought on by the pleasure and slight sting from the action. He groaned, a low rumble that gradually grew louder.

His body tensed, his dick flexed within. "Hell yeah!" he shouted.

They collapsed on the bed. She was too sated to care that he hadn't called her name. He didn't have to, as long as she got to do that again!

CHAPTER 22

Fredrick woke at six a.m. with Janiyah's head beneath his chin as she slept on his chest. The night before was perfect, better than anything he could have imagined. And he'd imagined sleeping with her more times than he cared to admit. After years of living in the "friend" zone with her, he couldn't push back or deny the male pride coursing through him after thoroughly putting it down. And he'd put it down. Front, back, and sideways, he'd had Janiyah in many of the ways he'd imagined, and still wanted more. The memory of her voice crying out his name instantly hardened his dick.

Insisting that she call him Fredrick was something he'd wanted to do since that day in his office. She'd always flirted with the nickname Freddy, said it in such a teasing way he couldn't help but accept it. But he hadn't wanted her teasing in the bedroom. He didn't want Janiyah to see Freddy, the guy who let her have free rein to his apartment and was on call to make ex-boyfriends jealous. He wanted her to see Fredrick. The man who made her body quiver as she screamed in pleasure.

She sighed in her sleep and snuggled closer. One of her legs rested across his thighs. It brushed against his erection with her movement, sending a rush of desire through him. He wanted her again.

Gently, he turned her onto her back and dropped his head to slip her nipple in his mouth. A low moan escaped her and her legs spread. He looked up, but her eyes were still closed. His hand slid between her thighs. She was hot and slick. He slowly spread her sweetness around her clit until her moans increased and her hips lifted from the sheet. When he dipped his fingers into her warmth she cried out; he smiled.

Satisfied that she was ready, he didn't hesitate to move over her and push into her with a long, slow stroke. They'd stopped with the condoms. He knew she was on birth control.

Her eyes opened, her lower lip clenched between her teeth. She put her arms around his neck and he lowered his head into the crook of her shoulder, hiding the adoration he felt at being allowed within her again. His movements began slow as he savored the feeling of her tight and oh so wet body around him. Her legs wrapped around his hips, she clenched her walls and he let go, sinking in and out, making sure she realized who was inside her.

His name became a cadence on her lips. He raised himself on his hands to watch her face. Each cry pushed him closer and closer to the release he wanted, but he held back, refusing to come before she did. He watched as she grew nearer. He could watch her come every day. Her face flushed, her eyes rolled to the back of her head as she twisted beneath him. Her cries grew frantic, her legs began to shake. She was almost there. Her eyes stretched as she screamed his name.

He finally let loose. He succumbed to the tightening in his balls, the rush of his release, and the thrill of being with her.

He tried to catch his breath as he watched her. She looked at him with a mixture of disbelief and uncertainty. The disbelief swelled his male ego even more. The uncertainty scared him. A night of great sex didn't erase her history of short term relationships. He might have sexually turned her out, but she'd emotionally put a hurting on his heart. He foolishly wanted all of her, would move heaven and earth to please her, and that scared him. She wouldn't want the same. Or for the time she did, she'd turn him into even more of a lapdog than he already was. Once that was gone, he couldn't go back to the friend zone.

The alarm clock buzzed. He was supposed to meet his realtor at eight. He had a date with Missy that night. They'd talked on the phone a few times, but because of their schedules tonight was the first time they were able to finally go out. He'd enjoyed their conversations about work and city politics for the most part, but he hadn't felt a spark. He'd hoped that their date tonight would change that.

Damn. In less than a day his life had become too complicated.

He pulled out and rolled over to turn it off. He didn't turn back to her, but the bed shifted as she moved away. He glanced over his shoulder to where she sat on the side of the bed.

The awkward morning after.

"I've got to head out early." He cringed when her shoulders stiffened. "You don't have to leave."

She peeked over her shoulder and smiled. "I don't usually get up this early on Sunday."

"I know."

She stood and pulled the sheet with her. After it was wrapped tightly, she turned back. "Are you busy today?"

"I'm looking at houses today."

"What?"

"I'm looking at—"

"I heard what you said. You're moving out?"

"We talked about this."

"Yeah, but that was before ... " She motioned to the bed.

He rubbed his face, then put on his glasses and stood. Her eyes dropped to his penis and her breathing hitched before they rose to his. That look made him want to pull her back in bed. Instead, he grabbed a pair of underwear out of the drawer and put them on.

"Before we slept together. Janiyah, last night was something that was churning between us since ... " He trailed off.

"Since I tried to get you in bed when I was seventeen."

He cringed. The day he tried to forget that was burned in his memory. Especially the part a few weeks later, when he'd caught her kissing someone else. His gut twisted now just thinking about it, and how it could easily be repeated.

He wiped away the memory, and the awareness the incident had awakened in him. "Yes, since then."

"And now you've scratched that particular itch, so you can move on."

"I could say the same about you."

"I can't believe this." She rubbed her forehead and turned away from him. "You think this was just some game for me, don't you? That now we can just go back to pretending as if it never happened."

"We have to. We work together. But most of all, we're too different. We don't want the same things. It wouldn't work."

She spun around and glared at him. "No, you're running scared again. You don't want to trust that we could make this work."

"Make it work how, Janiyah? I'm at the point in my life where I'm ready for a serious relationship. I've had my fun, and done the casual dating thing. My plan is to find someone who's ready to settle down. Someone who knows what they want out of life, and hopefully what they want is similar to what I want."

"Why can't that be me?"

"Because a few weeks ago you were talking to me about one guy and the next day you gave your number to another guy."

She stumbled back as if he'd struck her. He wanted to reach out and take her in his arms. He didn't want to hurt her, but he had to be honest.

"You think I'm that easy."

"No. I think guys are naturally drawn to you. I think you should go out and have fun and date whoever you want. But I know that what you want right now isn't the same thing that I want. If we keep doing this," he pointed to the bed, "one of us will end up getting hurt."

"You know what I think?" She snatched her dress off the floor and buttoned it with jerky movements. "I think that's your excuse to justify sleeping with me then moving on."

"Janiyah—"

She held up a hand. "I'm out of here." She ran from the room.

"Janiyah." He followed her but she was already out of the door.

With a groan he ran a hand over his face. What the hell just happened? Had he really been that guy? The guy that came up with some lame, morning after excuse? The idea made him sick to his stomach. No, he wasn't like that. This was for the best. They needed to end things before they got out of hand. They worked together. She was the complete opposite of the type of woman he needed in his life. He couldn't fall in love with Janiyah Henderson.

He was half in love with her already.

With a grunt, he went back into the bedroom. He took one look at the rumpled sheets and got a whiff of her perfume in the air and missed her immediately.

"Fuck!" He kicked the bed. Things were more complicated now than they'd ever been.

CHAPTER 23

Janiyah tried not to think about how pathetic it was to sit alone at a bar after the guy you loved told you it was a mistake to sleep with you, and it damn sure didn't help that they were playing Bruno Mars and she had to hear about sex and paradise. She wouldn't be experiencing that anymore. The bartender slid her a glass of Riesling and she downed half of it. It was official: tonight she was sad female cliché number one.

It was another young professionals mixer. They'd exchanged the artsy location for a wine and tapas bar. She couldn't even enjoy the better choice of music. Though the crowd was thinner than usual, the variations of blue, grey, and black suits were the same.

The dark colors were good. They matched her mood. Two days ago she'd gotten something she'd wanted for most of her adult life. Then Freddy tore her heart out by saying it was something they'd needed to get out of their system. In so many words, he'd put her in the same category as the asshole ex: someone it was fun to screw but not settle down with.

Freddy was the last person she expected that from. She'd believed him when he said he saw more in her than other people did. If that were the case, their morning after would have gone a lot differently. They'd be together, not awkwardly avoiding each other. He'd stayed out of the office all day today. When she checked his calendar, all of the appointments were marked private.

Liz came back from the bathroom and sat beside her at the bar. "Are you going to tell me why you look so pitiful or am I going to have to find someone else to entertain me?"

Janiyah looked up from her glass of wine. "I don't look pitiful."

"Puh-leeze! You do look pitiful, and I want to know why."

"Why, so you can lecture me about rushing head first into things without thinking them through?"

Liz placed her elbow on the bar and propped her chin in her hand. "Okay, spill it."

Janiyah took another gulp of wine. "I slept with Freddy."

Liz's chin dropped out of her hands. She jerked back up and leaned forward. "You did what?"

"I slept with Freddy."

"So that's why he canceled with Missy. They had a date last night and he canceled."

She was so upset she couldn't even feel satisfaction that at least he hadn't left her bed and gone out with another woman.

"Was it that bad? I thought he'd be good in bed."

Janiyah sat up. "Why are you thinking about him in bed?"

Liz lifted her hands. "You can't tell me you never thought it."

"Of course I thought it. But I never thought it would happen."

"How did it happen?"

She quickly gave Liz the rundown of the past few weeks with Freddy. Starting with their almost kiss and ending with Mrs. Driggers's pep talk.

"Liz, he was ... is ... the best I've ever had. It was ... I can't even describe it."

"Then why are you moping around if the sex was so good?"

"Because afterwards he basically said it was a mistake, the result of lust brewing between us, and we needed to move on."

Liz cringed. "Ugh, men are idiots." She reached over and took Janiyah's hand. "I take it you want more."

Janiyah took back her hand and toyed with the wine glass. "I don't know."

"That's a lie."

Typical Liz. "Okay, I do know. I want him, but he doesn't want me."

Liz scoffed. "How do you know that? I've always thought Fredrick was crazy about you."

"No, Freddy puts up with me. I'm his friend's little sister and nothing more."

Liz raised an eyebrow. "If that were the case I doubt he'd have sex with you."

"I know he's not interested in me." She downed the rest of her wine. "Let's just say this is the second time Fredrick Jenkins has thrown my affections back in my face. It's like he doesn't trust that I really want to be with him."

"Well, what do you expect?"

"Say what?"

"Come on, Janiyah, I love you to death, but you treat guys like accessories. You toss out your phone number as if it's nothing and aren't shy about the fact that you don't want a long term relationship. He's seen that for years. He may not believe you're serious about him."

She remembered the look on Freddy's face when he and Aaron walked in on her kissing that guy the summer Freddy first turned her away. He'd said he didn't want her, but there was hurt and jealousy on his face. She couldn't even remember that guy's name. He was classmate who'd tried to get with her all year. After Freddy's rejection, she'd called him up because she'd wanted validation that someone wanted her. She never forgot the look of disappointment on Freddy's face that night. The same look he had whenever she brought around another boyfriend.

No wonder he didn't expect much from her in the way of relationships. From the beginning she'd done nothing to show that she only wanted him. That she loved him.

No man she dated ever lived up to Freddy. No matter how interesting they might be, they didn't tease her, put up with her changing moods, or encourage her to do better the way Freddy did. The men in her past were more like a string of good friends than boyfriends. Freddy was always the constant man in her life.

"You're right. But is it worth trying to convince him that we belong together?"

Liz looked over Janiyah's shoulder and frowned. "You better decide sooner rather than later."

Janiyah turned to see who Liz was talking about and froze. She squeezed the wine glass in her hand so hard she was surprised it didn't snap. Freddy had arrived, with an attractive woman at his side. She did a quick examination of the woman: tasteful beige suit, short but stylish haircut, and flawless pecan skin. The type of woman she would picture with Freddy.

The woman placed a hand on his arm and leaned in to say something in his ear. Freddy smiled. Full on dimple, to this woman she'd never seen before! Had she been the "private" meeting on his calendar?

Technically they weren't together, so she couldn't play the jealous girlfriend. But to sit by and act as if it meant nothing to see him with another woman after he'd had sex with her two nights before was ludicrous.

"Excuse me," she said to Liz as she put down her wine glass and stalked over to them. "Hi, Freddy." Her attempt for a light airy tone came out more like a tight high-pitched squeak.

His smile melted away. She tried not to shift uncomfortably as his gaze swept over her. Memories of their night flickered in his eyes. It provided a modicum of relief. He wasn't the type to sleep with her then run into the arms of another woman. She hoped he hadn't decided to start today.

"Janiyah." His voice was even, as if it was no big deal to run into her with another woman on his arm.

"What are you doing here?" she asked.

"Networking." He turned to the woman beside him. "Shante, this is Janiyah."

Shante smiled and held out a hand. "It's nice to meet you, Janiyah."

Janiyah shook her hand and gave her a tight smile. "I'm his ... " Freddy stiffened at the woman's side. "His assistant."

Shante took her hand back and leaned closer to Freddy. "Good to know. I'm his realtor."

Janiyah relaxed and gave the woman a genuine smile. "Oh, good."

"Janiyah," Freddy said in a tense voice.

She ignored him. "Did he find a house?"

Shante looked between the two. "Actually, we were just discussing the one we saw last. I think he likes it."

Janiyah turned back to Freddy. "You're really moving?"

"I told you that."

"I just didn't realize you'd be looking so soon." Janiyah hated the hurt in her voice.

"No need to prolong the inevitable."

A tense silence ensued. Shante placed a hand on Freddy's arm. "Let's get a drink."

Janiyah's hand balled into a fist. "Freddy, can I talk to you for a second? Evan called and there's an issue in the office."

Freddy stepped out of Shante's reach. "Sure. Shante, thanks for your help this afternoon. Go ahead and call the other realtor about that house and give me a call tomorrow."

The note of dismissal in his voice made Janiyah want to do the Electric Slide. She couldn't help giving Shante a smug look. *That's right, girlfriend, he's all mine.*

"Alright, we can discuss their offer over lunch tomorrow. I know this great Italian place downtown." She smiled at him, then gave Janiyah a completely non-threatened smile before gliding away.

After she walked away, Freddy turned to her with a frown. "Do you have to butt into my business all the time?"

"Do you really want to have this out in front of everyone?" She spread her hand to indicate the crowd in the bar.

He turned and walked out. She followed him to stand at the side of the building, far enough away from the door so they wouldn't be overheard.

"I didn't mean any harm," she said.

"Really? You come over with murder in your eyes and question why I'm here."

"Well, what do you expect? I was in your bed yesterday morning."

He pinched the bridge of his nose. "I thought we agreed ... "

"No, you pushed me aside like a toy you didn't want to play with anymore."

A startled look came across his face before regret filled his eyes. "I know that what I said yesterday made me sound like a jerk."

"Try an ass."

"Fine. I was an ass. I don't think you're a toy that I can just toss to the side. I don't want you to think that what happened was just my way of getting a thrill. But, Janiyah, we both know that it can't continue. There are too many complications."

"Name three." She held up three fingers.

"We work together."

She dropped a finger. "We can keep our relationship a secret."

"We're incompatible."

She dropped another finger. "We balance each other out."

"You'll move on to another guy after a month." He held up a hand to stop her from responding. "I'm not playing the part in your show."

"What part?"

"Random guy filling in as current boyfriend."

She shook her head and reached for him. "It's not a show, Freddy."

He stepped out of reach. "You never had a problem replacing me."

"And none of them lived up to you. My dating history is just that, history. I want you, Fredrick." She used his whole name deliberately.

His gazed turned hot. He stepped closer, sending sizzling awareness across her skin. The wonderful smell of his cologne, mixed with the essence that was only Freddy, swirled around her. She trembled. Memories of calling out his name made her swollen and wet.

"But for how long, Janiyah?"

"Forever."

"I don't believe that."

She placed her hand on his chest, right over the pounding of his heart. "Are you telling me that yesterday meant nothing?"

"Come on, Janiyah, you know it meant something," he said in a quiet voice, as if admitting that was difficult. "It just doesn't have to mean everything. It's best if we move on."

He had to be the most stubborn, infuriating man she'd ever met. She snatched her hand away. "Move on. Really? Are you saying you'll be okay seeing me with someone else?"

His nostrils flared and jealousy flashed briefly in his eyes before he hid it and crossed his arms. "I expect to see you with someone else."

The cocktail of anticipation and edginess bubbled up. "Then prove it."

"I'm not playing games with you."

"Oh, this isn't a game. If you're willing to be so grown up and sensible then so am I. You want the other night to mean nothing, fine, prove it."

"How am I supposed to do that?"

Warning bells that she was about to do something foolish started, but emotions dulled the sound. "A double date. Me and the professor and you and Liz's boss."

He held up his hands, spun away, and laughed. "This is ridiculous," he said, facing her again.

"No, you saying we should act like the other night didn't happen is ridiculous. You felt the power of what was between us as much as I. You might say you're fine with moving and pretending it meant nothing, but I think you're a liar."

He rushed back over, and stood close enough for the aroused tips of her breasts to brush against his hard chest. Excitement flared between them. His pupils dilated as the heat from their bodies mingled and boiled like a deep fryer.

Her plan was stupid, a result of her impulsive side that her dad blamed as the reason she couldn't handle running the business—and though she'd never admit it to him, that impulsive nature had led to a few disastrous decisions. Freddy glared down at her. The discontent in his eyes drained the fight out of her. Forcing an awkward double date would do nothing to make him understand that her feelings were real.

"Freddy—"

"Set up the date," he said in a hard voice before stalking away.

CHAPTER 24

Janiyah walked into the restaurant on Gerald's arm with a ball of dread in her stomach. Her eyes scanned the room. She spotted Freddy sitting at a table with Liz's boss. The two had their heads close as they spoke. She tightened her hold on Gerald's arm and ran a hand down the side of the electric blue sleeveless dress she'd ordered off eBay right after Freddy agreed to her stupid plan. Her decision to buy fewer clothes went out the door when she'd realized Freddy wasn't going to change his mind. If she were going to do something stupid, she might as well do it in style.

"I see our party," she said to the hostess before leading Gerald over to the table.

Fredrick and Missy were laughing when they approached. She fought to keep the frown from popping up on her face.

"Well, it looks like you two are having a good time. It's almost as if you don't need us here," she said in a brittle voice.

Freddy looked up. He quickly scanned her body and she fought not to squirm. Her dress wasn't revealing, but she might as well be naked from way his gaze caressed her. He wore a dark orange shirt that flattered his light skin, and lightened the color of his brown eyes beneath his glasses. His tongue did a quick sweep over his lips. He'd done the same sweep with his tongue against her skin. She squirmed and broke eye contact before she made a fool of herself and begged him to end this craziness.

She looked up at Gerald with a forced smile. "Gerald, you know Fredrick. And this is his date ... " She finally made eye contact with his date.

"I'm Missy," she said with a warm smile. Her blue eyes danced with friendliness as she reached out a hand. Crap, it was hard to hate a friendly person.

"Hi, Missy, this is Dr. Gerald Westlock." She shook Missy's hand, which was slender and cool to the touch. An ice princess—definitely not right for Fredrick.

Gerald reached out and shook first Fredrick's hand then Missy's. "Nice you meet you."

Freddy stood and eyed Gerald from head to toe. He was shorter than Gerald, but far outshone him in Janiyah's eyes. His thickly muscled frame contoured perfectly to every important feature on her body. Her cheeks burned and a hot ache spread between her thighs. Her eyes dropped to his crotch and her lips parted with a silent gasp. Everything fit just right.

"Good to meet you, too. Have a seat," Freddy said, his voice thick.

She met his eye. She drew her lower lip between her teeth and his eyes darkened. So much for not wanting her. A small smile played at her lips, and in an instant, the desire in his eyes was replaced with defiance.

"So, Gerald," Freddy said when they were seated. "You and Janiyah have been out on several dates."

Gerald reached over to take her hand. He smiled warmly and she looked away. "We have. Each one better than the last."

Missy grinned at them both. "That's so cute."

"And poetic," Freddy said, bringing his glass of water to his lips.

Gerald cleared his throat and shifted in his seat. "How are things going with your firm, Fredrick? Pretty interesting, I'd guess, with all the new business you've gotten."

Janiyah snorted. "As interesting as watching paint dry."

Freddy's hand clenched the water glass. He threw a dirty look her way, and she only smirked. She could be just as much of a smart ass as him.

"It is, actually," Freddy said. "I'm trying to set up a meeting with the owner of the Satterfield restaurant chain to discuss doing business with them."

"I can relate." Gerald sat up in his chair. "My research is bringing in outside funding. I love my research, but the more money I bring in, the more weight I pull at the university."

Freddy glanced at Janiyah. "I bet."

She'd forgotten how pretentious Gerald could be. She turned to Missy. "So, Liz mentioned that you introduced her to yoga."

Missy smiled before flipping her hair over her shoulder. "I did. I love it. I try to go three times a week."

"Isn't yoga just stretching and stuff?"

"No, it's much more than that. It's about finding a mind and body connection along with relaxation and meditation. There is more to yoga than increasing flexibility."

Janiyah raised an eyebrow. "Maybe you can convince Fredrick to go. He could use help with the mind and body connection."

Freddy's eyes narrowed only slightly before his features relaxed. "I don't have a problem in that department."

Janiyah's insides clenched. This was her dumbest idea ever.

Missy leaned in to Freddy. "I'd love to show you how flexible I am."

The look in her eye turned Janiyah cold. She leaned closer to Gerald, hoping that the warmth of his body would soothe the iciness within her. "Good luck. He rarely trusts trying something new."

"I've always been open to trying new things. I just know that some things are better left alone," he said, the accusation clear in his voice.

Her back became ramrod straight as she sat up. "Sounds like fear to me. Heaven forbid you to step away from your well laid plans."

He turned away from Missy to glare at her across the table. "Sticking to my plans doesn't lead me astray. Knowing my boundaries keeps me from making foolish decisions. When I veer from my plans, I end up making mistakes."

Pain twisted her insides. Would he ever stop calling what happened with them a mistake?

She leaned across the table. "You don't always make mistakes. You enjoy yourself, but have to let go and give in to the," her gaze drifted slowly across his features, "pleasure. Give in to what could be if you let it. What you could have."

Freddy clenched his jaw. His Adam's apple bobbed in his throat as he swallowed several times. His direct gaze burned straight through her, his eyes as intense as they'd been when they'd made love. Focused, raw, and powerful.

Gerald cleared his throat. "Is there something I'm missing?"

Freddy's eyes came back into focus as he sat up. Janiyah shook her head. She looked at Gerald whose gaze darted suspiciously between her and Freddy. Missy's features were pulled into a frown.

"I don't think we're missing anything," Missy said. "I think it's pretty clear what's going on here."

Fredrick took a large gulp of his water. "There's nothing going on."

Janiyah sipped from her glass as well, but the cold water did nothing to cool her off. "I don't know what you mean."

"You two have slept together," Missy said matter-of-factly.

"What?" she said at the same time Freddy said, "No." Their eyes met briefly before they both reached for their now empty water glasses.

Gerald nodded slowly. "I think you're right, Missy."

Janiyah pushed aside her glass and turned to her date. "Hey, let's get out of here and go somewhere else. I'm more in a mood for sushi than Italian."

Gerald shook his head. "I don't think so. One thing I'm good at is reading people, and I definitely read that you'd rather be here as Fredrick's date than mine." He pushed back his chair and stood.

Missy jumped up too. "Hey, I'm in a mood for sushi." She rushed around the table to Gerald. "I know a good place."

Gerald smiled and took her hand. "That sounds great."

Janiyah's jaw dropped as they walked out of the restaurant together. As soon as the door closed behind them she whipped around toward Freddy. "See what you did? You've scared off our dates."

Freddy scoffed. "What I did? You practically announced that we slept together."

"I did not. I only *insinuated* that you needed to step out of the box more."

"Save it, Janiyah." He threw his napkin on the table. "We didn't order, so there isn't a bill. Let's just call tonight what it was—a loss—and move on."

"But, Freddy ... "

He shook his head. "Don't. Tonight's little game is just another example of why we wouldn't work. I don't play games. I never should have agreed to come in the first place."

"Then why did you come?"

"Because, when it comes to you I don't make smart decisions." He stood. "Good night, Janiyah."

She watched him walk out. His words felt like a slap in the face. What was she doing trying to convince Freddy they belonged together? If he didn't make smart choices when it came to her, then she was a damn fool when it came to him. She was tired of playing the fool.

You're a joke, Janiyah. For the first time the words rang true.

CHAPTER 25

Fredrick hung up the phone and ran his hands over his face. With his elbows on the desk, he massaged his throbbing temples. Once again his dad needed help, this time with the mortgage. The client he kept brushing off had finally given up and found someone else. Though his dad claimed to have another client lined up, Fredrick didn't believe him.

He counted to ten in a useless attempt to push back his frustration. It didn't matter that his parents' home could have been paid off ten times over if they would have managed their money better. Or that it was unfair his parents looked to him instead of his sister to support their frivolous lifestyle. They were his parents and he would help. It wouldn't burden him financially. But that didn't lessen the sting.

He wasn't much better. Janiyah had easily made him forget common sense and agree to her silly double date. Just like his dad, he was crazy over a woman and making bad decisions.

To make matters worse, she'd been right. He couldn't stand to see her on the arm of another man.

He jumped up from his desk and went to the door. Janiyah sat behind her desk, playing a game on her cell phone. In the short time she'd worked there she'd made the space her own. Colorful knickknacks, bright silk flowers in vases, and pictures of animals with funny phrases cluttered her desk. Again, she was the bright spot in the room. It was after hours. A few staff members were working late to complete assignments. She was done for the day, but always insisted on sticking around.

"Janiyah."

She jumped and slid her cell phone away. Despite their current strained relationship, he had to suppress a smile that she tried to pretend as if she were busy. He knew her work was done; he didn't care if she checked her phone.

"Please get me the latest draft of the audit on Congaree Practice, then you can go home for the night."

He turned away before she got up and went back into his office. She came in a few minutes later with the file. She placed it on his desk. He focused on that instead of looking at her. Every time he looked at her he had to force himself to remember why he kept pushing her away.

She still stood at his desk. "You'll find the first page the most changed."

He looked at the first page. It was a letter from Janiyah. Snatching it up from the rest, he read it quickly, his hand clenching.

"You don't have to resign."

"I think it's for the best."

"I don't want you to." He gripped the paper harder. That wasn't what he'd meant to say.

Her soft gasp meant she was just as surprised by his outburst.

He looked up at her. Her eyes focused on the wall above his head instead of him. She looked so resigned, so grown up, in a white button up shirt and maroon skirt. Since her dad's surgery she'd toned down her outfits. He missed the bright colors.

"Maybe we should talk," he said.

She finally looked at him. Her glare was as sharp as daggers. He deserved that.

"Now you want to talk? You've avoided looking at me for days."

He got up, walked around his desk, and closed the door. He could feel her watching his every movement, probably wishing she did have a dagger.

"I didn't know what to say. Janiyah, everything between us is all screwed up."

"Because of you."

He stalked over to the table instead of to her. He couldn't stand close to her. "This isn't all my fault and you know it."

She crossed her arms and shifted her stance. "Fine. I never should have suggested that stupid double date."

"I think we can agree not to do that in the future."

"I wouldn't have a problem doing it again, if you were my date."

"Janiyah ... "

He glanced out the window. It was growing dark outside. From the corner of his eye, he saw her come closer. "You're always so cold when it comes to me."

"I have to be." He silently cursed. Another blurted confession.

She came to stand beside him. She reached out as if to touch him, then pulled back. "I know that my idea was silly, but I can't act like what happened meant nothing. I can't pretend as if seeing your dimple pop out when you smile doesn't make my day, or how much I like it when you tease me about my dresses, because it means you've noticed me. I can't pretend like I'm not checking you out when you come home from the gym, or that I don't like it when you're all pumped up and sweaty. I can't because it hurts too much that you don't feel the same."

His heart used his ribcage as a punching bag, it beat so hard. Her confession weakened his determination. "Do you think it's easy for me to turn you away?"

"Yes."

The pain in her eyes hurt him. "It's not. It's hard as hell to pretend like I don't care when I see you with another man. Or that watching you walk around my apartment in your pajamas isn't the sexiest thing on the planet." Her eyes widened, and her full lips parted. "I pushed you away because I knew that after one taste of you I'd be hooked. I'd want you every day."

"Apparently there wasn't a need for you to worry. You got your taste and were happy to toss me aside."

"That's not true."

"Really, because you've done a damn good job convincing me that you don't want me anymore. That you don't want me now."

"I want to put you on this table, spread your legs, and fuck you so hard you won't be able to think tomorrow."

Her eyes widened and she gasped. He was full of the unexpected confessions tonight. It's what she did to him. Made him crazy. Made him say and do things he shouldn't. Made him the guy she wanted and not the guy he thought he was.

"Then do it," she said. True to form, she didn't back down. He let her slide her arms around his neck. He was surrounded by her essence, cushioned by her seductive curves. His body hardened with memories of their night together.

A second of sanity tried to slip in. "The office isn't empty."

Her knee slid between his thighs. "Do you want me to go?"

It was that speak now or forever hold your peace moment. He looked into her beautiful brown eyes, felt himself losing the battle, and spoke. "No, I don't."

She pushed him back until his knees hit the chair behind him. He sat, and she slid her right leg up to settle next to his hip on the chair. Unbidden, his hand came up to her hip and gripped tightly.

"You'll be sick of me in a month," he said, his voice hoarse with desire.

She lifted her other leg and straddled him, the heat from the juncture of her thighs pressing against his erection. "I haven't grown tired of you yet."

He placed his other hand on her hip and pulled her roughly against him. "I wasn't your man before."

She sucked in a breath. "You've always been my man, Freddy."

He frowned. It was true; she'd always had her hooks in him. No matter how foolish the idea, she always found a way to convince him. Terror gripped his chest. Right now he would do anything to have Janiyah, anything to make her smile.

He started to push her away but her head lowered. Her soft lips graced over his, sending sparks through his tense body. That's how it would work with them. She'd push forward when he tried to pull away. She always pushed for more, and because he was crazy about her, it was impossible for him to say no. The tip of her tongue flicked against his lower lip. Her arms wrapped around his neck, pulling him closer. His fingers flexed with the urge to take over, but he didn't. She started it; he'd let her lead.

She kissed him forever, their tongues gliding against each other. Each breath she took drew in more and more of him; who he thought he was and what he thought he wanted to be quickly diminished.

When she tried to stand, his grip on her waist tightened. "I'm not going anywhere," she whispered.

He loosened his hold and she eased off his lap. Slowly, she removed her blouse. Her breasts were encased in a blue bra with pink stars. He smiled; she hadn't given up all of the color in her wardrobe. She unzipped and removed her skirt, slowly revealing smooth cinnamon skin before taking off the bra and matching panties. He took his time looking at her. His mouth watered when he saw the wetness between her legs.

Unable to hold back, he put his hands on her hips and pulled her forward. Her breasts bounced before his face and he pulled one of the dark tips in his mouth. She moaned his name, igniting his need to sink deep within her.

"Spread your legs," he ordered.

Without question she hurried to comply. He used two fingers to part her juicy folds, now at eye level, and ran his tongue over her erect clit. She tasted sweet, delicious, and better than any damn cake he'd ever eaten. Her body stiffened. He leaned back to get a look at her beautiful wet treasure, before going in for more. One of her hands gripped the back of his head, the other his shoulder. Each one of her soft cries urged him on. He gently sucked the nub of her desire into his mouth. Another wave of her essence rained down, and he eagerly licked it up. His fingers dug into her hips; he couldn't get enough.

"Freddy ... Fredrick ... stop ... I'm going to ... "

He pulled back, watching with male pride as the lips of her sex quivered. Frantically, she reached down to unbutton his pants and pull his dick from where it strained against his zipper. He lifted his hips to push his pants to his knees, and fought to keep from coming when she straddled him again and her slick heat slid against his throbbing length.

Her warm hand clasped him, and a tense breath hissed between his clenched teeth. She rubbed his head against her wetness once, twice, then sat on him fully.

It was heaven.

Her tight body clenched and unclenched around him. Her soft breasts and hard nipples bounced against his chest, as her full lips pressed reverent kisses against his face and neck. Grabbing her hips he guided her movements, enjoying her moan and the way her head fell backwards with the movement. He pulled her swiftly back down on his dick.

"Oh, God, Fredrick, yes!" she moaned.

His dick got harder. He repeated the movement—long, hard strokes until his body trembled and sweat ran down his face with the effort to hold back his orgasm. His toes curled inside his shoes, his balls tightened with the need to explode. Leaning forward, he took her breast into his mouth, sucking hard on the tip. Her body trembled violently before he felt her walls clench around him. A new wave of wetness rushed as she squeezed him with her spasms. He let go. His body jerked as she continued to move, pulling everything out of him. He grunted, and groaned, and buried his face in the sweet valley between her breasts. It went on forever, each pull taking more and more, as Janiyah drew in his soul.

CHAPTER 26

Janiyah tried to catch her breath, but couldn't. She pressed herself closer to Freddy. He was still fully dressed. Embarrassment slowly replaced her pleasant afterglow. She was supposed to come in here, tell Freddy she quit, and that she wouldn't throw herself at him again. Instead she was naked in his office, with him buried deep within her, and no idea if anyone had overheard what happened. So much for keeping this a secret.

She squeezed her eyes shut and hid her face in his neck. Would she ever not be a fool when it came to Freddy? His hand trailed up from her hip to the back of her head. She shivered at the touch.

He turned to kiss her cheek. The smell of her was all over him. Heat crept to her face with the thought of what he'd done, and her sex tightened around him.

He groaned. "I'll need a few minutes before I can go again."

A small smile came to her lips. "We've done this before. You don't need that much time."

His chest shook as he chuckled. They stayed that way for a few minutes more. Her back became cold and her thighs ached from her position. She shifted to move, but he held her tighter.

"I don't trust myself with you," he said softly.

She lifted her head. His eyes were somber as they stared into hers. "Why not?"

"I don't make a single rational decision when it comes to you. You drive me crazy, and I don't like that."

Janiyah ran her hand along the back of his head. "Most people in relationships drive each other crazy at some point or another."

His lips quirked. "I don't feel like Fredrick when I'm with you. I'm Freddy, the boy toy at your beck and call."

She frowned. "I don't see you like that."

"You're the only one who doesn't see it that way."

"Are you crazy? My family says you're the only person I listen to. Whenever I make a remotely grown up decision Liz assumes it's because I've discussed it with you—and usually she's right. I've always looked up to you." She lowered her eyes. "It's why I asked you to be my first."

His head fell back and he stared at the ceiling before looking at her. "You were seventeen. I was twenty-two. I couldn't do that."

Her eyes flew back to his. "I know that now, but it hurt when you pushed me away. Ever since then I thought you didn't feel anything for me."

"I felt something." His hand lazily traced up and down her back, almost causing her to forget her train of thought.

"Then why did it take so long for us to get here?"

"I'm still trying to decide if we should be here."

Her warm afterglow completely froze over. "You're still doubting what's between us."

She pulled back. His eyes dropped to her breasts and he licked his lips. Unbelievable! He could throw out a line like that, then think about sex. She jumped from his lap to pick her clothes off the floor.

"I didn't mean it like that."

"Then how did you mean it?" she said as she jerked on her underwear. She whipped around to face him.

He rubbed the bridge of his nose and stood. "Can we just forget it?"

"No, because sex with you will be very painful if every time it's over you tell me how much of a mistake it was." Pain squeezed her heart as she looked at Freddy. "Am I out of your system now? You've had your fun and can move on to someone like your dental hygienist."

"No. I'd never treat you like that." He ran a hand over his head. "But I do wonder what we're doing. It's hard to believe that this is more than just a fling for you. I've hated being just your friend for years, watching you go out with one loser after the other. You take relationships about as seriously as I take those stupid VH1 countdowns. How do I know that you won't wake up three weeks from now and say dating Freddy was fun, but now it's time for something new?"

"Because it's not like that." She stepped toward him and he stepped back.

"I don't know that."

"But—"

"No buts, Janiyah. It's going to take a while for me to trust this."

She spun around to put on her bra while blinking away tears of frustration. "How can you not trust me?" She reached around to fasten it, but his hands brushed hers away and did it for her.

"How can I?"

She turned to face him. "Because I love you."

She held her breath. Surprise flashed in his eyes before he lowered them. Her throat burned. The second time in her life she'd told this guy she loved him and he looked away. It hurt before when she was seventeen, but now that they'd gone beyond just friends, the pain seared her heart.

She turned away. His hand shot out to grab her wrist.

He sighed. "I love you, too."

It wasn't a happy declaration. In fact, he sounded downright upset to say the words.

"You don't have to say it just because I said it."

He met her eyes. "I wouldn't."

"Is loving me really that depressing?"

He pulled her against him. She wanted to pull away, but his other hand made slow circles up and down her spine. She forgot about the chill in the room as the warmth from his body enveloped hers.

"Loving you is scary, but not depressing."

"I don't know if I should take that as an insult or a compliment."

"Definitely a compliment."

"If we love each other, it has to mean something. Freddy, I don't want to be a detour in your life plan, the girl you screw for a few weeks then forget once you go back to life as usual."

He lifted his head. "As if that could happen. You wouldn't let me forget you."

He smiled, full on dimple, and after a second she returned it. It wasn't a promise of forever, and there was still so much they needed to work out. But he loved her. So many couples didn't have that to build a relationship from. It had to count for something. Didn't it?

He kissed her, and she let her doubts slip away. They'd make it work. Somehow she'd show him she wasn't going anywhere.

CHAPTER 27

"It's about time you two came to your senses," Viola Jenkins said as she pulled Janiyah into a hug.

Janiyah gave a tight laugh and hugged her back. She lifted a brow as she met Freddy's eyes over his mom's shoulders. His stony expression didn't ease her discomfort. He could be annoyed with her all he wanted. What had Janiyah been supposed to do when she ran into Viola the other day and she'd brought up how much she wished Janiyah and Fredrick would get together?

She'd tried to think of a good reason why Freddy wouldn't tell his parents, one that wouldn't hurt her feelings, but drew a blank. They'd said the big L word to each other, though he hadn't repeated it. So she was officially outing them. Once she told Viola she'd told her parents. Who apparently already knew. Freddy had confessed to Aaron in order to be sure his friend was okay with it. She'd told him that was unnecessary, but he said he had to do it. Her parents weren't as surprised as she would have expected, though they were probably still distracted by her dad's recovery. She expected a full lecture once he was healthy.

Why he would tell Aaron and not his parents was a mystery. He seemed surprised when she said she'd told their parents. Except for telling Aaron, he didn't want to make a big fuss about them being together. She couldn't help but think it had to do with him admitting that he expected her to change her mind about them in a few weeks.

No matter what his thoughts were, she and Freddy needed to be outed. A month had passed since that night in his office.

A month of her trying hard to be the type of woman Freddy would be proud to have. She wore suits to work. Volunteered to help with the young professional mixer, and didn't go out to parties. She was reading the book he'd given her, and spending as much time with him as possible, all to show him that she was committed to their relationship.

Everything should be perfect, except she felt like she was going crazy. What in the world was her problem? She'd done it. She'd proved everyone wrong. She'd excelled at her job. She was in a stable relationship with a guy who was arguably the best catch in the city. She'd done what everyone wanted her to do, became grown up Janiyah. She should be happy, not bored with her job and afraid her relationship would shatter any second. Was this really the perfect life everyone wanted for her? Misery at work and walking on eggshells at home?

Viola broke the hug, but continued to hold Janiyah by the shoulders. "I was just telling Fredrick he needed to marry you."

Janiyah coughed. Freddy came over and peeled his mom's hands from her shoulders. "We're dating, Mom, not engaged."

Viola waved a hand. "It's just a matter of time."

Janiyah grinned from ear to ear. A few weeks ago, the thought of spending her life with one man would have her in the midst of a panic attack. The idea of being with Freddy forever warmed her heart.

She looked at Freddy, and her smile faltered. He was pinching the bridge of his nose. "Let's not get ahead of ourselves."

She took his hand. "Let's not rule anything out." He gave her a look that was both surprised and doubtful. Every time he did that it chipped away at her hope.

Viola clapped her hands. "Aren't they adorable, Christopher?"

Freddy's dad laughed, sliding his arm around his wife's shoulders. "Yes they are. Reminds me of us when we first got together."

Freddy's hand tightened on hers. She gave him a curious look, and he relaxed his grip, then smiled. The buzzer in Freddy's other hand went off, alerting them that their table was ready. In no time, they were settled with drinks and food ordered. Viola peppered Janiyah with questions about the furniture shopping she'd done with Freddy earlier in the day. He'd found a house, thanks to the pretty Shante, and was closing on it in a few weeks.

Freddy's arm rested along the back of her chair. She couldn't suppress the giddy smile from popping up whenever he absently ran his finger along her arm. He did that a lot when they were alone. Alone, he was affectionate. He'd touch her, hold her hand, or pull her against him. It was those small things that made her hold on to the hope that they could make this thing work, before she had to grin and bear it when he pretended they were only colleagues at the office.

Freddy jerked away. "You can't be serious?"

Janiyah and Viola stopped talking mid-sentence to look at Freddy and Christopher. Christopher's face was flushed beneath his tan skin. Freddy's shoulders were tense, his lips in a tight line.

"What's wrong?" Janiyah asked, rubbing her hand along his arm.

"My dad just lost another client."

Christopher held up his hand. "It's no big deal."

"It is. That was your biggest customer. How is the business going to survive?"

"We've had hard times before. Things will pick up," Christopher said in a less than confident voice.

"How will they pick up? What's your plan?" Freddy bit back.

Christopher looked around while twisting his napkin.

Viola came to her husband's defense. "Stop it, Fredrick. Your father has always found a way and he will again." She laughed. "You always were the worrying sort. Your father got that new client. That'll help."

Freddy's eyes slid to his mom. "What new client?"

Viola gave him a patronizing smile. "The one we told you about before the California trip. The one you both met with."

Freddy sat back, his mouth twisted with disgust. "We never met with that client. He lost him because of the trip."

Viola looked at her husband, then back at Freddy. "That's not what your dad said."

Freddy sat forward, his elbows braced on the table, and leveled his dad with a hard stare. "Tell her the truth."

Christopher sighed before taking Viola's hand. "It's true. I didn't want to upset you."

Viola's lips curved into a hesitant smile. "But things will be okay. We can still have the party next week."

Freddy tensed. "Party?"

Viola beamed. "Yes, after Janiyah told me you two were together I called her parents to plan a get-together to celebrate."

Janiyah frowned. "My dad's not really into partying right now." Her dad had barely wanted his kids to see him since the surgery.

"Your mom said that, but I insisted," Viola said.

"I really don't think it's a good idea," Janiyah said. The last thing she wanted was for her dad to compromise his recovery because of a party for her and Freddy.

"This is ridiculous," Freddy said, shifting in his seat. "You shouldn't be planning a party. You should be looking for ways to keep a roof over your head."

Christopher turned red, and Viola's mouth dropped. Janiyah looked between the three before taking Freddy's hand in hers and squeezing. She might be clueless as to what that statement meant, but it was clear this conversation had gone too far.

"This isn't the time or place. Why don't we change the subject?" she said, smiling at them all.

Viola straightened. Her smile remained, but now it wavered. "Excellent idea. Tell me about the living room furniture you looked at today?"

Janiyah looked to Freddy, but his lips were set in a firm line. No help there.

"We looked around and saw some nice items, but I thought we could go to Charlotte and check out some of the boutiques there. Freddy's new house is beautiful. Custom furniture would really make it shine."

Helping Freddy furnish his new house was another attempt at being a good girlfriend. They hadn't talked about how their relationship would change. If he'd give her a key. Whether or not she should bring any of her stuff over. If he even wanted her over as much. She didn't ask because she was afraid of the answer. Afraid he would say he was moving because he didn't want her around.

Viola's eyes lit up. "That's a wonderful idea."

"It's an expensive idea," Freddy said. "I don't need fancy furniture."

Janiyah laughed. "Oh please, Freddy, you can afford it, and it would look wonderful."

His body went rigid and his eyes narrowed with his frown. "Don't tell me what I can afford. I don't spend my money on frivolous things. Just because you buy things on a whim doesn't mean I'll do the same."

Pinpricks of heat traveled up her neck and cheeks. She slid away. "Thank you for making that clear," she said in a voice that mirrored his cold manner.

He looked instantly contrite. He lifted his hand to her, but she shook her head. Thankfully the waiter arrived with their food. They went through the remainder of the meal with Viola's attempts at lighthearted conversation, but it was a bad cover for the strain over the table.

A tense silence filled the car on the way home. She jumped out as soon as he parked. Slamming the door behind her, she hurried inside and up the stairs. The sound of his heavy footsteps followed. She went to the door of her apartment.

"Janiyah, you don't have to go to your apartment," he said in a regretful tone.

She glared at him over her shoulder. "I think I do." She went inside, then slammed and locked her door for good measure.

She leaned against it. The last of her optimism shattered when he'd snapped at her in front of his parents. For him to even imply that she cared about how he spent his money was ridiculous. She hadn't realized how little he really thought of her. The pain of her misjudgment burned like a million hot coals in her stomach.

A heavy knock shook her door. She squealed and jumped away.

"Open the door." Freddy's voice came from the other side.

She placed a hand over her pounding heart. After several deep breaths she answered. "Go away, Freddy."

"I'm not leaving."

"Then you can sleep on the other side. We don't have anything to talk about."

"Yes, we do."

"No, we don't. In fact, why don't we just cut our losses and end this. You don't trust me, and apparently believe I have an eye on your money. It's not very flattering to have the guy you fancy yourself in love with have such negative thoughts."

"Oh, so you fancy yourself in love with me now." His sarcasm was clear even though she couldn't see his face.

"You expect me to defend my feelings again? Why, so you can throw it back in my face? I'm not doing it, Freddy."

She placed her forehead on the door. She wouldn't look through the peephole at him. Seeing his face would crumple her resolve.

"I'm sorry about what I said at dinner." His voice was softer, closer. She pictured him leaning against the other side of the door. "The night we made love in my office I'd just gotten off the phone with my dad. He needed help paying the mortgage. That was the third time this year. Now that he's lost another client it won't be the last."

Janiyah stepped back. She unlocked the door to open it for him. Freddy leaned against the frame; his wide shoulders were stooped and sadness filled his eyes. She wanted to rush over and put her arms around him. Instead she hugged herself.

"I'm sorry about that, but it doesn't excuse what you said to me."

He straightened and came into the apartment. She tried to step out of his way, but he took her elbow and gently held her in place.

"Do you want to know why I'm scared to love you?" He kicked the door shut with his foot.

Instead of screaming yes, she lifted and lowered her head slowly.

"It's because of my parents. My dad will do anything to make my mom happy, even if it means the rest of the family will suffer. Growing up, I watched him blow money on cars, clothes, vacations, and jewelry for her, only to sit in his office the following week panicking about where the money would come from. My mom is oblivious, or at least she tries to be. She always laughs and says my dad will figure a way out of it."

She couldn't resist touching him anymore. She clasped the side of his face. "We aren't your parents."

"I know, but I feel that way about you." He pulled away to pace toward her couch. "Anything you ask me to do, I'd do it. I have for years, even when I hated it."

She frowned. "What have I asked you to do that you hate?"

He stopped and raised a brow. "Do you really think I enjoyed questioning your boyfriends before you went out on dates?"

"Well you sure as hell liked telling me how stupid they were afterwards." She put her hands on her hips.

"I hate watching gossip news shows, reality shows, and concerts on television."

"I know that. You gripe the entire time before burying your nose in a book and becoming completely oblivious to me or what's on television." She marched over to him. "I think you need to come up with something better, because I've never asked you to do something that would threaten your way of life. If anything, I've given up all that stuff to make you happy."

"I never asked you to give up the things you love."

"I know, but I did it. I gave up parties with Liz, and exchanged them for suits and pantyhose just to make you happy."

"Don't give up those things. Go out with Liz, *please*."

His emphasis on the please made her frown and take a step back. "Oh, you're tired of me already."

He hesitated, twisting his lips like the words were difficult to come. "We're always together, Janiyah," he finally said in a rush. "We live next to each other, we work together, we're sleeping together. It's too much."

She turned around and ran her fingers through her hair. He came behind her and put his hands on her shoulders. "I don't want to lose you, but we need space."

She jerked out of his hands. "Space ... space. I'm trying to be the woman you want."

"I don't want someone who doesn't do things she enjoys and spends all of her time forcing herself to like the things I do."

"Then what the hell do you want? I'm flighty, frivolous, and going to blow your fortune. But when I settle into a job and wear navy frigging suits every day I'm smothering you."

"I want you to be happy."

"I thought we were happy."

He took a deep breath and rubbed the bridge of his nose. When their eyes met there was sadness in his. "Are you really happy? Because I see you changing into someone I don't know and it worries me. That other person is who I fell in love with."

Her throat burned with the pain of what was coming. "You said yourself that you're afraid to love that other person."

"I don't know how to love that other person."

"I'm not another species. I'm not going to ask you to do something for me that will risk your business."

"But that's the thing. If you did ... I'd consider it. I'm not sure if I'm willing to risk that."

His words were like acid, stripping away the last of her fight. Tears burned, but she didn't let them fall. "Then you should go."

"Janiyah, don't."

"Don't what? Break up with you? It's what you wanted, right? You've been waiting for me to grow disenchanted with this. For me to wake up and realize ... how did you say it ... oh, it was fun dating Freddy but I'm through now. Well, I am through. Get out."

It hurt to say the words. Her knees wobbled with the need to buckle. She was through with trying to convince Freddy to love her. Fredrick would always stand in the way. He'd always second-guess her feelings. Always wait for her to somehow turn him into his dad, when she knew he was too strong, smart, and determined to let her or anyone else force him to give up his dream. If she asked him to give it up he might consider it for half a second, and then tell her he couldn't. But it wasn't a theory she was willing to test. Otherwise he'd never realize it himself.

"I do love you, Janiyah."

"But you don't want to love me, and that hurts more than you not loving me." Her voice cracked. A tear rolled down her cheek. He reached for her but she pushed his hand away. "Just go. And consider this my two weeks' notice. No need to make this harder than it is."

"You don't have to quit."

She imagined sitting at that desk watching him every day, eventually seeing him go out with another woman, and pain scorched her heart.

"Yes, I do."

CHAPTER 28

"You know I owe you a beat down," Aaron told Fredrick through the phone.

He'd called Aaron to see if he would help him move into his new house this weekend. Movers had already delivered his new appliances. Shante had recommended an interior decorator who'd picked everything out right down to the wall colors. The only thing left was to get all of his stuff out of the apartment. Start his new life in his new home. It was traditional, comfortable, and perfectly suited for the family he would have one day. Except every time he looked at it, he pictured bright pillows, or antique tables and chairs sprinkled in that Janiyah would see at some consignment shop and swear he needed—only to later realize she'd never visit.

"Why do you owe me a beat down?" Fredrick picked up the file for the Satterfield account. His meeting with them was in an hour. The proposal was perfect, thanks to Janiyah. It was the last thing she'd polished before walking out of his office the other day.

"Breaking Janiyah's heart."

Fredrick flinched. "She broke up with me, remember?"

"You didn't fight too hard to keep her."

"Her mind was made up."

His stomach churned at the memory of the tears on her face. He'd regretted what happened the moment he walked out that door. But every time he tried talking to her, she turned away. She said she didn't trust herself to listen to him.

"I really thought you would be the one she settled down with. I mean, she waited for you forever."

Fredrick took off his glasses and stared at the ceiling. "What are you talking about?"

"It was pretty obvious she was waiting on you to notice her."

"How could I not notice her? She was always around."

"You know what I mean, and don't think that because I never said anything that I don't know what she asked you to do years ago."

"I didn't touch her."

"I know, and she cried for days because you didn't, then went out with that fool to try and forget you. I thought she'd get over it, but she never did. Even though you did the right thing then, trust me, I noticed the way you looked at my sister."

"Then why didn't you give me a beat down then?"

"Because you kept your hands to yourself, and I knew you weren't just hanging around to gawk at Janiyah. I understand the reason why you stayed away from her before, but I don't understand why two people who've obviously held a torch for each other for years break up after a month."

"You wouldn't understand."

"Try me. Because you better have a good damn reason for breaking her heart."

"I wasn't trying to break her heart. I was trying to be honest with her. My dad risked everything to make my mom happy. I don't want to do the same thing with Janiyah."

"That makes no sense whatsoever. How would you risk everything for her?"

Fredrick ran a hand over his head. He tried to find the words to explain his fear, but they all seemed inadequate. "I hate to say this, but I seriously considered sleeping with your sister that first time." He heard Aaron take in a sharp breath. "It was wrong, but I wanted her, and not like the other girls I'd been with. I wanted her ... badly. I can't even explain. It struck me that I would risk my friendship with you, your dad's respect, and everything to have her. I hoped it would go away, but it didn't. It made me move in next to her, play nice with the stupid boyfriends she paraded around, and give her free rein to my apartment. All because of this thing I felt for her. It scared the shit out me."

"Fred, I know you. I trust you. Okay, you thought about Janiyah then, but you didn't do anything. And letting her in your life ... man, you're crazy about her so why wouldn't you? But to think that you'd risk everything you built because of that ... I disagree. You are not your dad. You already proved that by what you achieved, and despite Janiyah's tendencies, she's never stepped out of line. Mostly because of you." Aaron let out a dry chuckle. "You know what, I'm not going to kick your ass. You're going to beat yourself up when she meets someone else and really gets over you."

Aaron's words struck Fredrick like a bullet to the chest, blasting through the regret and killing his resolve. He was beating himself up for letting her go, and for wanting her back at the same time. Honestly, he couldn't imagine giving up his business or having his family worry about where the next meal came from. It wasn't in his nature. So what was his real fear?

"Fred, hold on a second. I got a call coming in." A few seconds later Aaron came back. "My dad's in the hospital."

Fredrick sat up and slid his glasses back on. "What's going on?"

"I don't know. That was Kareem. I've got to go."

Aaron hung up, and Fredrick stared at the phone. He looked from the phone to the Satterfield file and back again. Mr. Henderson was like a second father to him, but he didn't need Fredrick there. He had his own children there.

He looked at the file and thought of Janiyah. She loved her dad. If something happened to Mr. Henderson, she'd be crushed. They all would, but the thought of her crying, of her needing someone there to hold her, and him not being that person felt wrong.

There was a knock at the door. He looked up at Phyllis who was checking her watch. "You need to be getting ready to go meet the Satterfields. I've got all your materials ready." She looked at him and smiled. "I'm proud of you, Mr. Jenkins. This account will be the icing on the cake, and prove to everyone that you're the best accountant in the area."

He stood. "It will, won't it?" He powered off his computer. "Send Larry."

He hurried to the door. Phyllis grabbed his arm to stop him as he tried to go by. "Send Larry? Are you crazy? What could possibly be more important?"

"The woman I love." Her hand fell away, and he turned and rushed out.

• • •

Janiyah twirled a beaded necklace on the tip of her index finger. The green beads clacked against each other as she spun them faster and faster. That's how she felt. As if she were spinning in circles waiting for her heart to catch up with her mind. She was right for breaking up with Freddy. She deserved someone who loved all of her. It was going to hurt. Breakups usually did, but she'd get through this. She'd no longer see him now that her two weeks were over. And he was moving out of his apartment this weekend, which was good. Less temptation.

"You're supposed to be stuffing those in bags, not twirling them on your finger."

Janiyah jumped at Liz's voice behind her. Her twirling suffered and she hit herself in the nose with the beads. Liz laughed as she sat next to her on the couch.

"That wasn't funny," Janiyah said, dropping the beads on the rest of the pile on the coffee table and rubbing her nose.

"You didn't see it. Here take this." She passed over one of the two glasses of wine in her hand. "If you're coming here to drown your sorrows you need to really drown them."

Janiyah took the wine and swallowed. "I'm not here to drown my sorrows. I'm here forcing my friend to help me make goody bags for the young professionals mixer."

Liz was officially the best best friend out there. She'd taken the day off and offered her apartment for Janiyah to use to prepare for the next young professionals mixer, but was really there offering moral support in the face of Janiyah's heartbreak. Liz's couch had been her camping ground a lot since her break up with Freddy.

"Tell yourself that, but we both know stuffing beads and masks into these bags could have waited until the rest of the committee could help. You're hiding from Fredrick." Liz curled her feet on the couch and took a sip of her wine.

"If being here keeps me from being distracted while he takes his stuff out then it's a win-win situation."

"Janiyah, admit it, you're hiding."

"So what if I am?"

"You can't hide from Fredrick forever. He is best friends with your brother."

"Yeah, and I'll probably get the invitation when he finally decides to marry some goody two shoes who wears conservative clothes and coupon shops for groceries. I'll have to buy her pots from Williams-Sonoma for the wedding shower and RSVP me plus none to their perfect wedding."

Liz chuckled. "You're really going off the deep end over there."

"No, I'm not, and you know it. This will happen, and I swear I'm not going to the wedding and eating the cucumber sandwiches." Janiyah gulped the wine.

Liz took the glass out of her hand. "Maybe drowning your sorrows wasn't such a good idea. You're already drunk on love." She set both glasses on the coffee table. "Why don't you talk to Fredrick? You two love each other. That has to count for something."

"Yeah, but he doesn't want to love me, Liz. I can't be with a guy who doesn't really want to be there."

Janiyah waited for her friend to give her a *that's right, girlfriend* or something, but it never came. When she looked over Liz's lips twisted back and forth—something she did when she didn't know how to say what was on her mind without being rude.

"Spill it, Elizabeth."

"Fine. You changed when you were with him. All of a sudden you were trying to be this perfect woman—who was very boring I might add. That wasn't the person he fell for."

Janiyah groaned and reached for her glass of wine. "You sound like him. I don't understand. I tried to show him that I could be in a serious, long-term relationship."

"No, you tried to be someone else. He doesn't want a shell of Janiyah loving him. He needs the person you always are to love him. Otherwise, it looks like another persona you're trying out that we both know you couldn't do forever."

Janiyah slapped her hand on her thigh, then rubbed it when it stung too much. "I don't get it. You all wanted me to be different. You wanted me to be responsible."

"Hold up now. I never wanted you to do anything. From the very beginning I told you to do you and be happy. Your parents wanted you to change."

Janiyah picked up her glass to take a sip of wine. "I think Freddy did too, on some level at least."

"If he wanted someone else, he would have been with someone else. He dumped Desiree because you didn't like her. He dragged my boss out on an uncomfortable as hell date because of you."

"Does she hate you now?"

"No, I told her that was all you. Don't come to my office for a while."

"Gotcha."

Janiyah sighed and rubbed the cool glass against her forehead. "My life is more screwed up now than ever. I don't know what to do. I can't take another desk job; it was killing me. And I can't even think about dating, not even casually."

"You'll figure something out. You always do. Forget a new relationship; men are a dime a dozen anyway. When you're ready, you'll find one."

Janiyah sipped her wine, then gave Liz a half smile. "Say that when we're sitting here ten years from now and I'm still heartbroken."

"I have a feeling you won't be heartbroken for the next ten years. And the job stuff will work itself out. You've still got your virtual assisting clients."

"I do, and Mrs. Driggers did mention a friend who needs help promoting her business," Janiyah said nodding slowly. "At first I didn't have a lot of time to help, but I could now." In fact, some of the small businesses Freddy helped out needed help with small things like increasing their online presence and connecting with customers via social media. She could reach out to a few of them to see if they'd be interested in her help with that.

"See, things are looking better already," Liz said.

Janiyah thought about Freddy. How perfect they'd been when it was just the two of them. Away from the office they were comfortable with each other. Their relationship had seemed so easy in those moments. How could things be even remotely better without him in her life? Liz reached over and poked Janiyah's shoulder. "Stop thinking about him."

Janiyah shook her head to do just that. "I'm not."

"Liar." Liz pulled her over into a side hug. "If Fredrick's too dumb to realize that he was crazy about you just the way you were then it's his fault, not yours. I like him, but this whole breakup thing is all on his shoulders. Don't let him dump his hang-ups on you."

Janiyah finished the wine. She dropped her head back on the couch and turned to Liz with a smile. "I hate it when you're right. It makes you think you're such a know it all."

"Consider it my superpower."

"There's something seriously wrong with you," Janiyah said with a grin.

Her cell phone rang. With a sigh, and the truth Liz dropped on her weighing heavily in her chest, she crossed the room to get her phone out of her purse.

A picture of Kareem sitting on his motorcycle flashed on her screen. "Hello."

"Janiyah, Dad's in the hospital."

The strength left her legs. She collapsed against the wall. "What, when? Is he ... "

"We don't know what's going on. His temperature spiked. Mom and I brought him to the emergency room. They just admitted him. I've called David and Aaron. They're on the way."

She jumped when Liz's hand touched her shoulder. "Okay, I'm coming now."

"Don't cry. He'll be okay," Kareem said. She wondered if it were more for his sake than hers.

"I won't cry. Daddy hates that."

She ended the call and turned to Liz. "That was Kareem. Dad's in the hospital. I have to go."

"I heard. You're too shaken." Liz helped her get off the floor and took the keys out of her hand. "Come on, I'll drive."

She nodded and gave Liz's hand a grateful squeeze.

CHAPTER 29

Kareem was the first person they saw when they got to the hospital. He sat in one of the plastic waiting room chairs with his head in his hands. His dreadlocks were loose and spilled around his shoulders, blocking the view of his face. He was in all black, as usual, and in the hospital waiting room his normal attire had a more somber appearance.

Janiyah rushed over to him. She kneeled before him and wrapped her arms around him. Kareem jumped and tried to pull away, but she didn't let go. Now wasn't the time for his strong man routine. With a shuddered sigh, he relaxed and returned the gesture.

"Is he okay?" Janiyah asked.

He pulled back. "Yeah, he's fine." He rubbed his eyes with his forefingers. When he dropped his hands, he avoided eye contact, but it didn't hide the redness.

Janiyah sat back on her heels. "What happened?"

Kareem stood. He walked to the television hanging on the opposite wall and fiddled with the channels. Probably so she wouldn't hug him again. "We were slow at the shop so I went to check in. You could tell he wasn't feeling well, but you know Dad. He kept arguing with Mom and insisting he was fine. Mom asked me to talk some sense into him, but you know how that goes."

Janiyah nodded. She got off the floor to sit in the chair he'd abandoned.

"How did you get him here?"

"He tried to storm out of the room on me, but swayed on his feet instead. I had to grab him to keep him from falling." Kareem rubbed his eyes again. After a few seconds he continued. "He was burning up. I said that was it and brought him here. He's got pneumonia. They say it's common after bypass surgery."

Janiyah let out a heavy breath. A weight lifted from her shoulders and she clutched her chest. "But he can take medicine for that and be okay, right? I was afraid ... his heart was failing again."

"They're treating him for it. He may be here for a few days depending on his response."

Aaron rushed into the waiting room. The twists on his head were pointed in various directions as if he'd run his hands through them repeatedly. Janiyah rushed over to hug her brother. He tightly squeezed her shoulders. "What happened?"

He stepped away and walked to Kareem who started the story again. She was about to turn to them, when Freddy stepped into the waiting room. He looked so good in his dark grey shirt and pants that it hurt her chest. His light brown eyes stared at her with uncertainty before he held out his hand.

She didn't care about their breakup or the reasons they couldn't be together. She only wanted to be in his arms. He didn't hesitate to engulf her in his strong embrace. His shirt smelled like his laundry detergent, clean and fresh, but underneath she got the subtle hint of his cologne and the scent that was just him. She wrapped her arms around his waist, absorbing his strength as she let go of the fear that had clutched her heart on the way over.

He lowered his head and kissed her ear. "Are you okay?"

"I'll be okay."

As soon as Kareem finished filling Aaron in on what happened, David rushed through the door. Janiyah backed out of Freddy's embrace. Immediately she wanted to hold him again. The regret in his eye told her he thought the same. Liz came over and placed her arm through Janiyah's. Leave it to her best friend to save her from throwing herself at Freddy. She let Liz lead her back to her brothers. The sound of Freddy's footsteps followed them over.

David sank heavily into one of the waiting room chairs after Kareem gave him the update. He rubbed his chin before taking the movement over his closely cropped hair. It was the only sign of his agitation. He still looked as if he'd stepped off a runway in his wrinkle free tan slacks and button up shirt rolled at the sleeves.

"Where's Mom?" Janiyah asked.

"She's in the room with Dad." The corner of Kareem's mouth lifted. "He kicked me out for bringing him in."

Both David and Aaron laughed softly.

"Just like Pops," David said.

Janiyah lifted her head. "I want to see him."

"He looks pretty bad," Kareem said, leveling her with a hard stare.

Her lower lip trembled. Tears came to her eyes, but she blinked rapidly to hold them back. Her dad would kick her out if she showed one sign of crying.

"I can handle it." Her voice shook.

Aaron gave her a sad smile. "You don't have to see him now. You can wait a few more minutes."

She shook her head. "No, if I wait I'll imagine all types of things and I really will break down into tears."

"All of us can go," Aaron said.

David sucked his teeth. "Do you really want the man to go ballistic? Let Janiyah go first, then we'll go."

Aaron and Kareem exchanged looks then nodded. "Go ahead and check on Dad," Aaron said.

"What room?"

"Seventeen twenty-three," Kareem said.

She gave Liz a hug. "You don't have to wait on me. But I know you will," she said before Liz could reply.

"You know me so well. I'll get you some Doritos out of the vending machine," Liz said.

"Thanks." Janiyah turned to Freddy. "Please don't go."

He brushed the back of his hand across her cheek. "I won't."

With one last look at her brothers, she headed down the hall to her dad's room. She wiped her eyes and took a deep breath. With shaky hands, she opened the door and went in.

Her dad lay in the bed; her mom sat in the chair next to it. Their hands were clasped together as they watched the movie on the television. His eyes left the TV when she came in. They were glassy and bright from his fever. There was a grey tint beneath his dark skin which contrasted with the stark white sheets.

Tears instantly sprang in her eyes. They rolled down her cheek. Frantically she wiped at them, but it was useless as more replaced them.

Her dad's brows drew together. "What are you crying for? It's just a touch of pneumonia." Instead of the strong voice she was used to, he sounded hoarse and tired.

A touch of pneumonia. Of course he would say something that foolish. What in the world was a touch of pneumonia anyway?

Her dad could be as archaic as a cave man, but she didn't care. He was the man who'd raised her, was always there for her, and loved her. If he wanted to view her as his baby girl even when she was fifty, he could, as long as he stayed around.

More tears came. "I'm sorry, I just wanted to make sure ... you were okay. I'll leave." She turned to the door and fumbled with the handle.

"Come here, girl," her dad's scratchy voice said.

She spun around and hurried to the bed. Gently she sat on the edge and wrapped her arms around her dad. Sobs wracked her body. Her tears soaked his hospital gown. He felt frail beneath her.

Her dad. Frail.

The strongest man she knew. The man who used to lift her easily to carry her on his shoulders and scared men away with a look when she was in college now rubbed her hair with shaky weak hands. It was too much to bear; she cried harder.

"It's okay, baby girl," he whispered. "It's okay."

Eventually her sobs subsided. She was vaguely aware of her mom getting up and walking out. She continued to hold her dad, not wanting to let him go.

"I know you're fine, Daddy," she said.

He squeezed her shoulder. "Just fine."

She lifted and lowered her head before closing her eyes and praying that their words would be true. A few minutes later he made her sit up.

"I'm proud of you, Janiyah," he said.

With a shaky laugh, she wiped the tears from her eyes. "I think the fever has gotten to you. I quit my job and broke up with Freddy, remember? You were right. I'm too impulsive."

He rested his hot hand on hers. "I can sell a car to a complete stranger and know exactly what to say, but when it comes to my family my words are never right. I realize now that what I said sounded a lot like I didn't think you were smart enough to run Henderson Automotive. But that's not what I think. Running the company would have crushed everything that makes you special."

"What do you mean?"

"You're my baby girl, and I've spoiled you and indulged you because it meant you would always be my little girl. I know you got that job to prove a point, but you didn't need to. I always knew you were smart, and that you could do whatever you put your mind to. But being in charge of the company, dealing with the headaches, the quotas from the factory, the personnel issues, it would have smothered you. I watched it slowly drain the life out of David; I couldn't imagine it doing the same to you."

She tried to make sense of what he'd just said. Thought back to when he first said he was selling Henderson Automotive. He'd said she couldn't do it, yes, but he'd never explained exactly what he meant by that. Was that because he was afraid that it would take something away from her? That she'd grow resentful in the same way Kareem, and to some extent, David had?

"I thought you thought I was stupid, or silly, or a joke or something."

"My kid? Stupid?" He let out a hoarse laugh. "Impossible. I've always been proud of you. I know you think I'm old fashioned, and maybe I am. But one thing I love about you is that you know yourself. You're creative and have found ways to channel that. You're my beautiful little girl, and I love you."

Fresh tears cropped up. It was the first time her dad had ever said he was proud of her. Everything he'd said, combined with the knowledge that he was giving her a confession from his hospital bed, sent all of her emotions on a tailspin.

"Don't start crying," he said with mock sternness. "Or I'll kick you out."

She leaned over and hugged him. "I'd like to see you try and kick me out. Remember, I get my stubbornness from you."

CHAPTER 30

Janiyah's dad left the hospital several days later after his fever broke and his lungs cleared up. The family moved about in a frenzy during his checkout and subsequent re-settling back in the home. Fredrick stayed by Janiyah's side the entire time even though they hadn't talked about getting back together. He took some comfort that every time he tried to leave to give the family space she insisted he stay.

He entered the Hendersons' kitchen and dropped the bags of groceries on the counter. Mrs. Henderson had insisted on making spaghetti for dinner. As soon as she'd said she needed a few things, he'd offered to go to the store so the family could spend time together.

"Thanks for going to the store, Fredrick," Mrs. Henderson said, coming over and rifling through the bags on the counter.

"No problem at all."

She smiled. "You've always been part of the family, and always will be even though things didn't work out with you and Janiyah."

Fredrick flinched at the finality in her tone. The idea of everything being over between him and Janiyah irked him as much as that incorrect formula in the spreadsheet from weeks ago had. "I was afraid that would make things awkward."

Mrs. Henderson continued taking things out of the grocery bag. "I'll admit when she first brought it up I wasn't sure if it was a good idea. I was afraid she was trying too hard to be something she wasn't."

"Join the club." Fredrick sat at one of the chairs at the island.

Mrs. Henderson gave him a warm smile. "It's not as if she really needed to. I've seen the way you looked at her for years. You were crazy about Janiyah even when she dove into whatever flight of fancy came her way."

He shifted uncomfortably. "I never tried to change her."

"I know," she said, patting his hand. "But you also didn't tell her the reasons why you loved her for who she was. Maybe you ought to do that before you two reconcile."

"I don't know if we will."

Loretta raised an eyebrow. "Then I feel sorry for the woman who tries to fill her shoes."

Fredrick tried to imagine being with someone else and couldn't. Even his relationships before Janiyah had always been haunted by her presence. It's why he listened to her whenever she pointed out the other women's faults. Each one was inconsequential in the scheme of things, but compared to Janiyah they seemed insurmountable.

He escaped to the sunroom on the back of the house. He took off his glasses and rubbed the bridge of his nose. Guilt and regret bounced back and forth like a pendulum in his head.

Guilt: *you took out your insecurity on her.*

Regret: *you let go of the one woman you've always wanted over some foolishness.*

Guilt: *you watched her try to change to make yourself feel better.*

Regret: *you knew you loved her as she was, and instead of admitting that, let it tear you two apart.*

"Mind if I join you?"

Fredrick jumped from his internal guilt-and-regret tennis match as Roger approached. Once again he was startled by the change in the man's appearance. He'd lost weight since the surgery and illness, but the fierce glint in his dark eyes was still there.

Fredrick slid on his glasses. "Um ... sure, have a seat."

He moved his chair aside and pushed out the one next to him. Roger chose the chair directly across from Fredrick.

"You've been awfully quiet since I got home," Mr. Henderson said, staring straight into Fredrick's eyes.

"Everyone's been busy, making sure you're okay."

Mr. Henderson scoffed. "I'll be fine."

"I sure as hell hope so. You're like a second father to me."

"I'll take that as a compliment," Roger said. "Even though you have a good dad of your own."

"He's a good man." He meant the words. His dad was bad with money, and foolishly in love with his wife, but he'd never mistreated Fredrick or his sister.

"We all have our faults, and I know about Christopher's. No need to look so shocked. The business world is a small one, and debts are hard to hide. You're not your dad, Fredrick. If for one second I thought you wouldn't be able to take care of my baby girl, I would have expressed my concern the moment you two started dating."

"How did you know what bothered me?"

"I watch people. You have to if you're going to sell a person a car worth thousands of dollars. You know the ones who can handle the payments and those who can't. You can handle them. Remember that when you try and get her back."

Fredrick looked toward the door leading back into the house. He imagined Janiyah in the kitchen pestering the crap out of her mom while she cooked, her brothers lounging around the den laughing and joking. If they were together, she'd give him that sexy smile that indicated she was thinking of them making love. It would be so similar to other evenings he'd spent with them, but also drastically different because the woman in the room he'd always wanted would actually be his.

"If she takes me back."

Mr. Henderson rapped his knuckles on the table. Fredrick looked back at the satisfied smile on the man's face. "I think she will."

Janiyah skipped into the sunroom, a hesitant smile on her full lips. She wore a fitted plaid shirt and shorts that barely covered her fantastic backside. He tried not to stare at the enticing image she made. The ponytail she wore along with her exuberance over her father being home made her look delicious, further increasing his craving to taste the soft skin beneath the outfit.

"Daddy, can I talk to Freddy for a minute?"

Roger slowly stood and both Fredrick and Janiyah rushed to help him up. "Thanks," Roger said, though his voice sounded like he wasn't happy to need the help. "I'll go in the living room and let the boys pester me now."

"Do you want to talk out here?" he asked after Roger left.

"No, let's go to the pool house. Otherwise someone will interrupt us."

• • •

Janiyah shoved her shaking hands into the pockets of her shorts as they walked to the pool house. She could feel Freddy's gaze boring into her back on the way. She was not going to throw herself at him. She was not going to ask him to take her back. She understood his fears, and had realized that her trying to become what she thought he wanted was one of the reasons they'd broken up. She couldn't take another rejection.

But she did want to thank him for being such a good friend, and apologize for pushing things. Having him here made her realize she missed his friendship. She wanted that back.

The minute the door closed she second-guessed the location. They were too far away from everyone. She should have just stayed in the sunroom.

"Um ... I wanted ... want to say thank you for being here for my family. I know you missed the Satterfield meeting because of it."

"You don't have to thank me, Janiyah. I'll always be here for you, and your family."

She swallowed hard. He'd be here for her *and* her family. "I know, but I want you to understand that I appreciate it. You prepared for weeks for that meeting, then missed it because of me. I never wanted you to make that choice."

"The choice was easy."

"But *I* didn't want you to be in that position. I hope that despite what happened, we can still be friends."

"I want more than that."

She shook her head and looked down at her feet. "Don't say that. I've accepted that we won't be together. That we don't work."

"Yes, we do."

She turned away and paced back and forth. Her heart beat sporadically in her chest, shooting her up with that anticipation cocktail that made her rush into decisions.. She really wanted to believe him.

"No, we don't, remember? I'm a threat to your livelihood. I might tempt you to throw away everything you worked for. What happened with the Satterfield meeting is exactly what you were afraid of."

He took her elbow to stop her pacing. "What happened was that when I thought of you in pain and upset, nothing else mattered except being there for you."

"Fredrick, stop."

He pulled her close. "I won't stop. I messed up. I never should have said that to you. I used my dad's bad decisions as an excuse to push you away. The truth is, I wasn't worried about losing myself. I was worried about losing you. You wanted me once when you were too young to know what you were asking." He held up a hand. "Don't interrupt, because we both know if I would have taken your virginity back then, it would have been disastrous all the way around. After that, you teased and flirted with me, but you didn't show that interest again. You became this beautiful, fun-loving person who dated guys far more interesting than an accountant. Instead of admitting that I was jealous and unsure if I could make you happy, I put the blame on you. I'm sorry."

"You're the one I always come back to. I keep putting my feelings out there, and you keep tossing them back. I can't do that again. I'm nothing but a joke to men like you."

"You're not a joke. You're the excitement in my life, the person who reminds me that there is more to life than work." His hand lifted to her neck where his fingers lightly traced along the vein pounding on her throat. "We balance each other out. You shake things up and I'm your occasional voice of reason."

"I can't be the person I tried to be when we dated."

"I don't want her. I like the Janiyah who eats my cereal, changes the channels on my television, and helps our next-door neighbor sell sex toys."

"You know about that?" He couldn't have seen it in her budget; she hadn't charged Mrs. Driggers for anything. Mrs. Driggers said she'd find Janiyah at least two paying customers for all of the help she'd given her for free.

"I saw one of Mrs. Driggers's flyers in the common area. It had your design logo in the corner. I'm proud of how you helped her."

Her body hummed with the need to trust him. But they needed to be clear. She couldn't go down the same path as before.

"I'd never want to see you lose your business, especially because of me. I watched my dad build his automotive empire and work hard every day to keep it. I respect what he did, and I respect what you do. Why would you think I'd spend all your money? I couldn't care less about your money."

"I know. I shouldn't have implied that you did."

"You say that, but do you really mean it? You should think about this—away from me and my family—and be sure this is what you want."

"I know what I want" His voice was low, sure, and steady.

She took a deep breath and prepared to ask the hard question. "Are you still afraid to love me?"

He didn't blink, only moved closer and slid a hand around her waist as he stared into her eyes. "No. I am afraid of losing you." He lowered his head to kiss the side of her neck. He hit her spot, and her knees gave way. "Give me a chance to make this right."

She succumbed to the rush of anticipation flooding her system. This time she didn't question it. Her chin lifted, giving him better access. His tongue flicked against the soft skin of her neck, and any doubts quickly turned to desire.

"We haven't made up," she said.

His hands deftly unfastened the snap of her shorts. "We're getting close." He lowered one hand to the back of her shorts to cup her butt. He pulled her close until his dick pressed firmly against the front of her shorts.

"I'm serious, Fredrick." Her voice trembled.

He lifted his head and stared into her eyes. "That's twice you've called me Fredrick."

"It's how I think of you. When we're together like this. But my family is right next door."

He stepped back enough to unbutton and spread open her shirt. His eyes narrowed into seductive slits as he took in her breasts in a plain, white bra. Lust pounded through her veins, concentrating wetly between her legs.

"It's just us in here," he said.

He pulled her hair out of its ponytail and caressed her scalp. He went back to kissing her neck. Her hands gripped his hips. "I love the way you smell, Janiyah. It makes me want to lick every inch of your body. Say you'll give us another try, and I promise to do just that."

That was it. She was through talking. Her head twisted to kiss him. He groaned and pushed her shorts and underwear down. She quickly released the button and zipper on his pants to take his rigid flesh in her grasp. His body trembled, or maybe it was hers. It really didn't matter.

He made short work of removing her bra. Almost immediately he lifted her up and took one aching nipple into his mouth. Her legs wrapped around his waist, putting her slick center right on his erection. She twisted her hips, pleasuring herself and covering him with the sweat of her desire.

"You're like a dream come true," he said against her lips.

He gently lowered them both to the floor, and slid inside of her at the same time. Their lovemaking was fast. She wanted him so badly her orgasm was upon her almost as soon as his body joined hers. She writhed in pleasure, alternating between panting his full name and biting his shoulder to keep from screaming out like she wanted. When her body clenched around him, he came right after.

"I love you, Janiyah," he said into the crook of her neck, words he'd never uttered during lovemaking before.

CHAPTER 31

Fredrick watched Janiyah work the room at the young professionals mixer. Everyone in the room wore safari hats that clashed with their business suits. The Mardi Gras themed mixer she'd put together before was such a hit that they asked her to come up with a theme for each one. Even in her khaki dress and safari hat, Janiyah managed to be the brightest spot there. He was a big fan of her choice in dresses. Every time he looked at the V-neck his mouth watered to explore the soft swells beneath. The skirt stopped in the middle of her slim thighs. He let his gaze drop to the camouflage stilettos. She'd keep those on when they made love tonight.

She'd taken over the event planning for the group as part of the re-launch of her business. He wasn't surprised when she'd brought him a business plan to expand her virtual assistance work into a consulting service. Now she offered event planning, scheduling assistance, and document preparation for small businesses that couldn't afford to have someone in-house handle things. She said Mrs. Driggers gave her the idea when she referred her to a friend trying to start a business.

He'd never doubted she could do it, especially after she updated his office in a matter of weeks. If anything, he was proud she found a way to take her business to the next level.

"How's it going, Fredrick?"

He suppressed a sigh as Evan walked up. "Going well."

"Janiyah looks great tonight," Evan said.

They both watched her and Liz talking to a group across the room. Janiyah slid one of her new business cards out of the pocket of her dress and passed it to one of the ladies in the group. He smiled; she knew how to hustle her business.

"She does."

"Are you two still sleeping together?"

Fredrick turned from Janiyah to scowl at Evan. "Pardon me?"

Evan smirked. "I knew there was a reason you'd hire someone like her. Those after-hours perks are hard to deny."

"What perks?"

"Come on. I heard you two one night in your office."

Anger surged through every crevice in Fredrick's body. "I didn't realize you liked to listen at doors."

"I didn't have to stand too close. She's a firecracker, that one." Evan looked across the room at Janiyah. "Maybe send her my way when you're done playing."

He moved to block Evan's view of Janiyah. "I'm not playing with Janiyah. And if you ever talk about her like that again, I don't care where we are, I'll knock your teeth down your throat." His fist clenched to do just that.

Evan's eyes widened. He held up his hands. "I meant no harm."

"Neither do I. I'll look for your resignation tomorrow."

"You can't fire me."

"I can, and I just did. Good night." He turned his back on Evan and strode across the room to Janiyah.

He alternated between fury and disbelief. He no longer cared who knew he was with Janiyah. But to think that Evan, and probably other men, thought he was just having some fun made him want to break something. It was too close to the belief Janiyah had before they broke up. Inwardly he groaned. He'd once asked her how long they would be together. Even though they'd moved on, what if she still thought he felt the same?

He slipped his arm around her waist and pulled her close. Her eyes filled with surprise and then delight. It was time to break his rule of no public displays of affection. He'd end any whispered conversations about what might be going on between them.

"How are you?" he asked.

She placed a hand on his chest and leaned into him. "Great. I was just talking about my plans for the next mixer. I'm thinking a Vegas theme with card tables and door prizes from the businesses in attendance."

"Sounds like a great idea."

"She's going to make these events the highlight of the professional community," Liz said, grinning between the two. "Leave it to Janiyah to get everyone wearing Safari hats on a Tuesday night."

The group chuckled their agreement and touched their hats. He smiled down at Janiyah, making sure his dimple came out. "That's why I love her." Her lips parted and her fingers clutched the front of his shirt. He followed his instinct and lowered his head to kiss her quickly. "I'm going to leave early. I'll see you when you're done here?"

"I'll be there in about an hour. Are you sure you won't stay?"

He shook his head. "Long day, but you enjoy yourself. You can fill me in on everything later." He leaned down to kiss her cheek. "And I'll fill you in on what your legs and those heels are doing to me," he whispered in her ear.

She shivered and grinned at him. "I look forward to that."

He turned to Liz and the rest of the group. "You all have a good night."

He gave her one last squeeze then walked away. He glanced at his watch. It was getting late, but he had one last stop to make.

• • •

"If you check the time again I'm going to scream," Liz said, pulling off her safari hat and smoothing her hair back.

"There's nothing wrong with checking the time."

"What's killing me is that you're hanging around here pretending to have fun when you're dying to get to Fredrick's and follow up on that look he gave you. I'm totally hating because I'm in a dry spell, but it's hard to hold on to it when you're so obviously happy."

"I am happy. It's different this time. We're still us, but just together. If that makes sense."

"It doesn't, but I can see the difference," Liz said before tilting her head to the door. "Go on, have a good night."

Janiyah gave Liz a hug. When she pulled back she caught the eye of William, the guy she'd volunteered with at Conversions. She waved him over. Liz's eyes lit up while Janiyah made the introductions and William did a double take when Liz smiled at him. Bingo. Just as she'd thought, they were perfect for each other.

She stopped to talk to one of the committee members who put on the mixer on her way out the door and made up some excuse to leave. The knowing look in the young woman's eye meant she probably knew Janiyah was running off to be with Freddy. She knew there were rumors she was a fling for him, the up and coming successful businessman having fun with the young party planner. It didn't annoy her. Not much anyway. She knew there was more to her and Freddy than that.

"Oh, Janiyah, can you give me a second?" Diana stopped her.

Diana wasn't in a safari hat, and looked impeccable in a black pinstripe suit with her hair pulled back into a sleek bun.

"Sure, Diana, what's up?"

Diana shifted from foot to foot and studied her manicured nails. "I heard about your new consulting business and while I usually can handle things on my own, it never hurts to solicit help." She stopped shuffling and met Janiyah's eye. "Do you only work for businesses, or do you help individuals as well?"

"I've helped individuals."

"Normally, I can manage my schedule just fine. I'm just so busy with work, and the kids, and everything else. I tend to forget things like birthdays and anniversaries. My oldest wanted a party at the zoo and it just slipped my mind." Tears misted her eyes. "I'd like to avoid disappointing him again."

Janiyah pulled a business card out of her pocket and handed it over. "Send me all of the important dates. I'll forward a questionnaire about their interests and you can send more information to me as they come up. I'll schedule the parties, order the gifts, and get the invitations out. Don't worry, everyone can use the help of an assistant every once in a while."

Diana slipped the card in her purse and sighed. "If we can keep this between us. I don't want my husband to know that I can't keep up with this type of stuff."

"It'll be our secret," Janiyah said with a smile.

She left Diana and hurried to her car. She grinned all the way to Freddy's house. She was doing it. She was actually growing her business into something tangible. Maybe one day, she'd have a real office—with flexible hours. It felt good, and real. She'd gone from a joke to an entrepreneur, all on her own. Something she never would have thought she could do only a few months ago.

Surprisingly, Freddy wasn't there when Janiyah arrived at his house. Knowing him, he'd left the party and gone to the bookstore first. He was probably taking his time, thinking she wouldn't be there for a while. She wanted to take off her shoes and put on a pair of his pajamas to lounge on the couch. But his comment on her legs in her heels meant she was keeping everything on. It would be more fun to have him take it off later anyway.

She pulled a bag of grapes from his fridge at the same time his back door alarm chimed as he came in.

He grinned, full on dimple, and came over to pull her in his arms. "You're here already?"

"I can leave and come back later."

"Oh no, you're here and I'm keeping you."

He kissed her and she easily let her body melt into his. She would never get tired of his kisses.

"Mmmm, what was that for?" she said in a breathless whisper.

"A precursor to what I want to do later."

She grinned. "While I'm wearing these shoes?"

"Nothing but those shoes."

"Promises, promises." She kissed him again, then slipped away to get the grapes. "I'm surprised I beat you here."

"I had to make a stop."

She popped off a few grapes and chewed on the sweet fruit. "Another book?"

"Not this time. I needed something to celebrate this occasion."

"What occasion?"

He reached into his pocket and pulled out a jewelry box, a nervous laugh escaping his lips.

She clapped her hands. "You bought me jewelry! This is a reason to celebrate. What is it? Earrings, a bracelet, that dragonfly pendent I pointed out in the magazine the other day?"

"No, no, and hell no." He wiped his brow and twisted his head back and forth as if relieving tension in his neck.

She smiled. Guys didn't look that nervous unless they were ... Her heart rate accelerated. It couldn't be. Were they there yet? She searched her heart. Yes, she was there. She'd loved Freddy for years; there was no one else. But could he seriously be there?

He opened the box, and the light glittered off the most beautiful square cut diamond ring she'd ever seen. Holy crap, he could.

"Oh, Fredrick."

He swallowed hard before speaking. "Will you marry me, Janiyah? I know it's crazy, and unexpected. But I love you. I was too stupid and scared to let myself admit how much I love you, and it almost cost us. You're my light, my laughter, the one person I want to see every day. We make a good team ... couple ... team. Ah, hell. Will you?"

"Yes!" She jumped into his arms and kissed him repeatedly all over his face.

He laughed and pried her arms off him. "Will you put on the ring?"

"Who needs the ring? You want to marry me!"

"I don't think people will believe it without the ring, baby."

She fought back laughter and tears as he finally got her off him and slipped the ring onto her finger. It was a perfect fit.

"Daddy's gonna flip."

"I hope in a good way."

"He loves you, Fredrick, you know it."

"Do you want to call him now?"

She shook her head. "No, I'm not talking to him today."

"Why not?"

"David called. Now that he's getting better, Daddy's still talking about selling Henderson Automotive." The frustration she'd pushed away earlier tried to horn in on her happy moment. But family drama was for another day. Right now she wanted to bask in the happiness of knowing Freddy wanted to marry her. "I don't want to talk about Henderson Automotive right now."

"Then we won't. We'll talk about how crazy you're going to drive me while you plan our wedding."

Giddiness that made her want to skip and sing through every room in the house quickly chased away her irritation. "I'm already thinking silver and black, with crystals over everything."

He cringed. "I'm not wearing crystals."

"I'm talking about me. But maybe a diamond earring to give you some extra bling on our wedding day."

He tried glaring, but his lips twitched. "Janiyah, you can put crystals on everything if you never mention me getting an earring again."

"Do you know how many men look sexy with an earring?"

He took her arm and pulled her into his embrace. "Do you know how sexy you are when you spout foolishness?" He kissed her neck.

Janiyah wrapped her leg around his, love and happiness swelling inside her. "Why did it take so long for you to realize we belong together? You wasted so much time."

Freddy lifted his head. His smile was full on dimple. "That's why I'm marrying you. I'm not wasting any more time. I want the world know that you're the woman I want. Are you sure you want to spend the rest of your life with me?"

She leaned up and kissed him softly, gazing into the light brown eyes of the man she'd never thought would be hers. "Oh yes. I'm absolutely sure. You're just my type."

ABOUT THE AUTHOR

Synithia Williams has published over twenty-five novels since 2012. Her novel, A Malibu Kind of Romance was a 2017 RITA® finalist, she is a 2018 and 2019 African American Literary Award Show nominee in Romance. Her books were listed as Amazon Editor's "Best Book of the Month" in Romance. Reviews of Synithia's books can be found in Publisher's Weekly, Library Journal, Woman's Word, Kirkus and Entertainment Weekly. Synithia lives in Columbia, South Carolina with her husband and two kids. You can learn more about Synithia by visiting her website, www.synithiawilliams.com[1].

1. http://www.synithiawilliams.com

EXCERPT FROM LOVE'S REPLAY

David Henderson hated celebrating his birthday. But when faced with a pleading baby sister who insisted he'd regret not commemorating turning 30, he'd agreed to a small party with family and close friends. That was the problem with baby sisters: they made it difficult to say no. Janiyah was an expert at getting what she wanted—and at stretching the definition of a "small party."

His lake house was nearly bursting at the seams with people. The city's hottest DJ played all the hits from his set up by the pool where a fully stocked bar had four bartenders passing out drinks, and waiters in white coats maneuvered through the crowd handing out appetizers. Everyone who was anyone was there.

He should have known—his sister didn't do small when it came to parties. Especially one designed to help boost her new event planning business.

It wasn't as if he was against birthday celebrations in general. Just the reminder of the mistakes he'd made that came with his.

He smiled and talked to people as he made his way through the crowded living room to the stairs, stopping for the "Hey, David, check this out" from the fellas, or the "Hi, handsome" thrown his way by the women in attendance. He even accepted an appetizer and a drink from one of the waiters, and ate it with a guy he vaguely recognized. All in an effort to pretend he was having a good time. Each interruption delayed his escape to the quiet of the upstairs master bedroom.

Upstairs, he was stopped three more times before finally making his way to his bedroom. The music from the party became a dull thump when he closed the door.

"Finally, silence," he said. His feet didn't make a sound as he crossed the room, his footsteps absorbed by the thick, white carpet.

He checked the clock on the table beside the California king bed. He could probably spend a few minutes in here before someone sought him out to convince him he should bring in the next decade of his life with a bang.

When the hell had thirty crept up on him? It seemed like yesterday he was stepping out of his car onto the campus of Duke University as a freshman. Now, he was a man doing exactly what he never expected to be doing. He hadn't felt it was his responsibility to step in and take over the responsibilities of his older brother at Henderson Automotive. He was proud of their family business that had started with one struggling car dealership, and become one of the largest in the state. Somewhere over the past ten years he'd actually fallen in love with running it, and the legacy. Still, this wasn't supposed to be his life.

He ran a hand over his face. Thirty. Hell, next he'd have to marry and have kids.

A shudder went down his spine. Yeah right. He couldn't find a woman he wanted to stay with for more than a few weeks. How was he supposed to find one he would want to sleep with every day for the rest of his life?

A vision of hazel eyes, brown skin, and the whisper of a husky voice drifted through his brain. No surprise. He always thought of Sandra on his birthday. He'd lost her on his birthday. Part of the reason he never wanted to rejoice in the occasion.

His cell phone beeped on the nightstand with a text message alert. He raised a brow at the number on screen. It was his oldest brother Kareem, who, according to his sister, wasn't coming tonight, a revelation that neither surprised nor hurt David. He loved his brother, but sometimes he didn't like him very much.

Where u at? Kareem texted.

He sat on the bed and texted back.

Party. Upstairs bedroom. Why?

U alone?

He smirked. He wasn't always with a woman.

Yes.

David stared at his phone and waited for his brother to call. Instead there was a knock on the door, and Kareem walked in without waiting for an answer.

He closed the door and frowned at David, the movement making the scar on his upper lip more pronounced. "Why are you hiding up here?" Kareem asked.

"Not in a partying mood." He slowly eyed Kareem from head to toe.

His brother was in black, as usual. David didn't get his brother's need to channel Johnny Cash, but he'd long since stopped questioning Kareem's decisions. Though something was different tonight. Instead of a t-shirt and black jeans, he wore a black dress shirt and slacks. His dreadlocks were twisted back in a complicated style and ... wait a second ... he had on cologne?

"I know you didn't dress up for my party."

The stare Kareem gave him said shut the hell up. "I'm not dressed up."

"No, you've definitely polished the look." David sniffed the air. "And cologne, too. I'm flattered, brother."

Kareem scowled before turning his back on David. His shoulders were stiff as he paced back and forth. "Don't be. It's not for you."

Kareem's agitation was interesting. The only time Kareem showed discomfort was when their mom or sister tried to hug him. David stood and walked to the mirror on the dresser to check his appearance. He made a show of smoothing his hair and the beard around his lips to hide his interest in his brother's obvious discomfort.

"Then who is it for?" David asked.

Kareem continued to pace. "I've got a date. I invited her to your party."

David spun away from the mirror. "Not one of your reformed convicts."

Kareem froze and leveled him with a cold stare. If he weren't his brother, David would back off. Not many people outside of the family kept talking after Kareem gave that icy glare.

"Don't look at me like that. It's no secret you've been slumming for the past few years," David said, turning back to the mirror and smoothing the lapels of his dinner jacket.

"When did you become so stuck up?"

"After the last girl you brought to a cookout tried to steal mom's jewelry."

Kareem flinched. "That was over a year ago. I haven't brought a woman around since."

David faced his brother and leaned back against the dresser. "Why do you waste your time with these sorry women?"

Kareem crossed his arms. His thick legs spread in a defensive pose as he glared back. "You seem to forget the fancy women in your circle weren't interested after I got out of prison."

David scoffed. "Please. They were the main ones throwing themselves at you as soon as you got out. *You* decided to ignore their love of a"—he made air quotes—"thug, and go with these crazy women who see dollar signs when they see you."

"Dad's money."

David shook his head. "Your money. You're in the family, it's yours too."

"I'm making my own money."

"Whatever." David straightened. "I don't care that you brought a date. Just keep her away from the silver."

He turned back to the mirror to make one last check of his outfit. The burgundy velvet sport coat over charcoal grey pants was custom tailored. It was a little Hugh Hefner, but if he was going to have a big party to celebrate entering his thirties he might as well do it in style.

"She's not going to steal the silver." Kareem walked over to stand behind him in the mirror. "She's not like that."

"What's her name?"

"I can't remember. My boy Omar is bringing her here. She's friends with his girl and just moved to town because of her job. We're hooking up tonight."

David turned away from the mirror. "I'm surprised you're telling me. You don't need my permission to bring a woman to the party."

"I know that," Kareem said, as if the idea of asking David's permission for anything was crazy. "What I do need is for you to check her out for me. From the way Omar described her, she's more like those high class women you go out with."

David raised a brow and rubbed his beard to hide a smile. "So you're looking for advice on how to treat a classy woman?"

As expected, Kareem's expression darkened. "I don't need your advice when it comes to women."

David didn't bother hiding his smile now. It wasn't every day that he got to tease his brother. His relationship with Kareem was unique to say the least. They'd had a good-natured competition between them when they were younger, which had morphed into a true rivalry over time. Grades, girls, or games. It didn't matter. Both Kareem and David lived to outdo the other. Though David had always suspected the competition was less serious from Kareem's standpoint. Kareem didn't have a real reason to try and one up his younger brother. He had been their dad's pride and joy, the firstborn son that would one day take over the business. Until Kareem decided to rebel against the family and got into trouble.

At times like this, when David actually got to tease Kareem, he was reminded how much he missed the old days when their friendly competition wasn't colored by past mistakes.

"Oh, yes you do," David said with a grin. "Don't be shy; I can give you a few pointers on how to make a woman happy."

Kareem's lip twitched, and for a second David thought he'd get his brother to egg him on.

"I don't have time for your jokes," Kareem said. "Just let me know if you've seen her at any of those business luncheons you attend. Find out what you can about her. Omar doesn't run in your circles, so he wouldn't know if she's a waste of time or not. The only thing I got from Omar was that she was stacked."

"Sounds like all you need to know right there."

"Forget it," Kareem said, turning toward the door.

David started to let him walk out. But the fact that his brother had asked for a favor was monumental in itself.

"Hold up," David said. "I'll check her out. What's the name of the organization she works for? I may have some dealings with them."

Kareem shrugged. "Hell if I know. Like I said, Omar only pays attention to one thing when it comes to women."

David grinned. "Don't we all?"

That did earn a smile from his brother. They both made their way to the door. Kareem stopped before opening it.

"And for the record, if there was anyone I would ask for advice when it came to women it would be Aaron."

David held up his hands and stepped back. "Seriously? You'd ask our baby brother before me."

"Aaron has a woman in every city, and you know it." Kareem tapped David on the shoulder. "Maybe you should take points from him." He opened the door and walked out.

David shook his head as he followed Kareem. He hated to admit it, but Kareem had a point. Their younger brother started his own trucking company a few years ago, and he did come home with a story about a new woman he met after each trip. David was the one the family considered a playboy, but Aaron was just better at hiding his tracks.

David followed his brother into the hallway. Partygoers hung out in the upstairs hall, the long tails of balloons in the vaulted ceilings hovering above their heads. The music was louder than before, and someone had opened the large bay windows and French doors downstairs to ease the flow.

His smile tightened as he followed Kareem down the stairs. This was a far cry from his original plan to turn thirty sitting in the house drinking beer. Maybe indulge in a little reminiscence about Sandra. It was the one time of year he allowed himself to do that. The rest of the year he pushed those thoughts aside. Regret was a feeling indulged in by the weak.

When they'd met in college he'd taken one look at her and could only think about getting her in bed. Typical him at the age of twenty. Then she'd worked her way into his heart, and he'd fallen in love. He still couldn't believe how quickly love had hit him back then, while it eluded him now. But one night fueled by anger, angst, and selfishness he'd entered a bedroom with another woman and lost Sandra in an instant.

Many of the guests stopped him along the way. He shook hands with or gave a fist pound to a few of the guys. He brushed his lips across the women's cheeks, being sure to pull away when they leaned in for more. He wasn't interested in finding someone to spend the night with. That was his other rule: he didn't have hookups on his birthday.

He gazed around the room and caught the eye of Tanisha Cruz. They'd had a brief relationship the year before. The longest he'd had since college. Her full, pink lips glistened in the party lights as she blew a kiss across the room. Tanisha was prepped to attract attention in a barely there silver dress. Her olive skin and long dark hair sent a weak whisper of desire through him. Mostly a memory from what they'd once been. He wasn't interested in rekindling that flame.

He lifted his chin and quirked his mouth instead of smiling. Her sensuous lips curved upward as she flung the thick curtain of hair over her shoulder and wove her way through the crowd. He tried not to show his annoyance as she slid up beside him.

"What's up, birthday boy?" Tanisha said, slipping her arm around his waist. Her silky voice was filled with promise.

He chafed at the possessive way she clung to him. One of the many reasons they hadn't lasted. "I'm far from a boy, Tanisha."

She gave him a once over. "Oh, believe me, I know."

Kareem tapped him on the shoulder. "I see Omar. I'll bring her over in a second."

David nodded. "I'll be out by the pool." He tried to pull away from Tanisha, but she tightened her hold around his waist.

"I'll go with you," she said, giving him a seductive smile.

Inwardly groaning, he led her outside to a chair near the DJ. She finally released him when he promised to return with a drink. She pouted and squeezed his hand before letting go. He'd have to find a way to get rid of her later.

Though, if he thought about it, why should he? He was thirty, and more than enough time had passed since he'd made that mistake on his birthday in college. Shouldn't he move on instead of punishing himself every year? He glanced over his shoulder at Tanisha, who gave him a small wave of her fingers. Maybe it was time to truly put past regrets behind him.

He asked the bartender for a beer and a strawberry daiquiri for Tanisha. He rested his arms on the smooth marble surface to wait, when someone squealed behind him. He shook his head and grinned, instantly recognizing the voice. He turned as his sister ran over. There was a huge smile on her face and a bounce in her step. She always bounced with exuberance. It came with being the baby of the family and having everyone dote upon her.

"Oh my God, you're getting old, Davie!" She wrapped her arms tightly around his neck.

He quickly embraced her before pushing back. "Don't call me that in public."

Janiyah's eyes sparkled with mischief. She'd pulled her hair into a knot on the top of her head and wore a pink one-shoulder dress that stopped mid-thigh. "This isn't public."

He shook his head at her reasoning. "You know what I mean."

Janiyah clasped her hands behind her back. "Isn't this better than drinking beer alone on your birthday?"

He opened his mouth to say no. But the hopeful glow in his baby sister's doe-like eyes pushed back the comment. He smiled and nodded. "Yes, it is."

She clapped her hands. "Aaron is upstairs playing pool with Freddy," she said, referring to their brother and his best friend, her fiancé. "Want to join them?"

"I'll go up and join them in a second. I'm waiting on Kareem."

The bartender called out to him. He grabbed the two drinks and turned back to his sister. "Why aren't you up there? I thought you and Fredrick were joined at the hip these days."

Janiyah waved a hand. "I'm giving him a chance to miss me. It makes things so much better later."

He held up the drinks and frowned. "Please, please, please, spare me those details."

She grinned then reached out and patted his cheek. "Fine. Enjoy yourself, Davie. You only turn thirty once."

"Thank goodness for that."

Movement behind Janiyah caught his attention. Kareem came up and placed a hand on her shoulder.

"Kareem, you came," Janiyah said. She reached up to hug him, and Kareem indulged her for a quick second before pulling away.

"You did beg," he said.

"It's David's birthday, we had to celebrate," Janiyah said.

"Of course we did." Kareem turned to the people behind him. "Say hello to Sandra." He placed his hand on the lower back of one of the women in the group. "Sandra, this is my sister, Janiyah, and one of my younger brothers, David."

David took a sip from his beer before meeting the woman his brother was anxious for him to check out. When their eyes met his heart constricted, while the beer went down his windpipe with an icy burn. Fierce coughs were his only response to the shock of making contact with the hazel eyes that haunted him every year on his birthday.

He spun back to the bar and set the drinks on the surface. Rough coughs racked his body, and he pressed a hand to his chest to stop it. Hands hit his back. Voices asked if he was okay. But it was all background noise, drowned out by memories of her voice whispering his name in the dark, a secret smile directed his way, her soft body warm and welcoming beneath his.

It couldn't be her.

When the burn subsided, he took a deep breath and reassured his sister he was okay. He mentally braced himself before turning around. His heart beat harder than the bass of the music. He faced the group. It was her. Ten years had passed, and damned if she wasn't better with age. Cinnamon-colored skin; he used to call her his cinnamon bun. Damn, he was corny back then. He quickly let his eyes flick over her green dress. It stopped above the knee, and a black belt cinched her waist, accenting the flare of her hips. Black heels gave added height to her five feet nine inch frame. He remembered her exact height, the only woman that fit against him perfectly. Her hair was shorter now, in an asymmetrical cut, short on one side and long on the other. Nostalgia sent a drum roll of desire through his body.

She didn't appear surprised to see him. Her full lips curved into a smile that didn't quite reach her eyes. She wasn't happy to see him.

"Oh, wow, David Henderson." Her voice was low, husky. A reminder of nights spent in a twin bed in her dorm room while she moaned his name. "It's good to see you." A lie if he ever heard one. Her eyes were frigid.

Seeing her released a floodgate of memories. Memories he'd long suppressed and said no longer mattered. For a split second he considered reaching out to hug or touch her, pull her against him to confirm she was really there. Kareem shifted at her side. That's right, she was here for Kareem.

"Sandra Brevard. I haven't seen you since ... "

"College. You're Kareem's brother. Now I know why he looked so familiar." She turned to Kareem and smiled. "You've got the same eyes."

His stomach clenched. His eyes, what she used to call her favorite feature. Now she saw them in his brother. A raw and violent jealousy surged inside him at the thought of another man with her. That too wasn't new, but he'd lost the ability to act on it years ago.

Kareem put his hand on the small of her back. "I'm taking it you know each other?"

His brother's movement was a clear message. Back off.

"Yeah, he and I were in some of the same circles ... what ... junior year?" she said with a deceptively questioning tone.

She damn well knew what year it was. They'd been in the same circles? That's how she wanted to define it? It was far more than that.

"Yeah, we hung out a few times."

She turned to the woman beside her. "You remember Yvonne? She and Omar have been dating for a few weeks."

He reluctantly met Yvonne's smirk. Time hadn't been bad to her either. Her light brown skin and face full of freckles still made her look younger than she was. "Long time no see. What's up, Omar?" David said to the tall, lanky guy at her side.

He didn't care much for Omar—something about his shifty eyes. But he was a friend of Kareem, so David tolerated him.

"Sup, David," Omar said, pulling on the waistband of his ridiculously sagging jeans. Omar and Kareem were both thirty-two. And while he disagreed with his brother's tendency to dress in black everywhere he went, at least he didn't dress like some rap video reject the way Omar did.

Yvonne's lips twisted into a tight smile. "You always did do it big on your birthday."

Her voice was accusing. That wasn't a surprise. Yvonne hadn't liked him when he and Sandra were together, and she'd straight up hated him after he'd ruined things.

"No better way to celebrate than big," he said. No way would he admit to spending the past ten years sulking on his birthday.

He looked back at Sandra. If she was affected by Yvonne's reference to his terrible birthday years ago he couldn't tell. His gaze dropped to her hands. Of course no ring, though he would've expected her to be married by now. No nervous flexing of the fingers. He watched her face. No biting of the lip, no fidgeting. He couldn't get a read on her. He used to always be able to tell what she was feeling.

Their eyes met. The corner of her mouth lifted in a smile that said she knew he was trying to figure out what she was thinking. Back then she'd been an open book. When they first met, her nervous fidgeting had let on that she liked him even though she tried to pretend she didn't. They'd gone for the same book in the library, and when she refused to give it up, he'd known right then and there he wanted her. It didn't take long to win her over, despite her pretending like she wasn't feeling him. She was the girl he'd considered marrying—until he'd messed things up.

"Happy birthday, David. It's nice to meet you, Janiyah." She smiled fully at Kareem. "Show me around?"

Kareem lifted his chin. "All right. We'll see you around, David." He led her way, his hand still firmly on her lower back.

Yvonne gave him one last smirk before rolling her eyes and following with Omar. Her nasty sneer didn't matter. David kept his eyes on Sandra, waiting for her to glance back, or reach up and smooth her hair like she used to when thrown off balance.

She didn't. She couldn't really not care that they'd run into each other. How could she possibly be unaffected by seeing him?

Unless she'd expected to see him. Maybe she was using Kareem to get back at him. His jaw tightened. No matter what he'd done, he wouldn't let her play with his brother's feelings as a way to get revenge. Kareem had been through enough already without dealing with the hurt feelings from some woman David had wronged years ago.

"So, what's really between you two?" Janiyah asked. He started and cast a glance her way. "Yeah, I'm still here." She smiled.

He shook his head and took another sip of his drink. "Doesn't matter what was between us. I'm more concerned with what she's doing to Kareem." He patted Janiyah on the shoulder. "I'll catch you later." He walked away before she could question him more, and followed Kareem and Sandra.

ALSO BY SYNITHIA WILLIAMS

HENDERSON FAMILY SERIES

Love's Replay

Making it Real

From One Night to Forever

CALDWELL FAMILY SERIES

Show Me How to Love

Love Me as I Am

Trust Me With Your Love

SOUTHERN LOVE SERIES

You Can't Plan Love

Worth the Wait

A Heart to Heal